"*Anomaly* grabs the reader and refuses to let go. From the introduction to misunderstood anomaly, Thalli, to the boy she loves, one is never completely sure what is fact and what is a horrifying virtual reality. This is sure to be a favorite of teens everywhere."

—Heather Burch, author of the critically acclaimed Halflings series

"Krista McGee's *Luminary* . . . will please fans of dystopian lit as well as those who enjoy YA inspy romance."

—USAToday.com

". . . the first in what has the potential to be a fascinating trilogy of general appeal. McGee's simple narrative belies the novel's complexity, a factor that will make this intriguing book accessible to a wide variety of teen readers."

—*Booklist* review of *Anomaly*

"McGee blends the determination of faith, the malevolence of those who extol power over decency, and the assertion of individual integrity in a humane glimpse at youthful courage."

—*Publishers Weekly* review of *Luminary*

"McGee's versatility as an author really shines with this latest offering . . . *Anomaly* . . . should encourage inspirational romance readers who haven't yet tried out dystopian lit to give it a shot."

—USA Today.com

"McGee once again blends a Christian message within a horrific science fiction plot . . . death, torture, and confusing love triangles."

—*Booklist* review of *Luminary*

"McGee successfully asks readers to consider both what it means to act (or not act) on human emotions and the role such emotions play in relationships with God."

—*Publishers Weekly* review of *Anomaly*

ACCLAIM FOR KRISTA MCGEE

"McGee's debut novel is an absolute gem. Anyone who enjoys reality television and a well-told story shouldn't hesitate to read this great book."

—*Romantic Times* TOP PICK! Review of *First Date*

"[A] touching, fun, edifying, campy, quick, and downright delicious teen read."

—USAToday.com regarding *First Date*

"Good things come to those who wait—and pray."

—*Kirkus Reviews* regarding *Starring Me*

"An abundance of real-life problems . . . should keep this story relevant for many teens."

—*Publishers Weekly* review of *Right Where I Belong*

REVOLUTIONARY

OTHER NOVELS BY KRISTA MCGEE

THE ANOMALY TRILOGY
Anomaly
Luminary

First Date
Starring Me
Right Where I Belong

REVOLUTIONARY

BOOK THREE IN THE ANOMALY TRILOGY

KRISTA MCGEE

THOMAS NELSON
Since 1798

NASHVILLE   MEXICO CITY   RIO DE JANEIRO

Published in Nashville, Tennessee, by Thomas Nelson. Thomas Nelson is a registered trademark of HarperCollins Christian Publishing, Inc.

Published in association with literary agent Jenni Burke of D.C. Jacobson & Associates, an Author Management Company, www.DCJacobson.com.

Thomas Nelson, Inc., titles may be purchased in bulk for educational, business, fund-raising, or sales promotional use. For information, please e-mail SpecialMarkets@ThomasNelson.com.

Scripture quotations are from THE NEW KING JAMES VERSION. © 1982 by Thomas Nelson, Inc. Used by permission. All rights reserved. Also quoted: *Holy Bible*, New Living Translation. © 1996. Used by permission of Tyndale House Publishers, Inc., Wheaton, Illinois 60189. All rights reserved.

Publisher's Note: This novel is a work of fiction. Names, characters, places, and incidents are either products of the author's imagination or used fictitiously. All characters are fictional, and any similarity to people living or dead is purely coincidental.

Library of Congress Cataloging-in-Publication Data

McGee, Krista, 1975–
  Revolutionary / Krista McGee.
    pages cm. — (Anomaly trilogy ; book 3)
  Summary: "Unsure of everything around her, including her own identity, Thalli, who can experience emotions, doesn't know where to turn. She knows she needs the Designer, but he seems further away than ever. What she does know, though, is that if she doesn't do something to stop Dr. Loudin, the fragile world aboveground will be lost once and for all"— Provided by publisher.
  ISBN 978-1-4016-8876-9 (trade paper)
  [1. Emotions—Fiction. 2. Identity—Fiction. 3. Love—Fiction. 4. Revolutionaries—Fiction. 5. Christian life—Fiction. 6. Science fiction.] I. Title.
  PZ7.M4784628Re 2014
  [Fic]—dc23   2014002837

Printed in the United States of America

14 15 16 17 18 19 RRD 6 5 4 3 2 1

For my dad, Russell—thank you for adopting me
into the amazing Abney family.
I love you!

CHAPTER 1

My head is pounding. Images and thoughts fly into my brain, but I cannot catch them, cannot make sense of them because my head hurts so badly. It feels like hundreds of needles are being shoved into my brain. In and out. In and out. I moan and find that my throat is dry. The sound barely passes through. It sounds more like a bassoon, played with too little air.

Needles. Needles. That image looms in my memory. White space. A needle. Dr. Williams. Loudin.

I gulp in a lungful of oxygen. Pure, filtered oxygen. I force my eyes open, and the pain in my head intensifies, followed by

1

a dull ache in the recesses of my stomach. I am back in the State. In the Scientists' quarters. As my eyes adjust to the white walls, white floors, white bedding, the images floating in my brain begin to make sense. I was in New Hope. The Scientists came, they took Alex and Kristie and me back with them. Berk was yelling at them, demanding they release me or bring him. But they did neither. The door to the massive transport . . . what did they call it? The aircraft. It shut, separating us. Then Dr. Williams plunged a needle in my neck.

How long ago was that? Hours? Days? I see a cup of water on the table beside my bed. The need for hydration overwhelms me, allowing me to forget for a moment the pounding in my skull. I push myself up on my elbows. I force myself to move slowly. The room is spinning even with this slight movement. But I need water.

I fall back on the bed. I cannot get up. I do not even have enough energy to reach the water. I will die of thirst. The pain in my head intensifies, and I squeeze my eyes shut in a futile attempt to lessen that pain.

"You're awake." The voice sounds like it is magnified a hundred times over. I close my eyes tighter, wishing it were my ears I could close. "You need to drink this."

The cup is at my lips, and I open them. The cool water seems to evaporate on my tongue before it can even reach my throat. I try to drink more, but the cup is pulled away.

"Just a few sips at first." He waits an agonizingly long time before returning the cup to my lips. I lean forward to get more of it, and the water spills down my chin, cascading down my neck.

The cup is pulled away, and I feel fingers on my wrist. I

want to go to sleep. To wake up and be in my room back in New Hope, to find that this is all a bad dream. That I'm not in the State, that Dr. Loudin didn't bring us here, leave Berk and Rhen and Carey and all our other friends behind. But the pounding in my brain assures me this is reality. If I go to sleep, I'll just wake up here and start this agonizing process all over again. I ease open my eyes, wait for them to adjust. The blurry patches of white take shape. The man holding my wrist, checking my pulse, is Dr. James Turner.

John's son.

I look into his blue eyes—so like John's—and my heart aches even greater than my head. John is dead. I watched him die, held him as his life slipped away. If I had a father, I would want him to be just like John: kind, faithful, honorable. Everything his son, as one of The Ten, is not. Tears dry in my eyes as disgust takes over. How could this man have disregarded everything his father taught him? To reject the Designer I have come to love? Dr. Turner, as the head Geneticist, is responsible for the generations in the State, those of us created without real parents, created in his laboratory—after many tests failed—to be emotionless, unquestioning beings whose only purpose is to further the work of the State.

I was his mistake. I was born full of emotions, full of questions, full of doubts. An anomaly, I was scheduled for annihilation until Berk saved me, brought me here. Then John found me and taught me I was created by the Designer, loved by the Designer, given a purpose by him.

"You are not worthy of your father." John would not have wanted me to say this, but it is true. Dr. Turner's Adam's apple bobs. His fingers stop moving over his communications pad.

His blue eyes stare into mine. My head hurts too much to analyze the emotions passing over his face.

He does not speak as he turns and leaves the room. The door clicks behind him, the sound intensifying the sensation of needles in my brain. I close my eyes again, exhausted, wanting to escape. I feel myself slipping into unconsciousness, where the first sight I see is Berk.

"Berk." I see him, but I can't reach him. He is on the hill in New Hope. His bright green eyes flash anger and hurt. Jealousy. He stands tall, rigid. His lips are full and firm, his square jaw tight, fists clenched. I try to run to him, but I cannot move.

"Thalli." Alex's voice pulls my eyes from Berk. I turn around, and Alex is there, a breath away. I look up into his face and see so much emotion in his blue eyes. For someone so physically strong, Alex seems weak, helpless. I pull him into my arms and let him cry, the way he cried after his father died.

"It's all right." I reach up to run my hand through his silky blond hair. "I'm here."

"No." Berk is yelling, but he is even farther now. Standing by the pond where John died, Berk's shouts are taken by the wind and blown away. I cannot understand what he is saying.

Alex is crushing me, his arms squeezing air from my lungs. I cannot breathe, cannot think, cannot move. Berk is still yelling. Alex is still crying. I shove myself from his grasp and fall . . . and fall . . . farther, deeper.

I gasp as I awake to the reality of the sterile room, of separation. My head feels better, but my heart is still heavy.

"Alex." He is here. The fog of sleep lifts, and I remember again that Alex and Kristie were on the aircraft with me. Brought back to the State. Why are we here? Dr. Loudin told the people of New

Hope that he would be working with us, that New Hope and Athens and the State would be partners. But that is not true. Dr. Loudin did not work to create this underground State in order to share it with others. He did not push the button to destroy the earth forty years before so the few pockets of survivors could be part of the global leadership he wants to head. No, whatever his plans are, they do not include partnerships with the survivors.

I have to find Alex and Kristie, to escape. We need to get back to New Hope where we can talk with Berk and Carey and Dallas and Rhen. Together we can fight Loudin. Whatever he is planning, we can stop him. We must stop him.

I force my legs over the edge of the sleeping platform and close my eyes against the vertigo that movement brings. I cannot go back to sleep. I have to get up, to find my friends. I have to get out of here.

My legs feel like they will collapse beneath me. How long have I been on this sleeping platform? My muscles feel unused, shriveled up. I will myself to stand, one hand on the mattress so I remain steady. The door seems miles away. Like Berk in my dream, it appears to be moving farther from me. But this is no dream. I will put one foot in front of the other and I will reach the door.

I am grateful for the chair that sits by the wall, between the sleeping platform and the door. I take three unsteady steps to it and fall down, resting, breathing. Then I stand once again and reach the door in four steps. The door handle does not move. I push harder, lean my body against it, but it remains motionless.

Of course I am locked in. I am a prisoner. Abandoned. Alone.

I stumble back to the chair, refusing to lie back down, refusing to go back to sleep.

5

"Good afternoon, Thalli." Dr. Loudin's voice fills the room. I look to the wall screen and see him sitting in his laboratory, a thin-lipped smile on his face. The camera pulls back, and I see my friend beside him.

"Kristie!" I stand, falling toward the wall screen, touching, wishing I could break through it, reach Kristie.

"The medicine was a little stronger than we realized." Loudin's smile stays in place. His eyes look straight into the camera, appearing to bore right into my own eyes. "You have been out for three days."

Three days. "What are you doing? Where is Alex?"

Dr. Loudin is not looking at me anymore. An eyebrow raised, he is facing Kristie. "You see? She is alive and well."

"She is not well." Kristie's voice is tight, strained. She is staring at me with a pained expression. I must look terrible.

"Do not forget our agreement." His smile is gone.

"You said she would not be harmed."

"I said she would not be killed." Loudin looks beyond the camera and holds up one finger.

"No!" Kristie is standing, terror on her face.

"Do what I ask."

"Let her go." Tears well up in her eyes.

Suddenly an electric shock races through my body. I feel like every nerve is on fire. I am screaming, falling to the ground. I curl up and want to pass out, but I do not, and the pain increases. I hear voices, but I cannot make out the words. The pain is too awful.

Then it stops. I can only moan and maintain my position on the floor, feeling the effects of the shock still, fearing more.

"Do what I ask."

Kristie is sobbing, her breath ragged. I am losing consciousness. I feel myself being pulled under. In the moment before I surrender to the darkness, Kristie whispers, "I will."

CHAPTER 2

Sleep. All I want to do is sleep. Waking is horrific. Loudin always appears, Kristie behind him. He doesn't always shock me, but the threat is there. I know Loudin is using me to make Kristie do what he wants—likely repairing the oxygen-filtration system in the State. I should be strong, tell her to resist. What Loudin wants cannot be good, and if Kristie assists him, he will achieve that goal even sooner. Then he will annihilate her. And me.

I know all of this. But the pain is greater than that knowledge so I remain silent. I try to pray—praying I can escape, find Kristie and Alex, stop Loudin, return to the peace and safety of

New Hope. But my prayers seem to hit the ceiling of this pod and bounce right back. My head falls onto the mattress. Where is the Designer? I tried to do what he asked. I believed that truth sets us free, believed that I can walk through the valley of the shadow of death, believed that I can do all things through him. And how has he responded to that belief?

With silence.

So I close my eyes and sleep. Again.

Berk is always there, in my dreams. He is waiting for me, smiling this time. He sits by the pond in New Hope, food on a cloth beside him. A picnic. We had one of those here, in the State, before. Before we escaped and found New Hope. Before I traveled to Athens, met Alex. Before everything changed.

A harsh sound shakes me from my dream. I bolt up in bed. Too fast. My head pounds. I look at the wall screen, but Loudin is not there. It's blank. I release a breath. James Turner walks in the door, moving slowly. Bile rises to my throat. Seeing him reminds me of how he forced his own father to remain locked away down in the bowels of the State for forty years. Unable to actually annihilate John, James forced the old man to live alone, allowed to speak only to those scheduled to be annihilated. John was the best man I have ever known. James, then, is the worst.

"Thalli." His voice is not like John's. John's voice was like a cello—soothing, calming, deep and smooth. James's voice is high, forced, like too much air being blown through a muted trumpet. Other than his eyes, he looks nothing like his father. James is thin. Sickeningly thin, all sharp angles. His cheekbones seem like they could pierce his skin, his nose rises above thin lips, sharp and pointy. The white pants and shirt hang on his frame, sleeves too short, neck too large. "You are awake."

"Astute observation, Dr. Turner." No need to be kind. Not to him. He doesn't deserve it. A tiny pinprick of guilt lights in my stomach, but I ignore it, quench it. This is James Turner. He deserves no mercy.

"I understand how you may feel about me." He moves closer. Wrinkles crinkle around his mouth, bags droop under his eyes. He looks like a sheet of ancient music that has been crumpled and straightened back out.

I sit up straighter. "You are a murderous, heartless tyrant."

"I am." James has neither remorse nor pride in his voice. Just resignation. I do not know how to respond to that.

"Why are you here?" I grab the glass of water at my bedside, sipping slowly so my eyes can remain on James. "More torture?"

"No." He takes another step toward me. I scoot back, pull the bedclothes tighter. "I want to talk about my father."

My throat feels like it will close in on itself. I set down the glass and take a deep breath, forcing my lungs to inhale. He wants to talk about John? After keeping him prisoner for forty years? Leaving him alone to grieve? To live? James's eyes are sad, shoulders slumped. If I did not know what weighed him down, I might feel sorry for him. But it is right for him to feel that way. What he has done—the things I know of, anyway—are disgusting.

"Please." He stays where he is, his head down.

"You had decades to talk to your father." I think of John in his solitary room, on his knees. Praying, very likely, for James. "Seventy years in total. And you squandered them."

James pulls the chair from the side of the room and falls into it, as if the weight of his stick-like body is more than he can bear.

"You had a father, one who loved you so deeply. And yet

you created generations of us with no father. No mother. No feelings."

The look that passes over James's face is puzzling. I see guilt, but something else, something even deeper than that. I do not have time to analyze that look because my anger at what James has done bubbles over, spilling out, and I cannot stop it.

"You discarded what you were given, threw John's love in his face. You abandoned him."

James's Adam's apple bobs in his narrow throat. His eyes glisten. I am glad. He should feel pain for what he has done. But then I think of John, of who he was, what he taught me. He loved his son, and he would be disappointed at the way I am acting. He prayed for this man, longed to see him know truth. Am I now to be the answer to that prayer?

God, you stay silent, then ask this of me? I cannot think of anything I would like to do less than offer grace to James Turner, give truth to one of the men who raised me on lies. But if I refuse, am I any better than him?

"What do you want to know?"

CHAPTER 3

You have about twenty minutes before they discover this door is unlocked." James taps a code on the outside of my room and then turns to walk down the hall.

I release a sigh. Talking about John depleted the little energy I had. My head aches and my body feels as if it weighs three hundred pounds. But I have an open door and twenty minutes. I throw my legs over the side of the sleeping platform and lean my head into my hands to stop the spinning. I drink the last of the water from my glass. I stand. Slowly. I am nauseous, dizzy, weak. But Alex is here somewhere. Kristie is here. I do not know what is being done to them, but I know it is not good. We must reunite and escape. Right now, I am their best hope for that.

I force my legs to move, to walk, willing my unused muscles to wake up. I focus on the door, then the hallway. I look in each room. They have people in them, working. From their appearance, I would guess it is those from Pod B, the generation ahead of ours. If they notice me, they do not acknowledge it. They are focused on communications pads, tapping commands, completing tasks. I pass the final door and am stopped in my tracks. I go back.

The woman in this room looks very much like me. Just older. Though her hair is just above her shoulders and mine hangs halfway down my back, it is the same brownish blond, thick with waves, just like mine. She looks up from her communications pad, and my own eyes look back at me. My heart beats faster. Hers are as wide as I'm sure mine are—blue-green, framed with dark eyelashes.

But, unlike me, there is no curiosity in her eyes. They widened, I realize, not out of surprise, but because she needed to adjust her vision from the up-close interaction with her pad and the faraway interaction with me. She looked up just because movement caught her eye. She returns now to her work.

After months in New Hope and Athens, I have forgotten what people in the State are like, what "normal" is here. Programmed to be without emotions or curiosity, I was an anomaly. This woman behaved exactly the way the Scientists—James Turner—designed her to behave: working in her assigned field in order to maintain productivity in the State.

I walk on. I do not miss being around people who have no feelings. I do, however, miss my field, my job. As the pod Musician, I was able to play an instrument every day. I created music, played music written by others, mastered dozens of instruments. My music aided the others, increased their pro-ductivity, stimulated their brains. I am not sure why I am here now, but it is not as a Musician.

I shake my head to clear these thoughts. Five minutes have passed, and I am doing nothing but looking in windows at people who cannot help me, people who do not know that they need help. I need to find Alex and Kristie. I see the door lead-ing to a staircase. I push away thoughts of Berk and me in this staircase. I cannot be distracted by that now. But the images come anyway—Berk holding me, leading me out to the water reservoirs, me playing my violin for him. I do not know how memories can be painful and beautiful at the same time, but these are.

I reach the top of the stairs and pause. I am breathing too loudly. I have to quiet down before I move into the hall on this floor. I draw in a deep breath. In through my nose, out through my mouth. My heart slows to a normal rhythm. I open the door, allowing only my head through.

No one is in the hallway. These rooms are filled with what I am sure are those from Pod A. The first generation of the State. The Scientists must have moved everyone to their headquarters to conserve oxygen. Before I left, Pod C—my friends, my gen-eration—was annihilated because they were using too much of the precious gas. I swallow hard at the injustice of that. They could have been moved here. Or taken above. They could be at New Hope right now, living, breathing, working. But Loudin did not consider that. Did not allow for that. To him people are expendable. Replaceable.

All the more reason to find a way out of here.

I pass by the next-to-last door and look in, expecting to see yet another member of Pod A hard at work. But I do not see a member of Pod A. I see Alex.

I rush to the door and push the handle. Locked. Of course. But the movement causes Alex to look up. He moves to me so quickly, he almost falls over the tray of food on the floor beside his chair. He tries to open the door. I am sure he recognizes the futility in that attempt, but it is natural. His gaze finds mine and we both stop moving. Fear radiates from those crystal-blue eyes. But there is joy too. And relief.

"Are you all right?"

I can barely hear him through the thick door. I nod.

"Did they let you out?"

I shrug. "Not exactly."

Alex places his hand on the glass. I lift mine to his. "Can you get me out?"

I look around for something that would break the glass, but there is nothing in this sterile hallway. "I can't stay long."

Alex's eyes widen. "Why?"

"They don't know I'm gone."

There are too many questions in Alex's eyes. I cannot even begin to answer them all. "We have to find Kristie and escape."

"How?"

"That's what I'm trying to find out." I pull my hand away, then place it back on the glass once more. "I'll find a way out. I will."

Alex leans his forehead against the glass, closes his eyes. I cannot stop to do the same. I cannot allow errant thoughts and emotions in my mind and heart right now. I have five minutes to return to my room before I am caught. I turn from Alex and walk back down the hallway.

I am too late.

CHAPTER 4

The soft hands of a Monitor grasp mine and pull my arms behind my back.

"How did you escape?" The Monitor's voice is as soft as his hands. Could I overpower him? He is bigger than I am, but that doesn't mean he is stronger.

I lean hard to the left, and he loosens his grip. I fall to my knees, and his hands slip from mine. I crawl as fast as I can, ignoring the burning in my knees. I push myself up onto my feet and run, but he pulls at my ankles, and my chin connects with the floor. Bright-white dots flicker in front of me. I flip myself over onto my back and kick as hard as I can. The Monitor screams. When my vision clears, I see his hands covering his face, blood streaming from his nose. I roll over, push myself back up, and run to the door of the stairs.

Alex!

The Monitor is still covering his face. I rush to him and pull his communications pad from his shirt pocket. I see the image of this hallway in it. I press the Unlock button and hear a click. Alex has been watching from the window. He bolts out of the room the minute he can.

"Bring that thing." He points to the communications pad.

I place it in my pocket and lead Alex to the stairs. We run down, two and three at a time. I ignore the burning in my lungs, in my legs. I think only of Kristie. And freedom. Alex reaches for the door on my floor.

"No!" I pull him away and point downstairs. "They'll be waiting for us there. We need to go down one more floor."

We race down the next flight of stairs.

"Now what?" Alex looks from the door leading to the hall-way to the door leading outside.

I pause. "I don't know."

Alex looks through the glass into the hallway. "No one is there. We have a little time."

"No." I cannot get enough oxygen into my lungs. "They already know I am gone. They'll send more Monitors."

"Good decisions are never made in haste." Alex's royal upbringing is speaking now. I should listen, should slow down, but everything in me is screaming to run as fast and as far as we can. "Tell me the advantages of going into this hallway."

Alex's eyes are willing me to breathe, to think. He opens his arms, and I fall into them. "We could find Kristie. We could get supplies."

"All right." Alex's mouth is at my ear, his breath warming me. He rubs my back and I can breathe again. "And the disadvantages?"

I close my eyes. "It would be easier for the Monitors to find us and for Loudin to track us."

"And the other door?"

"It leads to the pods. But those are empty."

"That's good, then, right?" Alex pulls away, his hands on my shoulders. "It would give us time to think."

"I don't know if there is enough oxygen in them." I think of all the people from Pods A and B in these quarters.

I close my eyes again. *God, where are you? Tell me what to do!* Nothing.

"There are more places to hide out there." I point to the door leading outside. We can go near the reservoirs, where there are no cameras.

"All right, then." Alex squeezes my shoulders.

"We have to get Kristie out."

"Of course." Alex walks toward the door. "But we need time to strategize. We can't just run in. They'll overpower us."

I follow him out the door, half sure a Monitor or even Loudin himself will be waiting for us. But no one is there. "This is too easy." I look around.

"What do you mean?"

"There are cameras everywhere. Loudin always knows what happens. He even knew how to find us in New Hope. I cannot believe he is just letting us walk out."

"But you said this was the best place to go."

"I know. It is." Something does not feel right. But going back inside does not feel right either. "I don't know."

"Don't second-guess yourself, Thalli." Alex takes my hand. "Let's just keep going until we can't go anymore. All right?"

I look around, trying to remember the layout of the State, determining where we are. I see Pod A in the distance, to the west. The water reservoirs are east. "That way."

We walk in silence for several minutes, both of us alert, prepared to run or fight if our escape is discovered. *When* our escape is discovered.

"Did they hurt you?" Alex asks the question so quietly I can barely hear him.

The electric shocks . . . my body goes rigid with the memory. I shake it off. Alex does not need to know about that. He does not need to worry about me. We have to plan our escape. "They kept me locked in a room, and I do not want to be locked away ever again."

Alex sighs. "But they didn't hurt you?"

"No." I hate lying to Alex, but the alternative would be too painful. For both of us. "What about you?"

"They haven't hurt me." Alex walks faster. "They just keep testing me. They take my blood, put me in their strange box . . ."

"With images on it?"

"Yes." Alex nods, his blond hair hanging in a wavy strand down his face. "I'm on a boat, then in a city."

"Attacked by a ship."

"They put you in it too?"

I recall that testing before the escape. When Berk was there, trying to help me. "A long time ago."

"What are they trying to see?"

I shrug. "Loudin's expertise is in neurology. He is checking your brain to see how it functions. He's probably looking to understand the difference between your brain and ours, to see the effects of living above versus being State born."

Alex stops and looks at me, his hand on my face. "We're not very different, are we?"

There is more to that question than I can answer. And I do not have time to formulate a diversion because Alex is thrown to the ground. Four Monitors have surrounded us. I did not see them coming, did not hear them. It is like they appeared out of the ground. One is on top of Alex, pulling his arms behind with such force I am sure his shoulder will be dislocated.

"Stop."

Another Monitor pulls Alex up by his hair. I lunge at the man, but two of the Monitors stop me, one holding each arm.

"You just don't ever learn, do you?" Dr. Loudin walks between Alex and me. "You cannot run from me, Thalli."

I stare at him, hating the smile on his face, the confidence in his voice.

"You think you can save your friends? Save the world?" Loudin lets out a maniacal laugh. "I made you, Thalli. And I can unmake you. You would do well to learn that."

His green eyes narrow, then soften. I cannot read them, cannot figure out what is happening in his mind. But I will not give in to him. I will not let him win.

"Never."

CHAPTER 5

Alex is dragged away from me, back to the Scientists' quarters. Loudin is gone. I don't know where. I did not see him leave. I have so many questions for him. But he, of course, will not answer them. I am beneath him.

The Monitors are taking me to Pod C. I no longer have the energy to fight them. I am spent—physically and emotionally. I will fight again. I will escape again. I will find Alex and Kristie and return to New Hope. But I cannot do any of that now. Now I simply allow myself to be led back to my old home.

As we approach the pod, I am overwhelmed with memories. Berk and I scratching our names on the floor beneath the sofa. Rhen correcting me when I questioned too much. Meals together as a pod. We were not close—not in the way I have learned to be close to people above. But we were a family. We lived, ate, learned, and worked together. I grew up with those in this Pod. And now only Berk, Rhen, and I remain. The others were senselessly murdered by Dr. Loudin because they were consuming too much oxygen.

Anger animates me, and I fight against the Monitors again. The one on my left tightens his grip but he doesn't waver. The one on my right barely registers my fight at all. Neither looks at me or speaks to me. I am a prisoner, an anomaly that is unworthy of humane treatment.

The door to my pod opens and I am shoved inside, the door locked behind me. The furniture is gone. But unlike the last time I was here, there is no medical equipment either. Nothing. Just an empty space. I remember John speaking of Jesus' followers looking for him in the tomb and finding it empty. This reminds me of that. An empty tomb. But there is no angel here to tell me that there is hope. Just a hollow shell of the life I once had. Walls that hold memories, reminders of people I will never see again.

Why will the Designer not speak to me? Send someone to me? Why has he left me alone when I need him? Tears burn my eyes, my throat constricts, but I press on.

Every room is empty. All that remains is a sleeping platform in my cube. Loudin planned on bringing me here. I find three changes of clothes in the closet. I look over where Rhen's sleeping platform used to be, her closet. I miss her so much my heart aches. What is she doing in New Hope? Is she safe? Happy?

In those last days there, she was changing. Something

happened between her and Dallas, Kristie and Carey's grandson. She has feelings for him. I am sure of it. Rhen has feelings! The thought alone brings a smile to my face. Being around the people in the village, seeing the families and their way of life, seemed to release something in her, something beautiful and different. I want to know what that is, how it happened. I want to sit with her and hear about Dallas. He is so different from her, so different from any of us. He is relaxed, laughs all the time, jokes even in very difficult situations. Fun. That is the word Kristie used to describe Dallas. He is fun to be around. I have never known anyone like that. I cannot imagine anyone more perfect for Rhen than him. She needs fun. Deserves it.

My heart is lighter, and I stand to search more of my old pod. The memories become less painful. They almost feel healing. This was my home, my beginning. It was not perfect, but it is and always will be part of me. I stand at the door to the isolation chamber. I open the door and memories of my escape from there, of my first reunion with Berk outside after Dr. Spires died, fill my mind.

"Oh." My heart feels like it stops. There, on the chair in the corner, is my violin. *My* violin. I do not care what motives Loudin has for bringing it here, what recording equipment is watching me. I walk over and lift the instrument gently, the way I saw a mother in Athens lift her infant. I want to hold it to me. This is like a part of me that was missing and now is back. I am not completely whole. But with this in my arms, I am healing.

I place the violin under my chin and glide the bow over the strings, slowly at first, not really playing anything. I just want to hear the sound, to feel it. I close my eyes and find I have a melody, deep within, I have already composed, waiting to be played. So I play it. It is haunting at parts, discordant, cacophonous. But then it changes keys, changes tempo, becomes light, staccato. And then it changes again, an uncertain tune that stops and starts.

My fingers fly over the neck of the violin as note blends into note, my bow connects them, unites them, covers each string, over and back again. I realize that with all the changes in the song, the melody has remained the same. It may have been obscured, it may have been distant. But it is there. It has always been there.

CHAPTER 6

Thalli." The voice is vaguely familiar, though distant. I am too tired to discern whose it is. "Thalli, you need to wake up. Please."

The desperation in the voice forces my eyes open.

Kristie.

She is placing a circular object over my nose. The air coming from it is sweet, sickening. I reach to pull it off, but Kristie's hand pushes mine away. "There is very little oxygen here."

The object moves, conforming to my nose, and I am less aware of the air it is producing. As my eyes adjust, I notice Kristie is wearing one of these masks as well.

"You made these."

Kristie nods and helps me sit up. She places a small plastic square over my heart, and the wall screen lights up. My vital signs are all there.

"Am I all right?"

Kristie taps on the communications pad clumsily. "Where is the button for . . . ?"

I take the pad from her. "What do you need to know?"

"Everything." With a sigh, Kristie rubs her face with her hands. When she pulls them down, she looks at me, really looks at me. From top to bottom, in a way I have never been looked at before. "Are you sure you're all right?"

"I think so." I ease to my feet, my head pounding with the movement. "My head hurts."

"That is likely from the lack of oxygen." Kristie walks to the door and holds it open for me. "That should improve soon. Have you eaten lately? Had anything to drink?"

I follow her, but a million questions fight for precedence. "Why are you here?"

Kristie stops and turns around. She takes a deep breath, her brown eyes fastened on mine. "I am in Pod C to help keep you alive."

"Why was I brought here if there isn't enough oxygen for me?"

Kristie pushes me into a seat in the dining area and fills a glass with water. In the silence, I hear the answers she does not want to give.

"Loudin is using me to make you do what he wants."

Kristie places the drink in my hand, her fingers lingering on mine. "Yes."

"The electric currents in my room at the Scientists' quarters—he made you watch that to force you to complete his project."

Tears glisten in Kristie's dark eyes. She seems to have aged ten years in the days we have been here. I know she is older—Loudin's age—but in New Hope, she was so happy, her face so full of light, she appeared much younger. Now lines crease around her eyes, her mouth. Her cheeks seem to hang. She's lost weight since she has been here. The light has disappeared from her face.

"Whatever he is asking you to do, don't do it." My fist hits the table and water spills from my glass. "It isn't worth it. I would rather die than know I helped Loudin accomplish whatever it is he is trying to accomplish."

"You don't understand." Kristie's voice breaks.

"Then make me understand."

Kristie reaches over and strokes my hair. I saw her do the same thing to little Nicole, her granddaughter. She sees her children in me and doesn't want me hurt. But she cannot think like a grandmother right now. I need her to think like a Scientist.

"You have been away from Dr. Loudin over thirty years." I push away from the table, out of her reach. "As bad as he was when you knew him, he is worse now. He has had all these years to develop new ideas, to see his original plans come to fruition. I thought he meant well. And maybe in his warped mind, he does. But what he does is wrong. People should be free—like they are in New Hope. They are slaves down here. If you fix the oxygen problem, he will just make more slaves. You cannot help him."

Kristie wipes a tear from her cheek. "If it were only that simple."

"What are you not telling me?"

Kristie looks around the room. I could tell her there are cameras here—but I don't. The air is thick with tension. There is something she is not telling me, and I hate being unaware of what is going on.

"Where did they take Alex?" Perhaps changing the subject will encourage her to share more freely.

"I don't know." Kristie runs a hand through her close-cropped brown curls. "The Scientists' quarters, I suppose."

"Why did Dr. Loudin really bring Alex? I know why he brought you—to fix the oxygen. I suppose he brought me to punish me for leaving. But Alex? Why him?"

"I cannot say any more."

"Of course you can!" I am standing now.

Kristie stands and walks with me to the living area, now set up as a medical cube once again. "Please. I need to check your vitals, make sure you're all right."

"All right?" I pull away from her. "I am not all right. I won't be all right until you tell me what is happening."

"I cannot say more." Kristie repeats this slowly, looking around.

I walk right up to the wall screen. "I do not care. Do you hear that, Loudin? Do what you want to me. I would rather die than let you continue to rule down here. I have seen what life should be like, I have tasted freedom. And everyone deserves it."

"Thalli, please." Pain laces Kristie's every word. "You don't mean that."

"Of course I do." I face Kristie. "And so should you. What does Loudin have on you that makes you so afraid?"

"Don't answer that." I hear Loudin's voice before I see him.

The wall screen is alive, and his hideous face covers it. "Kristie, I believe your work here is complete for today. There is a transport outside waiting to return you to the Scientists' quarters."

Kristie nods and strides to the door.

"What are you doing?" I am right behind her, my hand on her shoulder, and turn her around. "Why are you obeying him?"

Kristie shakes her head, tears filling her eyes, then she turns and walks out the door.

I am momentarily stunned, feet frozen to the ground. When I finally make my way to the door, I find it is locked. I am, once again, alone in Pod C with no answers and no escape.

CHAPTER 7

Time for recreation." A Monitor stands at the door, motioning me out to the field.

After hours left alone in the pod, screaming for someone to talk to me, tell me what is going on, why I am isolated out here, this Monitor comes and behaves as if this is just another afternoon of recreation. That it is normal. But even she knows it is not normal. She has been living in the Scientists' quarters, not in Pod B, and she had no one to monitor because all of us from Pod C are either dead or escaped. She, of course, does not think about that. Does not question why she has been called to this pod after so long away. She simply completes the task she was given without question.

How could I have ever believed that was right? How could I have berated myself for not being more like that? I slip on recreation shoes—slower than necessary—and follow the Monitor out the door. I touch my nose. Kristie's invention is still there, allowing me to breathe normally. I decide to run hard and fast. I haven't pushed my body since I have been here. I was so active in New Hope and in Athens. We walked there much more than we do here. I rode horses. Of course, I also ran down stairs and through hallways and was chased by those who wanted to capture and kill me. I cannot allow myself to think all was ideal there. But it was far better than here. Freedom—even with its problems—is superior to the confines of life here in the State.

The Monitor stands at attention as I reach the track. I step on it and run slowly at first, then faster. If life were still as it were, I would have to run seventeen laps. One for each year I have been alive. Almost eighteen, as the year is close to ending. All of us in Pod C turn a year older when the calendar says a new year has begun.

I turn the corner on the tenth lap, and I see James Turner in the distance. I pick up speed. I do not want to speak to him. But I know he is coming for me. No one else is here. No one but the Monitor. And as I turn the corner on the eleventh lap, I see him stand beside her, point to the Scientists' quarters in the distance. She looks at me, then at James, and then she walks off. James stands in the spot she vacated. Watching me. His shoulders are slumped, poking out of his thin shirt and pointing at me like weapons. I keep running. I have six more laps to go, after all.

James walks toward the track as I slow down. "Will you walk with me to the greenhouse?"

It sounds more like a command than a request, and I bristle. My muscles are begging to be used more. I have missed the exhilaration of pushing my body. I enjoyed the last few laps when my mind could not focus on anything but running, all other thoughts gone.

"Please." James looks at me with those eyes, so like John's, and I acquiesce. We walk in silence to the greenhouse. He opens the door and allows me to enter ahead of him. Then he closes the door behind him. "I need your help, Thalli."

"You need *my* help?" I turn to face the older man. He is playing with the leaves on a bush at his side. The leaves are yellowed. Most of the plants in here are dead or dying. With no Pod C to feed, this greenhouse need no longer exist.

"I have been thinking about what you said about my father." He lifts his head and stares at a spot on the ceiling. "How he died . . . how happy he was. I allowed myself to forget who my father was. I needed to believe he was deluded and sick."

I take a step forward, wanting to hit him. But James is so frail, I am sure I would knock him down with just a touch. I do not know if John can see me, if there is a window from heaven to earth for those who have gone on. But if there is, I do not want him to see me mistreat his only son.

"He was neither delusional nor sick." I stare at James until he looks down at me. "John Turner was the best man I have ever known."

"Making me the worst." It wasn't a question. James closes his eyes and takes a deep breath. "I know that now. I am sorry I did not see that before. I can't tell you how sorry I am. It took almost dying to see what my life has become."

"Almost dying?" Is he trying to make me feel sympathy for him?

"Oxygen deprivation." His gaze flickers to Pod C. "My organs began shutting down. I barely made it . . ."

Waving my hand, I motion for James to stop talking. I don't want to hear any more. He is alive. His father is not. Pod C is not. They died so that men like James would have enough oxygen. He was saved because they died. And if Loudin gets his way, others will likely die as well. "So stop Loudin. Refuse to do whatever it is he has asked of you."

"It isn't that easy."

"I am tired of hearing that." I fold my arms tightly against my chest. "It is an excuse. Because you are afraid."

"I am no longer the only Geneticist. I may have the most knowledge, but there are others who would continue my work should I be unable to. It would take them longer, but they could do it. Eventually. My stopping won't solve the problem. It will only delay it."

"What is the problem then?"

James leans against the counter and sighs. "Loudin wants me to create another generation. That was always the plan. Every fifteen years, a new generation. He is moving the date up slightly, since Pod C was . . ."

"Murdered?" I want him to hear the word. Feel the truth of it.

"Yes. They were murdered." James twists a yellowed leaf from its bush. "The oxygen levels in the State have been compromised. Kristie is fixing that. Finally. We will be able to move the new generation into Pod C when their gestation period is complete."

"So you are going to create more people who will blindly follow Loudin?" I think of what Kristie said, how it took many attempts to perfect the State born, how babies were discarded, "mistakes" were righted. And James Turner was responsible for all of that. The thought sickens me.

"I can't." James seems to fall in on himself, his face crumbling. "It took forty years, but I see now that Loudin is wrong. That he has to be stopped. His plans go far beyond this State. He wants . . ."

"What?"

"Now that he knows there are survivors and he can locate them, he wants to rule them too. He isn't content to be in charge of the State only. He is looking toward his legacy. He had been confident we were all there were. When he discovered there were others . . . he set all this in motion."

"All what?"

"Everything."

My stomach feels like brass. "What do you mean, everything?"

James looks right into my eyes. "I mean, everything. You, Berk, Rhen, my father. He planned your escape. You played right into his hands. He watched you in Texas. He saw you were going to the other village. He waited for the right time to return for you."

The room begins to spin, and I lean both hands against the counter to steady myself. Loudin planned our escape? How is that possible? He watched us? Knew where we were? I thought God orchestrated that, that he allowed us to go. But it wasn't God. It was Loudin. Loudin the all-seeing, all-powerful? I don't know who I am more angry at—Loudin for doing this or God for allowing it.

"How do I know you aren't another part of Loudin's plan?" I narrow my eyes at James. "You could just be acting like you're sorry, pretending to want to help. Loudin knows how much I loved your father. He knows I'd be sympathetic toward you if you had a change of heart."

"I am asking you to help stop him." He straightens.

"Why are you asking me? Why not do it yourself?"

"Because, Thalli, he has a weak spot for you."

"Of course he does." I laugh at the ridiculousness of that statement. "That's why he tried to kill me, why he has me kept prisoner here."

"It is why he knew you would escape the annihilation chamber, why he watched with pride as you went to that other village—"

"Athens." I want him to know they are people. Real people. "And the other village is New Hope. The village where your father died. New Hope."

"All right." James swallows hard before continuing. "He saw you in Athens. He was delighted that you wanted to save the others—the people from New Hope. He did not intend for you to be an anomaly, but the fact that you were was another source of pride. Your intellect and courage were far beyond what they were designed to be."

"Why would he be proud of that?" I think of Loudin, so calculating, so rigid. Why would he enjoy seeing his plans not fulfilled?

"Because"—James takes a step closer—"Dr. Loudin is your father."

CHAPTER 8

What?" I am screaming, but my voice seems to come from somewhere else. I feel like I am somewhere else. A dream, maybe. Not reality. This cannot be reality. "I don't have a father."

"Everyone has a father." James sounds like a Monitor now. "All citizens of the State were created from the basic ingredients of life, stored here in the State from before the War . . ."

I cover my face with my hands, and he stops. I took biology. I know how children are created. I do not need a lecture on that. "I had a donor, but not a father."

"Dr. Loudin was your donor. He insisted that each generation have one of his children. You were his from Pod C."

I think of the woman I saw from Pod B, the one with my hair and eyes. My sister? The thought is beautiful and horrifying at the same time. As much as I long for family, especially after seeing the families in New Hope, I never, ever wanted to be related to Joseph Loudin.

"He takes pride in your unique qualities because he sees that his genes are stronger than my science."

His genes. Dr. Loudin's DNA is mine. His blood runs through my veins. I am like him? No. No, I refuse to accept that. I refuse to accept his pride. Now I wish I had been like everyone else, just to spite him, just to show him he is no one, nothing. My very existence has made him believe he is as great as he thinks he is. I have given him the confidence to look beyond the State to the world, to believe he can conquer all of it.

"You can use your relationship to him to your advantage." James sounds miles away, though he stands just feet in front of me.

"So I should manipulate him the way he manipulated me?" I move toward the door, wanting to run again, to forget what I just heard, go back in time so I would not ever have to know it.

"Thalli, you're the only one with that much power over him."

I push past James, open the greenhouse door.

"Wait, Thalli. There's more."

I run now. I don't want to know more. I wish I didn't know this. I run past the track, past Pods B and A, past the Scientists' quarters. If Loudin sees me, he isn't sending anyone after me. Did he hear that conversation? Did he orchestrate it? Maybe it isn't true. Maybe James is working for Loudin and he just wants me to believe this. Maybe he thinks I'll be more willing to listen to him now, to work with him.

I stop running because I have reached the end of the State. The massive water reservoirs remind me of time spent with Berk. When I thought being an anomaly was the worst thing that could happen to me. When I thought the whole world was confined to this State. I lean against the cool concrete and slide down, spent. Tears I was holding back burst out and I cannot stop them.

Why is this happening? Why is the Designer allowing it? Why give me a glimpse of him with my violin, a moment of peace, then strip it away, leaving me more hurt and alone than before, more confused? John said I can do all things through Christ who strengthens me. But this is too much. I cannot do this. I want to stay here. I want to fall asleep and never wake up. To go to heaven where there is no pain. No ugly truths. No confusion. I lean my head on my knees and drift to sleep.

I am shaken awake by a bony hand. Two blue eyes swim into my line of sight. James. Why can't he leave me alone? Why can't everyone just leave me alone?

"Thalli." James sits beside me, and I hear popping and cracking as he does so. "You need to know everything."

I put my head back down. "No, I don't."

James is quiet for a long time. Too long. I look up and find his gaze on me. "You weren't born the same way the people above were born. The way I was born. But you are a product of love."

Love? And Loudin? Those two words seem to be the exact opposite of each other.

"Joseph has always been driven." James looks out toward the pods. "Even when we were in college. He had to make the best grades, to be valedictorian. He had to get published first and most. We were all in awe of him. Myself included. He seemed so sure of himself. We knew he'd do great things. The rest of just followed his lead, happy to be around him. When the president chose him to head up what would be the State . . . Wow. He wasn't even thirty, and he had the most important job in the country. He was on the phone with the president daily. He got whatever he wanted, whenever he wanted it."

I want to stop listening, but I cannot help myself. I never thought about who Loudin was, how he became that man. I just know what he is. I won't allow myself to feel for him. But if he is my father—even the thought makes me ill—but if he is, I need to know this, to understand him. I do not want to make the same mistakes he did. I refuse to become like him.

"But what he wanted more than anything wasn't the State. It was a girl." James laughs softly. "Not even the great Joseph Loudin was beyond the sting of cupid's arrow."

Is he speaking of my mother? My mother. I have never in my life put those two words together. It is like another language.

"For a while it looked like he would get her. We weren't surprised. He always gets what he wants. But then he lost her."

"In the War?"

James raises his eyebrows. "No, Thalli. She survived the War."

"Like your father did? Was she here visiting him?"

"No."

"Then . . . ?"

"She was a Scientist." James waits for understanding to dawn on my face.

"Kristie?" I can barely say the name. "My mother is Kristie?"

James releases a long breath. "Yes."

CHAPTER 9

Relief and fear battle for my heart. Kristie is my mother. Loudin is my father.

"Kristie chose Carey," James continues. I try to still my mind so I can hear him. "Loudin was heartbroken. As heartbroken as he can be, anyway."

"What happened?"

"It was just a couple years after the War." James looks up, remembering. "When things started to slow down. For him. The rest of us took time off from the beginning. We had to. But Loudin can work for months on end without stopping. We couldn't. We'd have poker nights and movie nights, anything to clear our minds of all that was happening. Rebuilding a world was painstaking work. Exhausting. And we lived in constant fear that our safeguards would be compromised."

I want to sympathize, but I know they were not victims of the War. "But Loudin planned the War."

James takes in a loud breath. "How do you know?"

"Kristie."

"I didn't know." James shakes his head. "I swear I didn't. Neither did Kristie or Carey."

"I know." I bite my lip. "Your dad knew that too. He knew you weren't like Loudin."

James looks away and clears his throat. A minute goes by before he speaks again. "That's what ended it for Kristie. She was so angry with Joseph. He knew she would be. That's why he tried to keep it secret. But when she found out . . . I thought she would kill him. Carey held her back, calmed her down."

"I wish she had killed him." I feel a little guilty as soon as I say that. But I don't take it back.

"He meant well. Means well. He really thinks this is what is best for humanity."

"He is arrogant and homicidal." My voice echoes off the concrete. "Who cares that he means well?"

James laughs. "You sound just like Kristie."

Kristie's voice, like mine? The thought is so foreign but comforting somehow. "Was that when she left?"

"Yes, five of the Scientists left the State." James rubs his eyes. "Loudin was beside himself for weeks. Angry, hurt, scared. At that time he had no way to track them. We didn't know if they lived or died."

"So he made babies to get over her?" Loudin—whose idea it was to remove emotions—was completely controlled by his?

"I made the babies." James places his hands flat on the ground beside him. "I was the Geneticist . . . *am* the Geneticist. He came to me privately, asked that each generation have a product of Kristie and him. I thought it was just romantic. And I guess, at first, that's what it was."

"Something changed?"

"He looked in on the first child often." James shakes his head. "Until he saw he was functioning just like all the others, doing his job and nothing more. He did the same with the second generation."

"That one is a woman, isn't she?"

"Yes." James turns his blue eyes on me. "You've seen her?"

"Yes." The confirmation takes my breath away. A brother and a sister. A mother and a father. The words seem to float around me, circle me—caressing and choking me at the same time. *Brother . . . sister . . . mother . . . father.* My throat constricts and tears burn my eyes. *Brother, sister, mother, father.*

"She functioned normally as well."

"So I was the first anomaly."

"The first that came directly from Loudin, yes."

"There have been others?" People like me? Those who think and feel? Who spent their lives feeling like they don't belong?

"Those like Berk, who were chosen to be Scientists. I do not remove any potential cognitive or emotional functions from them."

"But you removed mine?"

"I treated your embryo the same as all the others, yes." James looks away. "Loudin insisted."

"And he watched me?" The thought is repulsive.

James sighs. "He was thrilled the first time he got the report that you were exhibiting unusual behavior."

"When was that?"

"You were barely walking. But you'd go the opposite direction from everyone else. The Monitors didn't know what to do."

"What happened?"

"Loudin observed you and blamed the Monitors for your behavior. He told them not to report anything again until you were past the preschool years."

"And then?"

"They reported your behavior then—you didn't complete assignments as directed and you argued with your music Tutors. He said the same thing. Wait until you were ten, then fifteen."

"But when I broke down in the performance pod . . . ?"

"At that point he had discovered the pockets of survivors and was planning to send emissaries to them. He determined that you would be the best person to send. You hid your differences for seventeen years, demonstrating an advanced intellect and adaptability. And you were his. Like I said, he is proud of you."

"He isn't proud of *me*." I think of this man who destroyed the world and killed people at his whims. "He is proud of his DNA in me."

"You're probably right."

"I am definitely right."

"But whatever reason, Loudin has a weakness for you that he doesn't have for anyone else." James stands, his bones cracking with each movement. "You can use that power to help your friends in New Hope, Thalli."

I don't say anything. I have too much to process. James seems to recognize that because he walks away, leaving me sitting at the edge of my world.

CHAPTER 10

I cannot stay here. I have to move. I have to do something.

I need to find Kristie and Alex. We have to get out of here. I do not care what James says, I don't want to work with Loudin. I don't want to be anywhere near him. I want out of the State, away from these memories. I want to go back to New Hope with Berk and Rhen, back to the little church and the horses and the orange trees.

I cannot just walk into the Scientists' quarters and grab Kristie and Alex. I don't even know where they are. And as soon as I leave this area, the cameras will pick me up.

I stand and walk around the water reservoirs. I recall being here before and seeing a button somewhere. An alert button. It was installed because there are no cameras here, before the communications pads were perfected. If I find it and press it, maybe I could divert the Monitors long enough to sneak into the Scientists' quarters.

There! It is high. Too high. Even with my arm stretched as far as possible, it's too far. I look around. There is nothing here to stand on. I jump, touch it, but I still cannot press it. I need a running start. I'll go back, race toward the wall, and then throw myself into it. The potential result outweighs the potential pain. I take several steps backward, then push my legs as hard as they can go. One step before I reach the wall, I leap.

A siren screams out my victory.

I ignore the pain in my knees, the blood flowing from where they struck the reservoir. I race to the Scientists' quarters. The doors open and Monitors pour out. I press myself against the side of the building. Monitors do not even look in my direction. They are running out to the reservoirs. Afraid, likely, there is a leak or some other catastrophe. Dr. Williams is out too, moving slower than the Monitors, strands of her gray hair coming out of the normally perfectly contained bun at her nape. She is typing on her communications pad, calling out instructions.

I remain plastered against the wall until the Monitors are out of sight, then I race to the door. In their haste, it has not been closed all the way. I breathe a quick prayer and sneak in as quietly as possible, then open the door from the stairwell to the hallway. Empty. But I still don't know where, exactly, to go. Alex is likely above, Kristie below.

I take the stairs down. It is riskier, going to where the Scientists' laboratories are. But Kristie will know better how to escape. My knees are aching and my lungs burning, but I keep going, until there are no more stairs. This hallway is empty as well, but full of noise. Muffled voices, mechanical beeps. The soft whir of machinery.

I will be a target if I simply walk out. My clothes alone will give me away. My once-white shirt and pants are wet with sweat, brown with dirt, red with splotches of blood that has leaked through the knees. I freeze as a female Assistant comes out one of the doors. An Assistant with a spotless uniform and a communications pad that opens every door.

I go back into the staircase, searching, hoping the Designer will forgive me for what I am about to do. I have no other choice. Nothing. I find nothing in here I can use, so I pull my shirt off and wait at the door. The Assistant walks by. I open the door, then shove it into her, knocking her off balance.

In the instant she reaches for her communications pad, I throw my arm around her neck and pull her into the stairwell. She is stunned. Nowhere in their training is instruction on how to respond when attacked. I use this to my advantage. Recalling the way the soldiers in Athens captured me, I pull her hands behind her back and use my shirt to tie her hands together. But I need her clothes.

Ugh.

I need her to be unconscious. Otherwise she will start fighting back instead of just staring at me, dumbfounded. I am crying as I force her down to the ground.

"I'm sorry. I'm sorry." Apologizing while trying to knock someone unconscious is ridiculous, but I cannot help myself.

When her eyes roll back in her head, I stand, watching her chest to make sure she is not dead. There. I see it. Slight, but there is movement, a rise and a fall. I turn her over, removing the restraints and taking her clothes.

I try to push away thoughts that this is terrible. That this is something Loudin would do. But what choice do I have?

I pull my hair back into a ponytail, use my old shirt to wipe my face and hands as clean as I can make them. Should I restrain the Assistant? I look at her, half naked, pale. I cannot do it. I can only pray she is out long enough for me to find Kristie and Alex and plan our escape.

Keeping my head down and my eyes on the communications pad, I open the door. My face stares back at me. A warning appears below my image along with a command to find and return me to the Scientists' quarters. I can only hope they assume I am too intelligent to be in the very place where they want me.

A Monitor comes out of a door halfway down the hall. I keep my head down, tapping on the pad as if I am engaged in a conversation. The Monitor passes me without a glance, hurrying to the elevator where he is, no doubt, going to try to find the girl whose face is on his communications pad.

I try to be as nonchalant as possible as I look in each window, left and right, down the impossibly long hallway. My heart leaps into my throat when I see Dr. Loudin in one of the windows. He is turned to the side, eyes on a screen. I start to move on, but a blur of blond hair stops me.

Alex.

Alex is behind Loudin. He is looking at the screen also, his arms folded. He is shaking his head and saying something—loudly—I cannot understand.

I need to get his attention without alerting Loudin. I look at my communications pad, at my face, surrounded by glowing red lines. A button below the image reads *Target located.*

I press the button, type in *Pod C greenhouse.* A loud beep comes from the screen in front of Loudin.

I rush to the next room. No one is here. I step in and look through the window. Loudin leaves the laboratory and walks toward the elevator. Alex is not with him.

I wait until the elevator door closes and then I make my way to Alex. He is not alone. Loudin has left a Monitor there to guard him. I take a deep breath, then open the door with authority.

"Dr. Loudin asked me to take the subject to Pod C." I pray the Monitor does not look up. He does not. But he does tap on his communications pad.

"I have not received that instruction."

Alex has seen me now, and he is moving toward me. He is far more familiar with strategy than I, so I try to communicate with my eyes that he needs to figure out a way for us to get out of here.

Alex stumbles—right into the Monitor, and the man's communications pad flies across the room. As the Monitor stands, Alex punches him hard in the face and he crumbles to the ground. I wince at the sight.

"Come on." Alex grabs my arms and propels me from the room.

"Kristie," I whisper. "We need to find her."

"Loudin sent her aboveground for the day to do some testing."

"Perfect." I race toward the stairwell.

"No." Alex pulls me back. "We don't have the equipment we'd need to escape. We go up there and we die."

I groan. I hadn't thought of that. The last time I escaped from here I was unconscious. Berk and Rhen did all the planning. I just went to sleep in the annihilation chamber and woke up outside.

I look into the room at the far end of the hall. An empty laboratory. I use my communications pad to open the door. It smells stale. Dust covers the surfaces. We walk farther in and see a small office. Dr. Spires's office.

"We should be safe in here." I close the door to the office and sit below the window. If anyone were to look in, all they would see is an abandoned room. "This belonged to a Scientist who died several months ago."

Alex sits beside me, his side pressed against mine, providing a warmth I wasn't aware I needed. "He's out of control."

"I know."

"You know?" Alex's sky-blue eyes fasten on mine.

"What do *you* know?"

"Loudin has an entire world-domination plan," Alex says. "He wants to go to every surviving village, gain their trust, connect the State to them."

"He told you this?"

"He wants to use me because I studied linguistics and can be a translator."

"For what purpose?"

Alex shrugs. "Not much different from my father's."

The word *father* makes me physically ill. I swallow back the bile that threatens to spill out all over Dr. Spires's dusty floor.

"What is it?"

"I don't have time to tell you now." I look away from Alex. "We just need to get Kristie and get out."

"He'll come back for us, Thalli." Alex places a hand on my knee. "We can't just run away. We have to stop him."

"Stop Dr. Loudin?" We can barely hide from him. How could we stop him?

Alex moves his hand from my knee to my shoulder, then pulls me toward him. I lean against him, so his face is inches away from my face. He caresses my cheek. "Oh, Thalli, I've missed you so much."

I close my eyes. I cannot discuss that right now. I cannot even process it. My brain is saturated with information—about Kristie, Loudin, James. "Alex, we have to do something. Help me."

"I'm sorry." He pulls his hand away. "You're right. Of course."

"Whatever Loudin is planning when he goes to the villages can't be good. Those people are like you. He calls them 'primitive.' There is no way he is all right with them continuing on the same way they've lived."

"You think he'll try to drug them?"

I think of Athens, how King Jason kept the people submissive through airborne pharmaceuticals. "Has Loudin asked you about Athens's drugs?"

"No." Alex runs his hand through his hair. "Not yet. He's been too focused on the 'meetings.'"

"What does he want you to say to them?"

"He hasn't told me." Alex stands and paces. "For a while I was just being tested on by those guys in all white."

"The Assistants."

"Right. But when he found out about my linguistics training, he brought me here, to his lab. Asked me all kinds of questions. When you came in today, he was showing me a map of the places he wants to go."

"Where are they?"

"All over." Alex keeps moving, though the office is so small he can barely take two steps without having to turn around. "At least one on every continent but Antarctica. Some continents have as many as ten or twelve."

Dozens of surviving villages. Places like New Hope and Athens. I am overjoyed and afraid at the same time.

"Loudin wants to start in South America. I am most comfortable with the Spanish language."

"Do these other places have communications?"

Alex shakes his head. "Not global communication. Some have electricity, like Athens. But it is localized. None seem to have developed capability to go beyond their borders. They probably don't see the purpose in it. If they're like us, and everything within hundreds of miles was decimated, they probably believe the whole world looks like that. Best to just rebuild what remained."

An idea is forming, improbable, almost impossible, but . . . "If Loudin were left there, in one of those locations, he couldn't get back."

"What?"

"If we could find a way to take the aircraft when Loudin is with the villagers, he would be forced to remain there. Right?"

"We'd have to overpower the Monitors, learn how to maneuver the aircraft, prevent everyone here who is loyal to him from going back after him . . ."

"But it is possible."

"Possible?" Alex stops. "Yes. I suppose it is possible."

I stand and hug Alex. The move is so unexpected that he almost falls over before reaching around and pulling me to him. He laughs in my ear and almost squeezes all the air from my lungs.

CHAPTER 11

T hey are in here." A Monitor pushes the door to the office open and speaks into his communications pad.

I jump back, out of Alex's arms, as three more Monitors converge into the tiny room, pushing us back into the desk at the far end.

"Take them to my laboratory." Dr. Loudin's voice whines from the first Monitor's communications pad.

Alex nods in my direction. I won't fight them. Not this time. We have a plan. I have no idea how we will execute that plan, how all the details of the plan will work out, but it is a beginning. And we have hope. If we can leave Dr. Loudin in South

America when he goes to make contact with the survivors there, then the State—and the rest of the world—will be free to live as they choose. I feel slightly guilty about forcing him on the survivors in South America. But without his resources and his followers, Loudin will not be a danger to them. I hope.

We are ushered into Loudin's laboratory, and I am immediately assaulted by memories. None of them good. This man—my father—a master manipulator and megalomaniac, must be stopped. He cannot be allowed to do to others what he has done to those of us here.

"Sit." A Monitor points to a chair in the center of the room. I obey with reluctance. Alex is seated three feet from me. As if we are too dangerous to be close together.

Maybe we are.

That thought makes me smile. They are a little frightened of me. And why not? I left an Assistant unconscious in the hall and escaped my pod. They lost track of Alex and me. Not for long, but still. To hide at all in this State is an impressive feat.

The silence in the room is oppressive. After several minutes, I feel as if the quiet has become a living organism, crawling around, suffocating me, tormenting me. But I will not speak. I cannot show weakness. Not to the Monitors, not to Loudin.

I try to focus on something else. I close my eyes and the first image that comes to my mind is Berk, standing in New Hope. The wind is blowing his light-brown hair, his face is tanned by the sun, and his smile is white. His green eyes gaze into mine, and I step into his arms. I can almost smell the soap on his skin, feel the fabric of his shirt against my cheek.

The joy I feel melts into an aching sadness. He is not here. I do not know when I will see him again. He could be sick. Hurt.

He could grow tired of my absence, of my insecurities and uncertainties. He could discover that the girls in New Hope are far more suited to him, far better for him than I could ever be.

I open my eyes. I prefer silence to those thoughts.

"Thalli and Alex." Loudin enters. His voice, a clarinet with a broken reed, dissolves the silence in the room. The Monitors stand straighter. "Quite a chase you sent us on. Clever. Fighting and subterfuge—are these the skills you have learned above, Thalli?"

I do not answer him, but neither do I look away. I will not cower in fear like the Monitors.

"Intellect and strategy—those are beneficial." Loudin stands directly in front of me. I look into his face and cannot help but search it for similarities to my own. My eyes are shaped like his—large, a noticeable feature. His mouth, though, is small, his lips thin. With the wrinkles in his skin and sunken cheeks, his eyes look even bigger. Haunting. Or haunted? "But not like this. And what were you trying to accomplish? Certainly you weren't planning to escape. You are too smart for that, aren't you? You know I'll just find you again, bring you back here. So what was it?"

"We just wanted to be together." Alex blurts this out in a voice that doesn't even sound like his own—high pitched, forced. "We were engaged in Athens."

I try not to let the shock register on my face. Our "engagement" was a ruse by Alex's father, who planned to murder me on our wedding night so his city would be incited to go to war against New Hope. But Loudin doesn't know that. I turn my face toward Alex, eyebrows raised. He responds with a sigh.

"I love her, Dr. Loudin." Alex shrugs.

Brilliant. The boy is brilliant. Now we seem like children given into emotions and not grown people plotting a coup. Admiration—that I pray looks like love—fills my heart.

"Is this true?" Loudin bends toward me, his foul breath spilling onto my face. "You love Alex?"

I swallow. John taught me there are different kinds of love. So I am not lying when I say, "Yes. I do love him. Very much."

Alex's smile widens and I bite my lip. He does not know I am speaking of a friendship love. Or perhaps, hopefully, he is simply playing along.

"You have forgotten Berk so soon?" Loudin straightens, but the stench of his breath remains. "I seem to recall you and he having secret rendezvous as well. Is your heart so liquid that you can transfer your affections from one man to another in so short a period of time?"

Is he thinking of Kristie or me? Or thinking that in this, I am like her? But she didn't choose Carey over Loudin out of a "liquid" heart. She chose him because Loudin's heart was so dark. She could not love him.

"Very well." Loudin's thin lips part, revealing perfectly straight, perfectly white teeth. "No need to escape or to injure any more of my Assistants. Alex may join you in Pod C. He can tell you about the adventure we are planning—a trip to South America. Perhaps he can even teach you a little Spanish. If you want so much to be together, then you may be together. I was thinking of bringing Thalli anyway, as sort of an ambassador to the other villages. You have lived in both worlds. You can tell the people the advantages of life above and life below. Right?"

It was not a question. But it is an opportunity. An invitation to go with him to South America? Time with Alex to plan that trip? Once, in New Hope, Berk brought me flowers—a gift, he said. Something unexpected and beautiful. This, though Loudin does not know it, is a gift. I look at Alex and smile.

"When can we begin?"

CHAPTER 12

Alex and I have been in Pod C for two days. It is odd, being here with him. But we have been busy. Loudin insisted that Alex teach me Spanish. Because Alex is unfamiliar with our learning pads, he requested paper and writing utensils. Those are rare here, but Loudin found some and gave them to Alex. But he insisted I teach Alex to use the learning pad as well, since the paper will run out before the lessons have been completed. So we have spent half our days on Spanish and the other half on technology. We have not spoken of anything but these assignments because we are being observed. We cannot allow Loudin to suspect that we have our own plans for this trip.

Alex has been affectionate since we have been here, even with the Monitors watching. I play along because they all believe we are in love. I am concerned, though, that Alex believes it too. I know he has feelings for me. Before we left New Hope, he proposed—not a proposal forced on him by his father, but an emotional one. He asked me to stay with him and help him as he takes over the throne left vacant by the assassination of his father, the king.

I did not respond, and we have not spoken of it since. But every time he touches me, caressing my cheek or pulling me close to him as we study, I am reminded of that moment. And I cannot deny I have feelings for Alex—deep feelings, borne out of shared experiences and mutual respect. Tragedies have melded us together in ways I have never known. Alex is not ashamed to feel, to express his feelings. I have never doubted him like I doubt Berk. I know what Alex feels, what he thinks, in ways I still don't know with Berk, even though I have known him since birth.

"Thalli?" Alex interrupts my thoughts and points back to the sentence he wrote. I would like to learn to write words. It is a beautiful thing to watch, this movement, the scraping of the utensil against the paper. Certainly it takes longer than typing on the learning pad, but there is something so personal about it, as if the words mean more when they are labored over, pressed into existence on paper that will yellow with age and become brittle, like the rare music I was occasionally given in the performance pod.

"Yes. *Sí.*" This language feels strange coming out of my mouth. But I enjoy learning it. It is like music, with its own cadence and key. "*Escucha.*"

"*Escucho.*" Alex corrects me with a wink.

"I am hungry." I stand and stretch my arms over my head. "Can we take a break?"

"I noticed the greenhouse behind us." Alex stands beside me. "Could we go there?"

"I don't think there is anything edible in there anymore."

Alex looks down into my eyes. "Could we just take a look anyway?"

The greenhouse is the perfect place. I should have thought of that two days ago. "Of course."

"You don't mind if we go there alone, do you?" Alex puts a hand on the Monitor's arm. "Just for a few minutes?"

The Monitor looks at Alex's hand as if it were a primitive disease, and Alex pulls it away. After tapping on his communications pad—asking Loudin, no doubt, for permission—he nods and moves into the kitchen to make himself a meal in our absence.

Once inside the greenhouse, Alex pulls me into his arms. "The Monitor may be watching. We don't want to look like we are plotting."

I lean my head against his chest and breathe in. Something about being near Alex calms me, slows me down. "So what are you thinking?"

Alex pulls back, and his blue eyes seem to darken a shade. "I am thinking you truly are the most amazing girl on the planet, and I want to spend every day with you—here, in Athens, in New Hope, South America. I want you by my side forever."

I pull away. "There aren't any cameras in here, Alex. We can speak freely."

"I am speaking freely." He cups my face in his hands. "I love you, Thalli. I'll do whatever we need to do to help everyone here, but when we're done, I want to marry you. In Athens. In front of my people. I want to take you on that honeymoon we were deprived of . . ."

I take several steps away, my face heating at his words, my throat constricting. "Alex . . . I can't. Loudin and Kristie . . . We need to focus." I can barely complete a sentence. I don't know what to say. I don't know how I feel. In our time here, I have forgotten who Alex is—King of Athens. And when this is over, if we are able to leave Loudin in South America and return to New Hope and Athens, Alex will resume his position. His responsibilities are immense, and he does need help and support.

All the emotions I felt at his first real proposal bubble back to the surface. All the reasons why marrying Alex is logical, beneficial to him and to others, assert themselves. The feelings I had for him—the feelings I *have*—are confusing. They make my mind feel as fuzzy as it did when I was under King Jason's pharmaceuticals.

"I'm sorry." Alex closes his eyes. "You are rightly focused on this task. Don't answer my question. Think about it. I will wait for you as long as it takes."

I blink back a tear. His sister was right—Alex deserves someone who truly, deeply loves him. Am I that person? Can I be?

Alex shifts into task mode and discusses what he has dubbed "The Mission." One of us must learn how to fly the aircraft. With everything here run by the most advanced technology, that duty falls to me. Once again I wish Berk were here. He would not have any problem flying it. I fear I will cause us to crash, leaving us dead or stranded in South America along with Dr. Loudin.

We also must lure Loudin and his Monitors far enough away so we have time to get the aircraft into the air. We are hoping the villagers will assist us. That they will trust us more than Loudin.

"Why would they trust anyone?" I look out the window of the greenhouse. "They are just like the people in Athens and New Hope. Suspicious of outsiders. They will be even more so since they have probably never even heard of the State."

"What we knew of the State made us *more* suspicious, not less." Alex shakes his head. "We heard the stories from the Scientists who escaped. We knew Loudin launched the first nuclear warhead. They don't know that."

That fact still makes me ill. Loudin—my father—didn't *respond* to the Nuclear War. He initiated it. Because of him, the world was destroyed. John's family and millions—billions—of families like his had been wiped out in seconds. I take a deep breath.

"Alex, I need to tell you something." I dig around in the dirt surrounding the dead plants, hoping that to the Monitor I appear to be looking for food. I do this also because I cannot look Alex in the eye when I tell him about Loudin and Kristie. I cannot bear seeing the pity there when he realizes the evil that lives in Loudin is inside me as well.

Alex moves closer to me as I tell him, his hand on my back. The pity I did not want to see in his eyes is there in his touch. But I find I need the strength that comes from that comfort to tell this story.

"You once told me"—Alex takes my filthy hands in his—"that

I am not responsible for my father's mistakes. Now it's my turn to say the same to you."

Tears I was holding back burst out. I cling to Alex and he holds me, whispering over and over again, "You are not your father."

CHAPTER 13

D r. Loudin requested that you both come to his quarters."
If the Monitor is uncomfortable at the sight of me in
Alex's arms, sobbing, he does not show it. I suppose he has
already been informed I am an anomaly, and Alex is earth born
so our behavior is expected to be abnormal.

I pull away and wipe my eyes, then wipe my hands on my
pants. I will not allow Loudin to see me upset. I will not allow
him to have that power over me. I take several deep breaths
before following the Monitor from the greenhouse. "Tell him
we are on our way."

Alex and I say nothing as we walk back to the Scientists'

quarters. I am struggling to regain my composure. I can only imagine what Alex is thinking. Considering yet another overthrow of a dictatorial ruler.

I approach the towering building. It is by far the largest edifice in the State, so wide I cannot see around it. It goes below the ground where I am standing, down to levels I never knew existed until I was taken to be annihilated. Kristie was here when this was built, Carey too. What had they thought as they oversaw its construction? Did they imagine they would live here, or did they assume it was just a precaution, that no one would really be so diabolical as to begin a war that would end the world as they knew it?

We step through the doors at the entrance of the Scientists' quarters. The Assistant whose clothes I stole is at the desk in the lobby. Her eyes widen when she sees me, but then she returns to her work at the desk, saying nothing, asking no questions, demonstrating no anger.

My shoes squeak as I walk on the newly cleaned floor, the sound echoing off the walls. We reach the elevator, and I press the button that will take us to the lowest floor of the building—Dr. Loudin's laboratory.

"Do you think he is ready to leave for South America?" Alex breaks the silence.

"Maybe." I do not say too much—they are certainly monitoring our interaction in here. "Though I do not think we are quite ready. My Spanish, you know, is poor. I will not be much help with translation."

The elevator lurches to a stop and the doors glide open, revealing the pristine white hallway that leads to Dr. Loudin's laboratory.

I see Kristie as soon as I open the door. I want to run to her, tell her I know she is my mother, that I am happy about that. But the look on her face causes my blood to cool.

She is terrified.

"No." The word comes out of her slowly, like a note sustained on my violin.

"Thalli and Alex." Loudin's thin lips curve upward.

"What is going on?" I do not walk farther.

Kristie is staring at me, her brown eyes wide. Loudin stands between us, blocking her from view.

"Kristie is having a little trouble completing the assignment she was given." Loudin's large eyes lock on mine. "Living in that primitive village has distorted her sensibilities."

I want to shout that he is the one distorted, that New Hope is not primitive. But I do not speak. He would only use that information against me. There is no benefit in him knowing how much I love the people of New Hope.

"Have a seat, Thalli." Loudin motions to a chair made entirely of metal. "Alex, you will be escorted back to your room."

A Monitor enters from a side door. Alex lunges for the man, but he is subdued when the Monitor plunges a needle into Alex's neck. Before I have time to scream, Alex falls to the floor.

"What have you done to him?"

"Alex is only asleep." Loudin motions for the Monitor to take Alex away. "Now, please sit."

Another Monitor forces me into the metal chair. As soon as I am in it, I realize I am attached. The chair is some type of human magnet. Too late, I realize that everywhere I touch, I stick. My back, my arms, are pinned helplessly to this contraption.

Loudin turns to Kristie. "Now, my dear. I believe you have some work to complete."

Whatever he wants her to do, she should not do it. The fact that she has refused until now convinces me that she should not. "No, Kristie. I'd rather be killed than see him cause any more damage."

"Cause damage?" Loudin stands directly in front of me. I look up, his breath, like sour apples, burns my nostrils. "I have done nothing but repair damage. I have spent my entire life repairing damage. I am the world's greatest ally."

"You destroyed the world!" I shout into his face, causing him to step back.

"I saved the world from itself." Loudin shakes his head. "If you'd only see the truth, Thalli. You have so much potential. Your mind is truly a beautiful thing. But you are sacrificing it on the altar of emotion."

"How can you believe that feeling—that loving—is bad?" I think of the way I have been changed because of the love of people like John and Kristie. Berk. I think of the love of the Designer, sending his son to die for me so I can live with him. The ultimate love from the ultimate Being. My anger dissolves to pity. "Someday you will realize how wrong you are."

"Enough." Loudin turns his back on me. "I did not bring you here to debate with you."

Loudin walks to Kristie and points to a screen beside her. "Complete this repair."

Kristie looks at me, and I shake my head.

The chair comes alive, and electricity courses through my body. The pain is so intense, I cannot even shout. I can barely breathe. I want to fall to the ground, to curl myself into a ball, but the chair keeps me sitting straight, refusing to release me. I am burning. I see black and white specks in front of my eyes. I long to pass out, for the Monitor to come to *me* with a needle as he did to Alex. But no one comes.

Finally it stops. But fear remains. Fear that the chair will turn back on, that the pain will return, worse this time. I cannot think of anything but being free of this chair. But the harder I try to stand, the more bound I become to it.

"All right." I hear Kristie, but her voice sounds far away.

"No tricks this time. No holes in the program. No mistakes. Thalli will remain right there until I am certain of the project's completion."

I groan. The chair holds my neck and my head, its back going above mine. I cannot even turn to the left or the right. My legs have been pinned to the sides of the chair in odd, painful angles—a result of movement when the current was running through me. And I have to remain here like this until Kristie finishes? If Kristie finishes.

Can I endure this until I die of starvation? Or until the electricity finally destroys my internal organs? It was easier to consider sacrificing myself when I thought death would be immediate. But this—endless torture—makes me reconsider, deletes the noble feelings I entertained.

Where is God? This Designer who delivered his people by parting oceans and bringing plagues to his enemies—where is he now? Why doesn't he intervene? I try to pray, but I cannot form words. I am too full of doubt—of anger. I have tried to obey him, tried to do what is right. And yet he is allowing Loudin to be victorious. Where is his power?

"It is finished." A minute, an hour, several hours . . . I

don't know how much time has passed. But Kristie's voice breaks through my thoughts, bringing with it two horrifying thoughts:

1. Loudin now has all he needs to create a new generation.
2. He no longer needs Kristie.

CHAPTER 14

t's time to go." Alex is in my room—in the Scientists' quarters.

I sit up in the sleeping platform and put my hands over my eyes. My head aches and my muscles feel weak. I have been in bed for two days, but my strength still has not returned.

Alex sits at the foot of my mattress, his hand on my leg.

"I can't."

"I think he wants to use your weakness to his advantage," Alex says. "Keep you too tired to do more than just what he asks you to do."

"Can't you stall him?" I open my eyes and Alex scoots closer to me. "I can't go like this. I don't even think I can walk."

Moisture gathers in Alex's eyes. He smoothes my hair, swallowing hard. "I'll help you."

I swing my legs over the side of the sleeping platform and my limbs feel weighted. How will I ever get to the door? Down the hallway?

"I'll carry you." Alex bends down to lift me into his arms.

"No." I push him away. I don't want to give Loudin the satisfaction of knowing how weak I am. "Just help me."

Alex places his left arm around my waist and holds my left hand with his free hand. He pulls me up, and I collapse against him.

"Let me carry you."

"No." I lift my head from his shoulder. "I can do this."

I release his hand, and his arm tightens on my waist. Though I do not want to admit it, I need him there. I cannot walk on my own. But I use my free hand to help balance myself. My legs feel so heavy that by the time I reach the door, I am out of breath.

Alex opens the door and I walk on.

"Where is Kristie?" I speak as quietly as I can.

"I'm not sure." He whispers as well. "He had her taken out right after you. Since then, Dr. Loudin has had me recording Spanish."

"How long have I been in here?"

"Twenty-four hours."

"Why does he have you recording Spanish?"

"Not just any Spanish—conversations we will need to have with the people there in South America. I think part of the reason is to make sure I say what he is instructing me to say."

"And the other part?"

"If he decides I am not longer valuable, he can just use those phrases to communicate with them."

I stop in the hallway and place my hand on Alex's chest. "No. He can't do that. He won't. How could he understand what they are saying if you aren't there to translate?"

Alex runs a finger along my jaw. "I appreciate your concern. I could be wrong."

I can tell by the tone of his voice that Alex doesn't think he is wrong. I turn away from him and step forward.

"Do you think Kristie is no longer valuable?" This comes out in a whisper because I can barely get the words past my lips.

Alex slows a little. "I don't think Loudin will kill her."

"Why?"

"Because, as messed up as he is, he loves her." Alex whispers this into my ear, his breath warm against my neck.

"I don't know." I wish I could have the same opinion as Alex, but I cannot. "Your father killed *your* mother."

"He didn't love her." Alex's voice is hard. "He didn't love anyone but himself."

"And you think Loudin is a better man than your father? You think *he* isn't as self-absorbed?"

Alex sighs. "There's no point in thinking the worst."

"You sound like John."

"From what I've heard, that is a compliment." Alex smiles down at me.

I release a breath. "It is."

We step onto the elevator, and I use the ride up to catch my breath. I want to slide down to the floor and rest, but I am certain that if I went down, I would not be able to get back up. The door opens too soon, and Loudin is waiting for us.

"Thalli." He glances at Alex's arm around me. "Nice to see you up."

I push Alex's hand away. "Where is Kristie?"

"She is enjoying some much needed time off." Loudin motions for me to walk ahead of him. "Her skills will be needed on another project soon."

"What project?" I don't like the tone of Loudin's voice.

"There is always work for a skilled Scientist." Loudin smiles a thin smile. "And Kristie, while rusty, is skilled."

The relief of knowing Kristie's life is not in danger gives me the energy I need to take the steps into Loudin's office on my own. I immediately collapse into a plastic chair though.

The wall screen turns on, and a map appears on it. A red line descends from the State to what I assume is South America.

"We will travel down to what used to be Ecuador." Loudin touches the ending point on the map, and the image changes to that of a live camera that appears to be several miles in the air. "Satellite imagery. We thought they were irrecoverable. But Dr. Williams and her team were able to restore them. Wonderful, isn't it?"

The camera seems to lower, and I see a village with houses and people. Many people. A long river cuts through the center of the village. I see people in the water, on transports. Families enjoying life as they have always known it, oblivious to the reality that their world will soon be disrupted.

Our plan to leave Loudin there suddenly seems cruel and unjust. These people do not deserve that. I try, once again, to pray. I force the words, even though I don't feel like they are being heard. I pray anyway. I pray that this village will be spared, that Loudin will be stopped, that the Designer will not make himself so distant when we all need him so much.

"What will you do to them?" I keep my eyes on the wall screen, refusing to look at Dr. Loudin.

"You ask the wrong question, Thalli. It is not what will I do *to* them, but what can I do *for* them."

"Do not think you can deceive me." I look at him now, wanting him to hear every word. "You do not want to help these people. You will disrupt their lives. You want to take people from there and bring them here, take fathers from their children, or children from their parents . . ."

"Or lovers from each other?" He arches an eyebrow and looks at Alex.

"Do not mock me."

Loudin smiles. "What if I took an entire family together? Would that help?"

"No." I slap my hands on my legs. "You don't understand how villages work. They don't live in pods, separated from everyone else. They live and work together."

"You presume to tell me how the world works?" Loudin's voice is louder than I have ever heard it. "You spent weeks in these villages. I spent years aboveground. Decades. The greatest gift I can give to these people is to separate them from each other. They may see it as a punishment, for a time, but that is because they are so compromised by their emotions and the superstitions that have been passed down from generation to generation."

"No."

"Yes, Thalli." Loudin's voice returns to normal. "And you have been infected by those ideas. I thought you were better than that. That you would form your own opinions and not blindly follow others'."

"What?" I stand from my chair. "How can you even say that? You expect blind obedience from everyone here. You annihilate those who think or feel."

"Not all of them." Loudin looks at me, his calm making me even more upset.

"You refuse to accept anyone's belief but your own."

"My 'beliefs' are scientifically tested and proven accurate." Loudin presses his lips together. "What about yours?"

An Assistant enters the room. "The aircraft is ready, sir."

"Excellent." Loudin turns away from me.

Alex looks at me, a smile on his face. He is proud of me for defending his people. But they aren't just his people. They are my people now too.

"Because we are bringing several people back with us, it will just be the three of us on the trip down." Loudin places his communications pad in his pocket. "I trust that will not be a problem?"

"No." A spark of hope lights in my stomach. "That won't be a problem at all."

CHAPTER 15

We are in the aircraft. Walking around, watching Loudin program the flight plan, exploring.

Something about this feels very wrong.

Loudin is intelligent and he anticipates everything. He knows how Alex and I feel about him. It is impossible that we will simply land in South America and leave Loudin there. I would like to believe it would be that simple. But I know better.

Alex is smiling, asking about how the aircraft is flown, how it lands. He appears confident that our plan is going to proceed smoothly.

I wish I could share his confidence, but a mounting dread fills me.

Being aboard this aircraft does not help. We are completely enclosed. There is a monitor at the front that displays a map, but there is no way to see the outside. I feel trapped. The same emotions I had walking into this aircraft back in New Hope are surging through me now. Loudin acted the same then, kind and happy, as if he were a benevolent leader who truly wants to help others. But that is an act. The truth is he is corrupt, calculating, and he will do anything to ensure his plans are accomplished.

"Smooth, isn't it?" Loudin sits in a large white chair toward the front of the aircraft. "The autopilot can detect where to find the pockets of air with the least amount of turbulence. And it can get there without us even feeling the change in altitude. It can travel for thousands of miles on one tank of fuel. And if it runs out, the solar panels can provide enough alternate energy to deliver us to our destination."

"Fascinating." Alex smiles at Loudin, and I am not sure if he is being genuine or playing along.

"What do you think, Thalli?"

A dozen retorts come into my mind, but none would be appropriate. Or beneficial. So I force myself to smile and say, "Quite an accomplishment by the Engineers."

"How do these compare to the airplanes from before the War?" Alex leans forward.

"What do you know of those?"

"Only what some of the older citizens of Athens have passed down." Alex shrugs. "But I have always been intrigued by them."

Loudin spends the next thirty minutes explaining the physics and mechanics of the primitive airplane versus the modern aircraft. If this conversation were music, it would be a tuba playing the same three notes over and over, as slowly as possible. I close my eyes and imagine playing my violin loud and staccato, the notes going over and around the tuba until it is muted and mine is the only instrument that can be heard.

I hear an A flat over the orchestration in my mind. It is sustained and synthesized. I open my eyes to see Loudin walking to the front of the aircraft.

"Strap yourselves in. It is time to land."

"Already?" I sit up and press a button on my right. Thin, translucent straps come out of the chair and wrap themselves around my body. "I had no idea the aircraft was that fast."

Alex leans as far forward as the straps allow, looking at the map at the front. "We aren't in South America yet."

"No, we aren't." Loudin sits in the chair that faces the map. "We are making a stop first."

"Why?" I look around. "Is something wrong?"

"Of course not." Loudin turns, and his profile reminds me of images I have seen on my learning pad of a vulture. "But I am hurt that you think me such a tyrant, Thalli. I want to show you that your suspicions are the product of an overactive imagination, not of reality."

Loudin's tone does not match his words. The dread that has been simmering under the surface spreads throughout my entire body. Something is very, very wrong. I turn to Alex. His eyes are wide, questioning. He knows, too, that this—whatever it is—is not good.

Alex speaks first. "Where are we stopping?"

Loudin turns back to the map and touches a slender finger to its surface. "New Hope, of course."

CHAPTER 16

feel nothing but terror. Loudin is returning to New Hope? What is he planning? I jerk forward, hoping I can free myself of the straps. But they are solid, unmoving. I press the button on my right, but nothing happens. I can only strap myself in. I cannot release the straps. Loudin has to do that at the control center. I maneuver myself to see if I can free one of my arms. If I can do that, perhaps I can slide through the center. Loudin is old and weak. If I can get to him, maybe I can knock him out, like I did to the Assistant in the Scientists' quarters. Once he is unconscious, I can release Alex and we can reroute the plane.

As much as I long to see New Hope—to see Berk and Rhen,

to tell Carey Kristie is all right, that we have a plan to see she and all the others are released—I cannot allow Loudin to come into that village again. He is too dangerous.

But I cannot pull even one arm out. The straps, though thin, are strong. And they seem to anticipate my movements. They tighten on my chest, making escape impossible.

"Don't worry." Loudin laughs. "The aircraft will land safely. The Engineers have developed the program to run on its own. I am just here to watch. And *if* something were to happen, Engineers at the State are ready to manually land it. We have lots of eyes on this aircraft. No need to panic."

He knows I am not panicking. He knows I am trying to escape. He probably also knows we were planning to overtake him. But that will be pointless. Why did I not consider there would be other eyes on this machine? I always underestimate this man, this State. Even if Alex and I were to leave Loudin in South America, the Engineers would not allow us to leave in the aircraft. They would know Loudin was not in it. They would shut it down.

I glance at Alex. His gaze is locked on me. He knows too. Our plans are useless. Our hope futile.

God! Where are you? I cannot defeat Loudin on my own, yet I feel like I have been abandoned by the only one who can defeat him.

I close my eyes and think. I will not give up. I will not allow Loudin to emerge victorious. I think of King Jason, of the moment when Alex and I realized the only way to stop that man was to kill him. This is where we are again. And though I do not feel the love toward Loudin that Alex felt toward his father, I do not think I can take a life. But what if there is no choice? If the only way to ensure the safety of New Hope and Athens—of the world—is to remove Loudin from it?

If he were dead, we could stay in New Hope.

But what about Kristie? The generations still trapped in the State? We can't leave them there. But if we returned, would the remaining Scientists try to annihilate us?

I open my eyes. I have no solution. No idea what to do. Unlike Loudin, who has planned everything, ensured that his plans succeed. It is not right that he should be allowed to accomplish his goals. I wish John were here. The Designer would listen to him. Or, at the very least, John would know what to do in the face of the Designer's silence.

I feel so very alone.

"We are here." Loudin stands and moves toward us. "You didn't even feel it, did you? Not like airplanes of old. Those landings were rough, and your ears would ache from the change in pressure. All that has been corrected, thanks to our Scientists. I do hope, Thalli, that you come to see how beneficial our advancements have been."

I say nothing. I do not even look at him. He touches something above my head and the straps release. I lunge toward him, but he holds out a device. I don't need him to tell me what it is. My body responds before my mind does. I lean back. It is a weapon that dispenses electricity. All he has to do is turn it on and I will feel its effects, as will Alex.

"Of course, I do not wish to use this." Loudin releases Alex from his restraints. "But I cannot take any chances."

"Of course." I look at Loudin now, not hiding my anger. He does not fool me. I know exactly who he is. The fact that who he is, is part of who I am makes me ill. But Kristie is also part of who I am. And the Designer, though he seems so far away, is ultimately the one who made me. He did not create me to cower to this man.

The door opens and the first face I see is Berk's. Every other emotion disintegrates. Only love remains. Berk is there, waiting for me, smiling at me. I run down the ramp, into his arms. He lifts me off the ground, spins me in circles. I lean into his shoulder inhaling his scent. He lowers me and places his hands on my face, his eyes searching mine.

I am home.

CHAPTER 17

Loudin clears his throat, and I step away from Berk. Behind him, Alex is staring at me. I cannot determine if he is angry or hurt. Or both.

"Why are you here?" Berk pulls me to his side, his arm around my waist. Alex turns away and Berk tightens his grip on me.

Loudin places the weapon in his pocket and folds his arms. "As you can see, Thalli has missed you. I thought I could remedy that by stopping here and inviting you to come with us."

"No." I step away from Berk, but he refuses to release his hold. "You didn't say anything about bringing Berk."

"It was a surprise." Loudin shrugs. "I thought you would be grateful."

"Grateful?"

"Unless, of course, you did not wish your time with young Alex to be interrupted." Loudin motions toward the aircraft where Alex stands, his face flushed. "Women are fickle, Berk. When one man is gone, they find another to take his place."

"That's not what happened." I turn to Berk, his eyes full of questions.

Loudin steps forward. "She *was* engaged to him, after all."

"Because his father tricked me—" I stop talking. I am reacting exactly the way Loudin wants me to react. I cannot do that, cannot make this easy for him. I release a long breath and pull away from Berk. "You're right. I am fickle. But they are both wonderful young men."

All three sets of eyes stare at me. Alex knows what I am doing—playing along with Loudin instead of reacting to him. I do not know if Berk sees what I am doing. He suspected I had feelings for Alex. When I left New Hope, I still was unsure of what those feelings were. Even now, though I love Berk, I feel a pull toward Alex. But I cannot sift through any of that right now.

"They are." Loudin's lips curve into a smile. "Exactly my thoughts. And I, too, have missed Berk. He was one of my most promising young Scientists."

Berk stiffens beside me.

"Which is why I am inviting him to join us. And why he will return to the State with us and resume his training."

As much as I long never to be separated from Berk again, I don't want him to come with us. I don't want Loudin to be able to use him against me the way I was used against Kristie. He needs to stay here where he is safe.

"I would be honored to join you, sir." Berk leans into me, his shoulder touching mine. His touch warms me in ways that make it difficult to think clearly, rationally. I step away.

"No." I do not look at him. I cannot. "I am sure Berk is needed here more than he is needed in the State."

"And I am sure that is not your decision to make." Loudin narrows his eyes. "You will come with us, Berk. You have one hour to gather your belongings. Thalli and Alex, you have the same amount of time to visit whomever you choose."

For the first time, I look to the crowd that has gathered. I was so intent on Berk I did not even see them. I see Rhen and Dallas and Carey. I recognize a handful of people from Athens mixed in among the New Hope residents. I want to know everything that has happened since I have been gone. I want them to know everything that has happened in the State. One hour is not enough time.

"May we not spend the night here?" I look to Loudin. "I can assure you, the sleeping platforms in the pods here are far more comfortable than those in the aircraft."

Loudin walks to me, bends his mouth to my ear, and whispers, "Both you and Alex will be monitored wherever you go. Everything you see, I will see; everything you hear, I will hear. You will not now nor will you ever keep a secret from me. Do not even think about it. I am not like Alex's father. I will not be overthrown. I will not be tricked. Do you understand?"

A knot forms in my stomach, and I nod once. Loudin pulls away.

"You have one hour." Loudin returns to the aircraft where, apparently, he has the ability to view Alex and me.

Berk once placed a microscopic camera on Loudin's lapel.

I look down at my shirt. Do I have a camera on me? Or is there something inside me, placed there during one of my surgeries? How much does Loudin know? How much has he really heard? I have no doubt he can lie as easily as he can speak the truth. But he cannot possibly observe everything all the time. It is entirely possible he has not heard Alex and me discuss our plans. But it is also entirely possible that he has. And we have no way of knowing what he knows.

"Thalli, where is Kristie? Is she all right?" Carey interrupts my thoughts. His face is lined with worry.

"The last time I saw her she was all right. Dr. Loudin told me she was resting in preparation for another project."

"What other project?" Carey runs a hand through his thinning red hair. "What did he make her do?"

"He requested she repair the oxygen system in the State." I try to keep my voice level, to somehow communicate that I cannot speak freely. "She was able to complete that repair. I am not sure what her next assignment will be."

"Has he hurt her?"

"No." I cannot tell him Loudin hurt me to make Kristie do what he asked. I cannot tell him that Kristie is my mother, though I suspect he knows. Before we left for the State from New Hope the first time, Loudin spent half an hour alone with Carey and Kristie. They came out with disbelief on their faces, and then Kristie agreed to come aboard the aircraft without a fight. I did not understand it then, but now I see—if Loudin revealed the truth of who I am, Kristie would do whatever he asked. "She is all right. And Loudin says that once we complete the work he has for us, he will allow us to return to New Hope."

"You can't believe him, Thalli. We'll find another way to rescue Kristie. You can't get back with him. We'll stop him."

"No."

"How many does he have with him?" Carey looks at the aircraft, then out toward the crowd.

Loudin's weapon is agonizing. He will use it on anyone who comes near him. "We cannot stop him."

"We are uniting with Athens now. We have—"

I put a hand up to stop him. Loudin doesn't need to know any more about Athens than he already does. "I do not have much time. Let me just enjoy being here."

I can tell Carey is confused, but he nods and I walk past him, wishing the last few weeks never happened.

CHAPTER 18

Thalli!" Rhen hugs me. She hugs me. That has never happened. Rhen was always so normal, never displaying emotions. New Hope has changed her. She pulls away, and I see a bright smile on her beautiful face. "I have missed you."

"I missed you too." I smile back at Rhen. "You are so . . ."

"Perfect?" Dallas, Kristie and Carey's grandson, wraps a muscular arm around Rhen's shoulders. She looks up into his face and seems to glow from within. I close my eyes and open them again. Is this really Rhen?

"Dallas." Rhen shakes her head. "Perfection, as you know, is impossible."

There's the Rhen I know. "So you two . . . ?"

Dallas winks at me. "Rhen is crazy in love with me."

"What?"

"Dallas." Rhen pulls away, but her cheeks turn pink. "Dallas and I have developed a friendship. Not unlike what you have with Berk."

"Really?" Even Rhen's manner of speaking has changed. Some of her words are accented the same as the others in New Hope. She has changed so much in the weeks I have been away. I want to know everything, but I don't have time.

I watch Dallas watching Rhen. Dallas—my mother's grandson. I do not know what, exactly, that makes him, but he is a relative. We share the same blood. I want to ask him a million questions. I want to go to his house, speak to his parents: my brother. His wife. The thought makes me hear a dozen violins, playing in harmony. But I stop myself. I bite my lip. Loudin is watching. I do not want to share that moment with him.

"But we want to know about you." Rhen places her hand on my shoulder. "Are you all right? What is happening in the State? Have you returned to stay?"

I sigh, shaking the thoughts from my mind, tuning out the violins. *God, get us back here without Loudin so I can know this family.* There is still silence when I pray, but I do it anyway. "I cannot say everything that is going on. But I am all right, and I do hope to return."

Rhen frowns. "I have come to realize that Dr. Loudin is much more dangerous than we ever imagined."

If she only knew how well I know that. But, of course, with Loudin listening to our conversation, I cannot do anything but nod. "I cannot stay long. Can we walk to the pond? I want to see it before we leave."

"Of course." Rhen begins walking.

"I'll give you girls some time alone." Dallas remains where he is standing. "So you can talk about me."

Rhen laughs and again her cheeks turn pink. Dallas winks at her and walks away—confident and slightly off balance.

"You and Dallas. I saw a connection before I left but . . ."

"I never could have imagined it."

"How did it start?"

"It really started with John."

We reach the top of the hill, and I see the pond below. The sun is reflected off its surface, and the smell of soil and grass makes me ache to stay here. Life below, in the State, seems even more of a prison when I am here.

"John?" My gaze goes automatically to the spot where he died, at the edge of the pond.

"I thought he was crazy at first." Rhen slows her pace. "All the talk of a Designer, of love. It went against all we have ever been taught."

"I know." I had the same thoughts when John first started speaking to me.

"But the more I listened, and I watched him, I began to see the logic in his beliefs." Rhen stops at the edge of the pond and we sit. "And I began to see some of the holes in the Scientists' logic."

Rhen picks at a blade of grass. She is thinking. I look at her, blond hair loose around her face, the wind blowing it in all directions. She is so relaxed. So different.

"The love that John spoke of began to make sense." Rhen

looks at me and her blue eyes are bright. "And the Designer . . . he made sense too. In fact, the more I thought about it, the more I saw that the Scientists were just mimicking who the Designer was—they were creating and ruling. They attempted to know everything, but they couldn't. We saw that in the power outages and the oxygen depletion and the anomalies. Even the Scientists were imperfect."

I lie back in the grass, closing my eyes and feeling the sun warming my face. "Go on."

"So I began asking questions." A smile manifests in Rhen's voice. "I sounded like you. But you were in Athens at the time. I wanted to tell you when you returned. But . . ."

"Dr. Loudin came."

"Yes."

"So tell me now." I sit up. "But quickly. I have to return in a few minutes."

"No, Thalli." Rhen's eyes widen. "You just arrived."

"No arguing." Never did I think I would say those words to Rhen. "I want to hear the rest of your story."

"John gave me the Designer's book. He told me the answers to my questions were there." Rhen pulled a worn book from a bag at her side. "I began reading it. I have not read it all, but I have read much. It is amazing, Thalli. This Designer—God—he is . . . real. He exists."

"I know."

"And knowing of his love has allowed me to love others." Rhen smiles. "And to be loved."

"So Dallas . . ."

"Rhen!" Nicole, Dallas's sister—another relative—jumps into Rhen's arms. Her dark hair is thick and curly and wild, her olive skin smooth. Her brown eyes, so like Dallas's, are bright. "Guess what?"

"What?" Rhen smiles into Nicole's face and lowers the young girl onto the ground.

"I just—" Nicole notices me and her eyes get wider. "Thalli! You're here."

"I am here."

"I'll tell you too." Nicole reaches into her pocket and speaks so quickly I have trouble understanding all her words. "I lost a molar. It's so cool. And I didn't even need any help. I pulled it out all by myself. Wanna see it?"

I get down on my knees and look into the girl's face. Her smile is wide, revealing white teeth with an adorable gap between two. What would it have been like to have grown up with Dallas and her here in New Hope? To have watched her as a baby, seen her take her first steps and say her first words. I want to make up for those lost moments. I want to enjoy every moment I have with her—with everyone. "I would love to see it, Nicole."

Nicole slowly opens her hand. The molar, still pink with blood, sits proudly in the center of her palm. Rhen and I clap and tell Nicole how brave she was to have pulled such a big tooth out all by herself.

"We have to go." Berk is behind me. I turn and see resignation in his eyes.

"Not yet." I look out over the pond, up into the sky. I want to spend more time with Nicole, with Dallas. I want to talk with Carey and learn more about Kristie.

"I'm sorry." Berk reaches for my hand and pulls me up. His hand stays in mine, warm and strong. I stand and Rhen follows. "Dr. Loudin has given me only five minutes to return with you."

I want to delay, but Loudin will use his weapon if I do. And I don't want the people of New Hope seeing that or worrying for me. So I keep up with Berk's long strides and too soon I am standing at the ramp leading up to the aircraft.

"I have decided"—Loudin is standing at the entrance—"that I would very much like to study your friend Dallas. And you as well, Rhen. So much change in so little time. You should not have been able to develop feelings, and yet you have. Your logic should have overridden the primitive teachings you have been exposed to, but it did not. Why is that?"

"Because the Designer is greater than you." Rhen speaks calmly, authoritatively.

"Nonsense." Loudin laughs. "But I would like to see where I went wrong. More specifically, where James went wrong. It is obviously a hidden anomaly. And it must be rectified before the creation of the next generation."

"No." I stand between Loudin and Rhen. "We cannot take Berk and Dallas and Rhen and still have room for the people in South America you want to bring with us. The aircraft isn't large enough."

"I am well aware of the limitations of this aircraft." Loudin pierces me with a stare. "Which is why we will return to the State. We can postpone our trip to South America. Knowing what has changed Rhen is more important."

"Why Dallas?" Rhen places her hand in his. "You don't need him."

"I don't *need* him, no." Loudin remains, unmoving, in his spot at the entrance. "But what a contrast to Alex, is he not?

Both born and raised here, sixty miles from one another. One, the son of a king, the other, grandson to Scientists. But what are the differences between Alex's brain and Dallas's? These are questions I want to answer."

"You're going to experiment on my brain?" Dallas looks from Loudin to Rhen.

"Enough talk." Loudin motions for us to come aboard. "There are seats enough for all of you. And Thalli can tell you that any attempt to disobey my wishes will result in a most unpleasant experience."

"He's right." I hate to say those words, but I do not want anyone hurt.

"You're not taking them." Carey pushes his way forward, moving faster than I thought possible for someone as old as he. He takes two steps up onto the ramp and then falls on the ground, groaning in pain.

"Stop." I bend down to Carey, but I cannot touch him. I can hear the electricity flowing through him. If I touch him, it will transfer to me as well. "You will kill him."

"He deserves no less." Loudin releases the button on the weapon. "But I will show mercy. Now come aboard."

A crowd that has gathered behind us begins to murmur. They are good people. They will follow Carey's lead in trying to stop Loudin. But they will fail, as he did. I cannot let anyone else get hurt.

"He will do that to anyone who tries to stop him." I raise my voice so the crowd can hear me. "You have to let us board."

Rhen turns to the people. "God delivered his people from far worse than this man. From lions and fire, from slavery. There is nothing he cannot do and there is no human who can overpower him. Pray for us, that God once again shows his power to those who would try to usurp it."

The people nod at Rhen's words, and we board. I am amazed at Rhen's faith. I wish I were as confident. But I am not. I am frightened. Fear is crushing my faith. The door closes, and with it, my hope that I will ever see freedom again.

CHAPTER 19

I am seated between Alex and Berk. We do not speak. Rhen and Dallas are across from us, Rhen's head on Dallas's shoulder, both asleep. I do not understand how they can rest. Loudin is bringing Rhen and Berk back to the State, bringing Dallas there. I know what his cerebral testing is like, how Loudin can make virtual worlds seem real, how he can strip away senses, memories, anything.

Alex and I were so sure our plan was going to work, that Loudin would be left in South America, that we'd return to the State and free the people and finally go back to New Hope and Athens. What a ridiculous notion. I cannot believe I allowed myself that dream. How could I have ever thought it would be that easy?

"We'll be all right." Berk places a hand on my knee. Alex's gaze immediately goes to that hand.

"Loudin is taking us to the State." The muscles in Alex's jaw flex. "We have no guarantee we or anyone else will be all right."

"There's no reason to think the worst." Berk squeezes my knee.

"No reason to think the worst?" Alex's voice reverberates around the aircraft. "I can give you a dozen reasons right now. Nothing good happens when Scientists are in charge."

"No?" Berk pulls his hand from my knee and folds his arms against his chest. "Of course not. You prefer the rule of kings, right? Because that obviously worked well in Athens."

"I am not my father." Alex hits the seat, the sound echoing around the transport.

"And I am not Loudin." Berk speaks softly, but there is so much anger behind his words. I have never heard him sound like this. "But I do care about the State, and I care about New Hope. And Athens."

Alex tenses beside me. I need to find a neutral topic, to remind us we are all working toward the same goal.

"How are things in New Hope?" I ask Berk. "I saw some of the Athenians there. Are they all right?"

Berk sighs. Several moments pass before he speaks. "The Athenians have been very helpful." Berk nods toward Alex, a slight concession. "They did just as you asked—they are seeking peace with us. In return, the farmers in New Hope have not only given food to the Athenians, they are also training them to be farmers."

"That is good." Alex speaks softly, but I hear the relief in his voice. He cares deeply for his people.

"There have been some minor skirmishes, but that is to be expected."

"My people have been at war a long time." Alex leans forward, his elbows on his knees. "It will take a long time to convince them that mentality is no longer necessary."

"*Your* people?" Berk says. "They belong to no one."

"You have been there a few weeks." Alex's nostrils flare. "Don't presume to speak on their behalf."

"Beg your pardon." Berk frowns. "Your Majesty."

"Berk." I cannot believe he is acting like this. "Enough."

"They are working on developing a council with members from each village," Berk continues, ignoring both Alex and me. "They are hoping you will return in time to lead that council."

Alex says nothing. We both know our lives are in Loudin's hands. But his ears are everywhere, and we will not give him the satisfaction of knowing our fears.

Dallas opens his eyes and smiles at the three of us. "Hey, guys."

"Dallas." I cannot help but smile in return.

"So, Alex." Dallas leans his head to the side. "I heard some good stuff about you."

"Thank you." Alex is still tense, and his eyes look everywhere but at Berk.

"The folks aren't too happy with your dad though." Dallas's accent is so odd I find it hard to concentrate on what he is saying. "Stuff's coming out about him that is making the people pretty mad. But they aren't mad at you. Don't worry about that.

They see he mistreated you the way he mistreated them. And I'm real sorry to hear about your sister."

Alex turns white at the mention of Helen. Killed by order of the king, her murder blamed on Berk and me. Everything surrounding her death is painful to Alex. He has not spoken of it at all since he left Athens.

"Your sister?" Loudin is suddenly standing beside us. He has been seated behind the controls since the aircraft left New Hope. "I was not aware you had a sister. I thought I extracted everything from that brain of yours. You must have buried her deep in there."

"I do not wish to speak of her." Alex's every word seems to take monumental effort. I reach over to take his hand in mine, but he pulls it away and folds his arms across his chest.

"Helen and Alex." Loudin ignores Alex's request. "Very stately names. Very Roman."

"I *do not* wish to speak of her." Alex's words come out as a growl. He begins to move forward, but Loudin is surprisingly fast. He presses a button, and the straps across Alex's chest tighten.

"Have you not yet learned that fighting me is futile?" Loudin shakes his head. "Enjoy the rest of your flight." He walks away, laughing.

"That guy needs to be punched," Dallas says.

I am not sure what a *punch* is, but I hope it is painful, and I hope Dallas can find a way to deliver it.

CHAPTER 20

W hat an excellent opportunity to test Kristie's work on our oxygen system." Dr. Loudin stands at the door to Pod C as Rhen, Dallas, Alex, Berk, and I enter. The living space has been returned to its original state—with couches and chairs replacing the medical equipment that had been here. I walk down the hall and see that three cubes have sleeping platforms, but the rest have the medical equipment that had been in the front.

"You will live here." Loudin looks at each of us. "Together. Try to function as much like a pod as you can."

Another experiment. Of course.

"All these emotions under one roof." Loudin walks the length of the living area, speaking more to himself than to us. "I have not seen this since before our rogue Scientists left us. It's a danger, of course. But a controlled danger." Loudin motions to the kitchen. "There are provisions for you. And learning pads. I have decided not to send in Monitors. Assistants will come throughout the day. There are some tests I want to run . . ."

"And what if we refuse?" Only Dallas would ask such a question.

Loudin steps within inches of Dallas's face. "Refuse?"

Dallas does not back down or turn away. I bite my lip to keep from smiling.

"Refusal is not an option." Loudin takes a long breath. "Your only options are to obey willingly or to be forced into obedience."

Dallas grunts but does not move. Loudin pulls out his communications pad and types. "Get some rest tonight. Tomorrow will be a full day."

The door shuts behind him, and we are all silent. Dallas slams his hand against the door. "This is ridiculous. We're just stuck here, doing whatever he says, whether we like it or not?"

Rhen puts a hand on his shoulder. "The State is very different from New Hope."

"No kidding." Dallas shakes his head. "I can't believe you lived like this for seventeen years."

"I lived in *here* for seventeen years." Rhen looks around. "This was all I knew."

"Because it's all that jerk let you know." Dallas hits the door again. "He lied to you about survivors, and he tried to make you into his own version of a house pet."

"Don't forget he is also single-handedly responsible for

destroying the world in the first place." Alex slumps down on the couch.

"Right." Dallas leans against the door. "There's that too."

"He is also very likely listening to every word we are saying right now," I remind them.

"Good." Dallas raises his voice. "I hope he is. I hope he knows we see through his act. We know he is a lying, twisted, evil man."

"Calling him names will not benefit our cause." Rhen speaks quietly, but all of us turn toward her. "We need to think about this logically."

"I am being logical." Dallas straightens.

"You're being emotional." Rhen's voice remains soft. She walks toward Dallas and places her hand in his. "And Loudin is expecting that. I believe he wants nothing more than to see us divided. He thinks he can demonstrate the dangers of emotion by placing us in a petri dish of sorts. We start out angry at *him*, but that anger will spill over into our relationships."

"I could never be mad at you." Dallas wraps his arms around Rhen's waist and leans down to kiss her forehead.

He is so open with his affections. In this, he is very much like Alex. But I am not like Rhen. I cannot look at Alex the way Rhen looks at Dallas, cannot reciprocate emotions in that way. I cannot even evaluate my emotions. Not with Loudin, Berk, and Alex all in the same room.

"Rhen's right." Alex leans forward. "Loudin seems to love playing with people's minds."

"And in people's minds." I feel the tiny hole in the back of my head.

"Well, I won't let him play with mine." Dallas releases his hold on Rhen.

"Then don't let him get you angry," Rhen says. "Let go of your anger toward him. Forgive him."

"Forgive Loudin?" I am shouting now. "He almost had both of us killed, Rhen. He manipulated us, tricked us. Did you know he watched every step of our escape? He planned it? He watched us in New Hope? Dallas is right, Loudin is evil."

"I understand how you feel." Rhen's quiet voice is no longer soothing. It is annoying. "And I am not suggesting you excuse Loudin. He will face judgment for what he has done."

"You better believe he will." Dallas strikes his fist against his open palm.

"But we are not the executors of that judgment." Rhen raises her eyebrows at Dallas. "God is. He has commanded us to forgive our enemies."

None of us says anything. I don't know what the others are thinking, but I am amazed at this change in Rhen. Just a few months ago she called anything to do with faith "primitive." Now she is telling us to make decisions based on that faith. And as much as I want to agree with Dallas, to stay angry and do whatever I can to see Loudin face punishment for his crimes, I feel the truth of what Rhen is saying deep in my being.

"We should pray." Rhen holds Dallas's hand and then reaches for mine. "There's a scripture that says where two or three are gathered in his name, he is there in the midst of them."

The Designer. He has felt so far away. When I have prayed, I have felt nothing in response. But maybe Rhen is right. Maybe when we pray together, he will hear me, he will answer. Berk takes my other hand, and Alex and Dallas close the circle. Rhen leads us in a prayer for wisdom. And for deliverance.

CHAPTER 21

Grandma!" Dallas rushes to hug Kristie, who has just come into Pod C. "Are you all right? What are you doing here?"

"I just need to check a few things." Kristie returns his hug, her hand rubbing circles on his back. What would it have been like to grow up like Dallas in New Hope, surrounded by family who loved me? Kristie pulls away from Dallas and looks at me. Her brown eyes bore into mine and she smiles. "You know."

I swallow hard. Nod.

Dallas's forehead wrinkles. "Know what?"

Kristie releases a long breath. "Let's go outside."

"But Loudin ..."

"I don't care what he hears." Kristie's voice is soft but confident. Dallas and I follow her out the pod doors. She is silent for a long while, her gaze going from Dallas to me and back again. "There are things about my life I wish I could change. Coming here, following Loudin ... I wish I could go back and erase all that we did."

"But you left," Dallas says. "You and Grandpa risked your lives to escape because you knew what was going on here was wrong."

"But that was after we had done so much..." Kristie motions toward the State walls. "We made it possible to live down here, to have air and water. We allowed Loudin to achieve his dreams. We enabled him."

"You wish you hadn't done that?" My heart feels heavy in my chest.

Kristie places a hand on my arm. "John and I talked about this. He taught me that God allows good things to come out of even the worst situations. You are proof of that."

"You said Thalli knew something." Dallas steps closer to Kristie and me. "What does she know?"

"Dallas." Kristie's smile lights up her face. "Thalli is your aunt."

I laugh at the look on his face. "My aunt?"

As Kristie explains, Dallas's jaw drops. "So there are more?"

"I have a brother and a sister," I say. "I've seen my sister, briefly, though I didn't know at the time we were related."

"You knew this?" Dallas asks Kristie.

"Not until Loudin came to New Hope."

"That's why you came." It isn't a question. "It's why you did what Loudin asked you to do."

Tears glisten in Kristie's eyes. "Thalli is my daughter."

The words sound like music, beautiful music. Then a minor chord intrudes. "But Loudin is my father."

Kristie takes a deep breath. "He is not all bad. Joseph is a brilliant man, passionate, driven. When I first met him, I was swept off my feet. I thought he could do anything."

I glance at Dallas—what must he be thinking? "But he destroyed the world."

Kristie sinks onto the grass outside our pod. Dallas and I join her. Her eyes are looking far off in the distance, toward the water towers. "I'll never forget where I was when that happened." She wipes a tear that has fallen onto her cheek. "I had just gotten out of the shower when we got the call to come to the headquarters right away. I threw on some clothes and ran down. My hair was very long back then. By the time I got to the headquarters, the back of my shirt was soaked. It was dripping on the floor, and Carey slipped in the puddle when he arrived."

"My grandpa could slip on anything." Dallas shakes his head. "Not the most graceful man."

Kristie smiles. "Very true. Nevertheless, he was not happy with the mess I'd made, and we started to argue. Then Loudin turned on the screen."

Kristie closes her eyes and her shoulders shake. Dallas scoots beside her and pulls her into his arms. I want to join them—my family—but I cannot move. I just watch, an observer, and my heart seems to sink lower in my chest. I need to hear what she will say next, but I dread it.

"Cameras were everywhere then, on all the street corners, in every major building. We were used to turning them on and observing. 'People watching' it was called. Usually it was an escape. We'd see angry pedestrians yelling at cars or mothers chasing toddlers down the sidewalk. Just life among the regular people." Kristie sighs. "We'd laugh at them and congratulate ourselves on being so much more valuable than they were. So much better."

Dallas rubs Kristie's back the way I have seen her rub his. "You don't have to talk about this."

"Yes, I do." She looks at me, her eyes wide, full of pain I wish I could remove. "We cannot ever allow what happened that day to be forgotten. You need to know about it."

"What did you see?" I can barely get the words out. I do not want to know. But Kristie is right. I need to know.

"It happened so fast." Kristie's lips tremble. "One minute we were watching the sidewalk in front of the Capitol building in Washington, DC. Tourists were taking pictures and lobbyists were picketing. An average day. Then it all stopped. We saw a flash of light and then the people were gone. Just—gone. Everything was gone. I thought the cameras malfunctioned."

"It was the nuclear bombs." Dallas holds Kristie tighter to him.

"Joseph switched to other scenes: New York City, Chicago, LA." Her voice is shaking. "Then overseas: London, Paris, Tokyo—they were all gone. I started screaming. I knew the nuclear threat was possible on paper. But I never imagined it would happen. Never."

The ground seems liquid, and I place my palms flat on the grass to steady myself.

"We begged Joseph to check the smaller towns, rural places—we needed to see that there was still life." Kristie runs a hand through her short brown hair. "Those images were worse."

"I thought everyone died when the bombs hit." I repeat what I was always taught.

"Everyone died, yes. But not all died immediately. Some of the people, in outlying towns, were suffocated because the firestorms removed all the oxygen in the air. Many burned to death. So many. And the ones who managed to survive that..."

Kristie can't continue. Dallas's eyes are hard, the muscles in his jaw tense. We sit for several minutes.

"The ones who survived that died horrible, excruciating deaths." Kristie shakes her head. "We couldn't help but watch the screens. We'd switch from big cities to small towns. Malls and office buildings. Everywhere people were bleeding and screaming. And then all the cameras shut down. The screens went black. The last images we saw of the outside world were of people with blood streaming out of their eyes and ears, skin literally melting off bone. It has been forty years, and I can still see those images as clearly as I did that day."

"And Loudin is responsible for it," Dallas bites out, hate lacing every word.

"We didn't know that then," Kristie says. "But even he wasn't prepared for what that would look like. He didn't speak for days. We were all in shock, but Joseph . . . he was worse than any of us."

"Because he pushed the button. *He* pushed it."

"Yes, he did, Dallas. And he has to live with that every day of his life." Kristie's voice is sad as she continues. "When he finally broke his silence, he was a different person. His humanity seemed to have been destroyed with the world above. What was left was ... what you see."

"An evil man drunk on power." Dallas stands and wipes debris from his pants.

Kristie takes my hand in hers. "But he wasn't always like that."

She is asking me to feel compassion for this man? Never.

: : :

"Could I speak with you?" Berk leans his head into my cube.

We slept late this morning. After talking to Kristie last night, I needed to be alone. And then I needed to be with the others, to know I am not alone.

We ended up praying together late last night. We sat and talked about the Designer, reminding ourselves that he is sovereign, he is good. That Loudin is not the final authority. Each of us heard the Designer in different ways—me through music, Rhen through the logic of his Word, Berk through the complexity of the earth. Alex is still unsure of what to believe. He listened to us, asked us questions. We all understand his doubts. We had them too. We will answer whatever questions he has to the best of our abilities and trust that he, too, will hear the Designer and choose to believe in him.

I pull my hair back into an elastic band, slip into some shoes, and follow Berk down the hall, past the kitchen, into the isolation chamber.

"Am I in trouble?" I try to make the moment light, but it is not. Berk and I have not had a moment alone together since I left New Hope.

He opens the door and allows me to pass through first. I sit on the couch and Berk sits beside me. We are not touching, not even looking at each other. The space between us on the couch seems as wide as the distance from here to New Hope.

"We never really got to speak of what happened in Athens." Berk breaks the silence. His voice sounds tentative. I have never heard Berk sound anything but confident. I look over at him, into his eyes, and see insecurity there too. I know he is asking me about my feelings for Alex.

I close my eyes. No one on earth knows me better than Berk. Not even Rhen. Berk has always understood my differences. He has always appreciated them. Even when we were separated, he never left my thoughts, never left my heart. When I was taken to the Scientists' quarters, it was Berk who protected me. He saw me as more than an anomaly. He loved me. Loves me. When I was scheduled for annihilation, he planned the escape from the State. He gave up everything for me.

But so much changed in Athens. *I* changed in Athens. I discovered I do not need to be rescued. The Designer showed me, through the difficulties I endured there—the drugs and the manipulations, the false accusations and imprisonment—that he can give me strength when I have none, that I can walk through the valley of the shadow of death and not be afraid. That I can come out of those valleys stronger and better than I was when I entered. Love for God rushes through me as I am reminded of what he did in me during my weeks in Athens. He will do the same here. I can trust him.

"Thalli?" Berk's voice shakes me from my thoughts. He is still waiting for an answer about Athens.

I open my eyes and tell him everything—from the first

time I saw Alex on his horse outside the city walls to meeting Helen, visiting the city, meeting King Jason. I tell him how our engagement was announced, and how confused I was, how I tried to fight it but the drugs the king used to manipulate people's minds kept me from thinking clearly.

I don't need to tell him the next part. Berk knows about the imprisonment—he was there, captured with me in an attempt to rescue me. I tell him how I returned after we were released and how Alex knew that his father had to be stopped, had to be killed, or all of New Hope would be destroyed.

I tell him of Peter's sacrifice—killing the king to avenge Helen's death. Tears cascade down my cheeks as I recall helping Peter to Helen's room so he could die there, near her. And I tell him how Alex is ruler now, if we ever escape and are able to return. He is King of Athens, and he is alone. He is frightened. But he will make a wonderful king. He will rule with compassion and wisdom.

"But he does not wish to rule alone." Berk is not asking a question. He does not need me to answer this. He knows. His jaw clenches, and his eyes focus on something in the distance.

"There is so much to be done." I think of all that the Athenians have been taught—about New Hope, about their rulers. "It is similar to what will need to happen here. The people have been slaves for years—the pharmaceuticals their Scientists devcloped kept the people completely submissive to the king. I felt the effects of those drugs. I saw the effects of them on the people, and on Alex. They are strong. And now the people are breaking free from that and seeing reality for the first time. It will be chaotic."

Berk leans forward, his elbows on his knees, head in his

hands. "I knew Athens had more advancements than New Hope. But I didn't know how like the State it was."

"But they are free now." That knowledge fills me with joy. "Alex will not rule like his father."

"Back to Alex." Berk sits up and his gaze meets mine. He still doesn't touch me, doesn't take my hand or even brush my shoulder with his. But the look in his eyes is full of heat, his breath is quick. He releases a long sigh before he speaks. "Do you love him, Thalli?"

The pain in his voice makes my heart ache. But I have to be honest with him. He will know if I am anything but. "He needs me."

"No, he doesn't." Berk moves closer to me and his leg touches mine. In that touch, there is electricity—but the opposite of what I experienced from Loudin's weapon. This spark is pleasant and beautiful. It leaves me wanting so much more. But I cannot say that. Not now. I drag my gaze back to his as he continues. "Alex *needs* the Designer. He *wants* you."

"You don't know him." I stand and walk to the other side of the room. "He watched every member of his family die. His father was responsible for his mother's and his sister's deaths. He lives with that knowledge. He won't admit it, but I know he also lives with a fear that he will be like his father. That's why he does not want to rule alone. He wants someone there to keep him from becoming like his father."

Berk walks toward me. He takes my hand in his. "And that someone is you."

I lower my head and swallow back tears. "Yes."

"But do you love him?"

That question is so complicated. I feel like a timpani being struck over and over again with two mallets. Alex. Berk. Alex. Berk.

Berk pulls me toward him, and I cannot resist. I lean into his chest, listen to his heartbeat, smell the scent that is Berk, enjoy the current that runs between us. I close my eyes and relax into him, my arms around his waist. When I am with Berk, he is the one I want. The one I love.

Do I feel the same when I am with Alex?

I don't know. I cannot even process all these feelings. I feel the tension in Berk's muscles. He is waiting for an answer. *Do you love him?*

The door opens before I have to respond.

CHAPTER 22

There you are." Dallas enters the isolation chamber. "Hate to intrude, but we are being summoned by Dr. Loudin. His big, ugly face just popped up on the wall. He wants us all in the living area right now."

I pull away from Berk, avoiding his eyes. He places a hand lightly on my back as we exit the chamber and make our way back to the living area. Rhen and Alex are already there. And, as Dallas said, Loudin is on the wall screen, his smile too wide.

"Excellent." Dr. Loudin's white teeth fill the center of the screen. "Alex, it seems there is much you did not tell me. I am disappointed. The news of your sister is not all that intriguing, though it sounds as if her death was quite dramatic."

Alex takes a step forward, as if he could reach Loudin through the wall screen. Dallas pulls him back.

"Now, now." Loudin smile remains firmly in place. "No need to get upset. I do not wish to know about your sister. I do, however, wish to know about your father. More specifically, about those drugs your father used. To subdue his people? Fascinating. Our Scientists, I am sure, developed that. Emile was *my* Pharmaceuticals Expert. I felt his loss deeply when he left. But we didn't have time to train someone in that field. It didn't seem as important as maintaining the oxygen and securing the infrastructure. Those five deserters left us operating at a loss. Unlike you, I find I cannot possibly forgive them."

He heard everything. Our discussion in the living area last night, Berk's and my conversation in the isolation chamber today. Every word I told Berk went straight to Loudin. Bile fills my throat and I swallow it down. Angry at Loudin for invading our privacy and angry at myself for not knowing that he would. I have allowed my emotions and my exhaustion to cloud my thinking.

"I know I said you would stay there in Pod C, but I am afraid I will have to rescind that offer. You are needed here. All of you. A transport is being sent as we speak. Gather whatever belongings you need and be prepared to depart in five minutes."

The wall screen goes black, but the five of us stand where we are, staring at it.

"How did he know about my father's pharmaceuticals?" Alex looks at each of us. "I purposely kept silent on that during my testing."

"It is my fault." Berk's jaw clenches, the words coming out like a growl.

"No, it's mine." I walk to Alex. "I told Berk about it. The isolation room has always been camera-free. I assumed it still was."

Alex punctuates each word with his hands. "I've been here a few days, and I know better than to assume Loudin isn't listening to every word we say."

"She's lived here her whole life and never knew that room to be monitored." Berk narrows his eyes as he steps toward Alex. "It's an honest mistake."

"And now the most diabolical man on the planet knows about my father's pharmaceuticals." Alex does not move. "All because *you* made her talk."

"I'm sorry." I step between the boys. "Truly."

"It seems as if the Designer is giving us many opportunities to practice forgiveness." Rhen smiles at me, and I feel even guiltier because of the kindness she is demonstrating.

The door to our pod opens, and Monitors enter. Rhen moves quickly to our cube. The rest of us walk outside, and the transport is waiting. I look beyond it. I want so badly to escape. To run as fast and as far as I can. But even if I did, there would be no real escape. There is no way out. Not while Loudin monitors our every word and our every move. He cannot be overpowered. He cannot be outwitted. How can a man so evil be permitted to rule? Images of the Nuclear War fill my mind, and I feel a renewed fear at what Loudin was—and is—capable of doing.

Rhen joins us, carrying a worn book in her arms—the words of the Designer she has been reading. I look at the ancient tome. I should read it too. Reading its words has certainly helped

Rhen. Changed her. Perhaps it can bring light into the dark places in me.

The five of us are silent as we step into the transport. I look up as we travel, and I see one of the viewing panels. There, far above us, I see the sun. Evidence of the Designer, a reminder that there is a world above waiting for us, a world where there is freedom and love. I think of John, lying beside the pond, eyes looking up toward that sky, smiling at the unseen. I think of the water he loved so much, the baptisms he performed in that water—the cleansing, the new births those represented.

Rhen stands beside me and follows my eyes. She opens the ancient book and points to a section that is underlined. My eyes are momentarily blinded from looking into the sky, but as they adjust, the words come into focus: *"Nothing is impossible with God."*

CHAPTER 23

Wﾟhat do you mean you do not know how to make it?"
Loudin is yelling at Alex.

We have been brought directly from Pod C to
Loudin's office. Alex was right. Loudin wants King Jason's pharmaceuticals. I push down the feelings of guilt that threaten to choke me.

"I have told you everything I know," Alex yells back.

"Liar." Loudin lowers his voice, almost to a whisper. "You have withheld plenty of information from me. You were taught well. Your father may have been less evolved than I, but he certainly understood leadership. And he taught you what he knew because he wanted the Athens he ruled to be strong when you became ruler."

"He did not know how to make the pharmaceuticals either."

"How could he not know something so important?" Loudin is louder again, pacing the floor. "The Scientists could have chosen to use that knowledge against him. They could have subdued your father and taken over the throne."

"They would never do that."

"Why?" Loudin stops in front of Alex and curls his lip. "Because they are loyal?"

Alex does not answer.

"No." Loudin raises his eyebrows. "They were not loyal. Of course not. Your father was well aware of the dangers of his subjects. He knew what all those opinions and emotions could lead to. That's why he had the drugs developed in the first place."

Alex's jaw tenses.

"But if they were not loyal, then what was it that made those Scientists do what your father asked?" Loudin smiles. He knows. Or he thinks he knows. And Alex believes Loudin knows because his face is turning red, he is breathing in short puffs of air, barely keeping himself contained.

"He threatened them." Loudin claps his hands together. "He threatened those they loved."

Alex closes his eyes.

"Yes, I do believe your father and I would have gotten along very well. It is an excellent plan. Use those dangerous emotions to your advantage. Do what I say or I hurt someone you love. So they did whatever he asked and they never considered betrayal."

Alex opens his eyes. They are hard. "My father died at the

hands of one of his subjects. He was not as successful as he imagined."

"Yes, but that subject had no one left, am I right? I heard all about it, how poor Peter loved your sister."

"Peter was a better man than you will ever be." I cannot remain silent.

Loudin waves me off, refusing to take his eyes off Alex. "When your father had your sister killed, Peter was angry, wasn't he? And as soon as he knew his own sister was safe from the king's men, he returned to seek his revenge. And he could because there was no one left in Athens he loved. No one left to threaten."

Alex looks like he is going to burst out of his skin. I want to go to him, comfort him. But I cannot show weakness and neither can Alex. I pray he is able to resist Loudin's taunts.

"And that was his error." Loudin shakes his head. "Peter felt the freedom to kill the king because it was only his own life he was putting in jeopardy. He was gladly willing to sacrifice himself, especially since he lost the only woman he ever loved."

The door opens and Kristie is brought in, a Monitor on either side of her, holding her arms.

"I know what it is like to lose the woman you love." Loudin looks at Kristie. "Your father was wise not to love your mother. He was very wise to kill her when he discovered she was not faithful to him. Had she been allowed to live, who knows what damage she could have done? People may have even used her against him. She herself may have tried to defy him."

The look in Loudin's eyes makes my blood freeze. He walks to Kristie and holds a strand of curly brown hair between his fingers.

"No," Loudin says quietly. "No good comes from loving a woman. It is a weakness that must be destroyed."

Kristie's eyes widen. "You were not always so cruel."

"No." Loudin releases her hair. "But the man you knew—the man you pretended to love—he died long ago."

"I did not pretend." A tear falls down Kristie's cheek.

"Yes, you did!" Loudin shouts so loudly that I jump. "You pretended to love me, and then you gave that love to Carey. And you plotted with him and the others to leave. You abandoned our dreams. You abandoned *me*."

"You changed." Kristie fights to remove herself from the Monitors' grip, but they refuse. "What you were doing to those babies . . . I couldn't . . . we couldn't . . ."

"Weak," Loudin shouts. "You were weak, and you wanted to make me weak. But I would not let you then and I will not let you now."

Loudin pulls the weapon out of his pocket, taps something into the control panel at its side, and then points it at Kristie.

"No!" I lunge toward Loudin, but half a dozen Monitors rush in to stop me and the others who are also moving forward. We are all shouting—Rhen, Alex, Berk, Dallas.

"Enough." Loudin raises the weapon in the air and we are silent.

"This is the power a loved one has over others." Loudin's gaze pauses on each one of us. "Chaotic, yes, but necessary in a world where emotion reigns. You would do anything to save her, wouldn't you?"

We all nod, pretense gone in the face of pure terror.

Loudin pauses in front of Alex. "This is what your father

knew. A threat against a loved one is far more powerful than a personal threat."

I look toward Kristie. Loudin will keep her alive. To keep us submissive. And he is right—we will do whatever he asks in order to see she is safe.

"And that is why I brought all of you here." Loudin smiles to himself. "I saw your gathering last night. Holding hands and praying to your imaginary god, talking of forgiveness and kindness. It was quite interesting, really. Like the old television shows—'reality TV' they were called. People watching other people. We learn from that, you know."

I can barely swallow down the bile rising up into my throat.

"I have learned all of you love each other." Loudin says the word *love* like it is a disease. "You have not yet learned what I learned—that love is destructive. It holds you back. It creates weakness. I will not be weak. But I will use your weakness to my advantage."

Loudin points the weapon toward Kristie. I kick at the Monitor holding me, but he is strong, and his grip only gets tighter.

Loudin motions for the Monitor holding Alex to step forward. "I will not make the mistake your father made. I will not allow any of you to be a Peter. But I will follow his example in protecting myself."

Loudin presses a button on the weapon and a bolt of blue light rushes out and pierces Kristie's chest. Shaking violently, she falls to the ground, then curls up on her side. The light from the weapon is gone as quickly as it came. The setting was different from what he used on me. It was quick and deadly. Kristie rolls onto her back and tries to take a breath.

Everything around me seems to slow down. I see the Monitors moving away, Loudin stepping back. I walk toward Kristie, but it is like I am walking in deep water, so slowly, my ears filled with a rushing sound, my lungs struggling to take in enough oxygen.

I crawl to her side, lift her head onto my lap. Her face is so pale, her pupils dilated. Dallas kneels beside me, his hand holding Kristie's, his tears falling on her white shirt.

"My children." Kristie's voice is soft, labored. "I am so proud of you."

I shake my head, my eyes and throat burning. This cannot be happening.

"John taught me well." Kristie smiles. "I will see you again."

"No." I push her hair from her face. "You'll be fine."

"Tell Carey I love him." A tear forms in her eye, and I reach up to wipe it away.

Loudin stands over Kristie, his face hard.

She looks up at the man who is responsible for her death. "Remember who you once were. You can be that man again."

Loudin spins on his heel and leaves the room.

Kristie's eyes focus on something above us—far above us. She smiles, closes her eyes, and she is gone.

CHAPTER 24

Dallas runs from the room, Rhen following him. I cannot leave the spot where I am sitting, Kristie's head on my lap. I place my fingers on her neck, praying, hoping she isn't really dead. That she is just unconscious. But seconds pass, a minute, and I feel nothing but her cooling skin.

"Thalli." Berk is behind me, his arms wrapped around my waist.

I lean back into him, but I do not feel comforted. I feel empty. Like part of my heart has been ripped out. How can this have happened? My mother, killed by my father. Parents I didn't even know I had until days ago.

I had dreams of sitting with Kristie, sharing with her my hopes and dreams, telling her more about my childhood, learning about hers—her life with Carey in New Hope. The children they had together. I wanted memories with her, years with her. I look at her face, trying to memorize every part of it. Her black eyelashes, curling at the ends, her skin, shades darker than mine, marked with lines around her eyes and lips—lines etched from years of laughter and joy. I want to see her smile again, to see her eyes, hear her voice.

I turn my head into Berk's chest and cry, my sobs echoing throughout the room, shaking my body, soaking Berk's shirt. I hear the door to the laboratory open and shut, but I do not look to see who is here. I do not care. I cannot feel anything but grief.

I mourned when John died. I still miss him, his wisdom and love, his warm smile, his laugh. But he was so old and longed so much to go to the Designer. But Kristie is not as old as John. And she was not ready to go. She has children and grandchildren to love, a husband. She has a village full of people who love her and need her. Fresh tears fill my eyes. I can't bear to tell Carey and Nicole and the others that Kristie is dead.

Berk's arms tighten around me, his head rests on mine. He doesn't speak, and for that I am thankful. No words could comfort me now.

I do not know how long I stay there, on the ground. But eventually my tears dry. Berk releases me and helps me stand. Alex is in a chair against the wall, his head in his hands. Dallas is not here, nor is Rhen. But Dr. Turner is here. He stands by the door, his eyes red. Has he been crying too?

"I am so sorry, Thalli." James walks toward Berk and me. "I

did not know what Loudin was planning. I would have never imagined he would do . . . this."

"We have to take her before Loudin does." I look back at Kristie. "I will not allow him to touch her."

"He will want to examine her before she is cremated," James says.

"No." I stand between Kristie and the door. "I will kill him myself before that happens."

The door opens and Rhen enters, followed by Dallas. His gaze goes to Kristie and a sob erupts. He turns away and slams his hand into a metal table.

"We need to take her to the cremation chamber," Berk says softly.

"Cremation?" Dallas turns around. "No. We bury our dead. We don't burn them."

"We cannot bury them here." Berk walks to Dallas. "The ground is too shallow."

"And Loudin would dig her up even if we tried." I hold my arms against my stomach in an attempt to soothe the pain there. "We need to cremate her now, so he cannot touch her. Ever."

Dallas looks from me to Kristie. The muscles in his jaw flex and the look in his eyes is fierce. "Fine."

Berk moves toward Kristie's body, but Dallas stops him. "I'll carry her. Just show me the way."

Dallas bends down and lifts Kristie into his arms. Her head falls to the side, and he cradles it with his elbow. Alex stands from his chair and opens the door. Berk leads the way, then Dallas follows with James, Rhen, and me behind him. None of us speaks as we go down the hall, into the elevator, up to the top floor, and through a hallway that leads to a locked door.

Berk looks to James, who steps forward and places a finger on the panel beside the door. I hear a click and we enter.

The room is hot, and there is a white cylinder in the center. The cylinder is taller than Berk and just as wide, and a wide tube—almost two feet in diameter—extends from the top of it into the ceiling. This is where my podmates were taken. Every one of them annihilated and then cremated, their remains passing through that tube into the air above.

"I can't put her in there." Tears stream down Dallas's face and onto Kristie's cheek. "She doesn't deserve this."

"She was a beautiful woman." Rhen places her hand on his shoulder. "In every way. She helped me overcome the conditioning I was given by the Scientists. She told me I could be more than just what Loudin told me I was. More than just logical. She showed me the beauty of emotions. She told me her story, how she and your grandfather left the State and came to New Hope because they didn't want to help Loudin accomplish his goals. She was a woman of great strength and character."

Dallas nods.

"She risked her life to escape from Loudin," Rhen continues. "I am confident she would want us to do this—to cremate her body—so Loudin cannot benefit any further from her death."

"I can't . . ." Dallas pulls Kristie closer to him.

"She is gone." Rhen rubs Dallas's back. "Even if we could bury her, her body would eventually return to dust. But her memory will stay with us forever. The lessons she has taught us, the life she lived, that will never die. And we know we will see her again. She is with John, with Jesus, whole and happy, in a new body that will never die."

The struggle wages on Dallas's face, and I understand. Rhen

is right—logical—but the emotion of placing someone you love into the ground seems much less painful than placing that same person into flames. I recall seeing Helen burning in Athens, the sounds and the smell. It was terrible.

But allowing Loudin to have access to Kristie—to open her up and study her as he would a rat? We cannot permit that.

Dallas knows this too. After several minutes, he nods, and James presses a panel on the side of the chamber. A sound like a tuba playing an eighth note fills the room. It is followed by such a rise in temperature I begin sweating immediately.

"We should pray." I think of the service we had at the church after John died. We read from the Designer's book, shared stories of John's life, and we prayed together. We may not be able to bury Kristie the way we buried John, but we can celebrate her life in the same way. She deserves that.

We gather around Dallas and Kristie and close our eyes. I pray, then Berk and Rhen. Dallas cannot speak, but I have my hand on his shoulder and I can feel his muscles relaxing. When we finish, Dallas looks toward the cremation chamber and nods. James presses the panel again and the room is silent.

The chamber hums and a narrow shelf comes out of it. The shelf is rounded on the sides and is just wide enough for a body to be placed on it. Dallas lowers Kristie onto the shelf. He straightens her shirt and places her arms across her chest. He leans down and kisses her cheek, smoothing her hair from her face.

"I love you." Dallas wipes tears from his eyes and steps back.

James presses the panel again, and the section of the chamber just above the shelf opens. The flames are so hot I can barely breathe. They are so bright I am momentarily blinded. When my eyes adjust, I see Kristie being pulled into the chamber, the flames hiding her body, the smell just as I remembered from Athens. Sickening. Terrible.

The chamber closes and the shelf disappears.

Kristie—my mother—is gone.

CHAPTER 25

The door opens and Dr. Loudin steps in.

"Too late," I say.

Loudin's smile is thin. "Don't be so smug. I knew you were here—I watched the entire episode from my communications pad."

I wipe beads of sweat from my forehead. "You are lying."

Loudin turns his communications pad toward me and presses its screen. I see the six of us praying together over Kristie's body. I push the screen away. My chest feels heavy, like I cannot breathe. To think that, as we said our good-byes to this amazing woman, Loudin was watching, waiting, right outside the door, is revolting.

"You think me so cruel." Loudin drops the pad into his pocket. "But I chose not to interrupt this little gathering. I allowed you to cremate her. I admit, the possibility of examining her would have been interesting. I'd like to know the effects of living above on the organs and the blood, especially the brain. But I will, no doubt, have plenty of other opportunities to make those observations. So you were permitted to say your good-byes."

I take three steps to Loudin and push him as hard as I can, keep pushing him until he loses his balance and falls to the floor. Monitors enter, but not before I have the satisfaction of seeing pain on his face.

Berk pulls me back, away from Loudin. I am shaking. I have never felt this much emotion. I have never wanted to hurt someone the way I want to hurt Loudin.

"James." Loudin wipes dust from his shirt. "You are dangerously close to following Kristie. Do not allow misplaced emotions over your father to prevent you from accomplishing our goals."

James says nothing. He walks past Loudin, out of the room.

"Alex, we need to make a trip to Athens so we can recover the formula for the pharmaceuticals your father used." Loudin motions for a Monitor to bring Alex to him.

"Never." Alex shakes off the Monitor's hand.

"Did this"—Loudin motions to the cremation chamber—"teach you nothing? Do I really need to kill someone else for you to do what I ask?"

I turn to Alex. "It would be better for all of us to die than for him to get what he wants."

Loudin grabs me, his hands around my neck. Monitors move into the room to subdue the others. "You first, then."

"Fine." I can barely get the word out, Loudin's hands are tightening on my neck.

"No." There is an apology in Alex's eyes. "Don't hurt her. I'll go."

Loudin releases me.

"Don't do this, Alex. He'll use those drugs on your people and on all the other colonies. We can't give him that much power."

"Too late." Loudin walks to the door. "I already have it. Did you hear nothing I said in my laboratory? You cannot stop me. You cannot defeat me. I am, however, still willing to permit you to join me."

I say nothing. He may be determined, but I have that same determination and something more—I have heart. Kristie gave that to me. Loudin leaves with Alex behind him, flanked by two Monitors. Berk, Rhen, Dallas, and I remain.

"Can we get on that aircraft?" I look to the door. "Or follow them on another one? If we can get to New Hope, we can stop him."

Berk puts a finger to his lips and points to the wall with his other hand. Then he steps beside me, his lips at my ear. "I will disable the cameras after Loudin leaves. Then we can talk openly."

I turn to him, trying to keep my voice to a whisper. "We cannot allow him to go to Athens."

"We have no choice."

I pull away. *We have no choice.* That is a reality of a world I want no part of.

I take one last look at the cremation chamber and I leave the room.

"You are to return to Pod C." A Monitor is waiting in the hallway.

Dallas is too dazed to do anything but take Rhen's hand and follow her out. I motion for Berk to go ahead of me. The Monitor leads the way. Behind us is another Monitor. I slow down, creating a distance between Berk and me. I stop to adjust my shoe and the others turn the corner. I come up quickly and throw my elbow into the Monitor's stomach. He doubles over, but not before he reaches into his pocket for his communications pad.

I race past him and find a doorway that leads to a stairwell. But there is no door that leads above, and the aircraft is above. Loudin has a private elevator from his office that leads to a door outside. But that cannot be the only way out. I press on the walls as hard as I can, hoping—praying—there is a secret entrance. Nothing but solid, unmoving concrete is beneath my hands.

I groan and sprint back out the door. A line of Monitors move toward me. I duck back into the stairwell and run down the stairs. I do not know where I am going, but I refuse to give up easily. I run past level after level, until my lungs burn and my legs refuse to continue moving. I am sure Monitors are waiting outside this and every door leading from the stairwell to the hallway. I cannot escape them. I sit on a stair and catch my breath. Running made me feel better. I am less likely to try to attack a Monitor anyway.

It was a terrible idea, but I had to do something. I had to fight back. It felt too much like my pre-New Hope life, acquiescing to Loudin's demands, going where the Monitors told me to go. That Thalli is dead.

My heart is heavy as I think of Kristie, hating that my last memory is her on the shelf, going into the cremation chamber. I close my eyes and think of Kristie in New Hope, sitting with

Carey in their house, talking with us, smiling. I want those to be the memories that come to mind when I think of her.

The door opens and I lift my eyes, prepared to see an angry Monitor. "James?"

"Come with me."

CHAPTER 26

C an you take me to the aircraft?" I ask James, running to catch up with him as he makes long strides down the hallway.

"No. I can't do that." He turns back to look at me. "But there is something I *can* do."

We continue walking until we reach an elevator. We ride down three more floors, to Level F. I have never been on this level. I have passed by it on the way down to H, where Loudin's laboratory is housed. The doors open, and a rush of cold air makes me grip my arms, rubbing warmth into them. It must be twenty degrees cooler here than it was in the cremation chamber.

"This is my laboratory." James presses a panel that opens a glass door. His laboratory, like Loudin's, is white. But every wall is filled with cooling appliances. They are taller than I am and only about a foot wide. The sides are some sort of metal, but the panels on the front are made of a thick glass. The glass isn't transparent, so the objects inside seem blurry. They are some type of containers, but I cannot see what kind.

Metal tables appear throughout the laboratory as well. Some tables have microscopes and other tables house instruments whose uses I do not know. Every surface glows—no dust, no fingerprints, nothing out of place. And the smell is different—a pungent, too-clean odor that makes my eyes water.

"All the ingredients for life are stored here." James motions to the cooling appliances. "I began gathering these before the War. I went all over the country, taking samples, talking with other Geneticists, determining how to store and create. I learned from the greatest minds in the country, and I had the newest technology. I even patented some of my own. Had the War not occurred, I would have been very rich."

"Are you sure you should be telling me this?"

James smiles. "Do you think Berk is the only one who can disable the equipment in here?" He sits on a chair by one of the tables and motions for me to join him.

I pull the chair out so I can sit across from him, the metal under my hands cold. "So no cameras?"

"I programmed the image to repeat." James shrugs. "All Loudin will see is an empty room."

"What if he looks for me?"

"You're subdued in a medical chamber." James weaves his

fingers together. "The lights are out, so the image might be slightly unclear."

"What about the Monitors looking for me?"

"They received a communication from Dr. Loudin that the search was successful and they should continue on with their previous assignments."

How did he do all that in the time since he left the cremation chamber? And what does he have to show me? I lean forward.

"As I said, these are all the ingredients for life." James leans back. "I have made more babies here than I can count. 'Designer babies' was what they were called before the War. The technology had developed rapidly, and parents were desperate for it. In my parents' day, all they hoped for was that their children would be born healthy. But by the time I completed graduate school, good health was practically guaranteed. Unless someone had a child without the help of a Geneticist. But that was becoming more and more rare."

I have never heard any of this history. It landed, I suppose, under the "primitive behaviors" section—too many strange ideas and practices to be listed for us, too unnecessary for us to learn.

"My parents were not pleased with my career choice." James looks down. "They thought I was playing God. But, of course, since I didn't believe in God, I didn't listen to them. I listened to Loudin. He had such vision, such intelligence. I had never met anyone like him. He was just a few years older than I was, but he seemed so much older than that. No one was surprised that the president chose him to build this place. Loudin certainly wasn't surprised. And I was so honored to be part of it.

I'll never forget the first time I came down here. It was beyond anything I'd ever seen before. An engineering marvel, a scientific marvel. There was literally nothing else on earth like the State."

I cannot imagine what he is describing. The State was all I knew for seventeen years. It was not marvelous. It was a cage. It *is* a cage—one I desperately want to be free of. I prefer the "primitive" life of New Hope and Athens to this sterile, oppressive environment.

"Once I came here, I was hooked." James sighs. "I told Loudin I would do whatever he wanted me to do, if only I could be part of it."

"What did your parents think of that decision?"

James looks at me, his blue eyes so like John's. "They tried to be supportive, but I knew they were disappointed. I was turning my back on everything they taught me. At the time, I just felt sorry for them—Loudin called people like my parents 'underevolved.' He said they were too mired in the old systems of belief that they could never come out, their minds were fossilized."

"Your father was an incredible man." My face warms, despite the temperature in the room.

"I know that now." He shakes his head. "But it took forty years for me to see it. It took you, Thalli. Seeing you—one of my designer babies, a product of Loudin himself—break out of the mold I had designed for you. I can't describe it."

"What do you mean?"

"There had been anomalies before you." James looks at the cooling appliances. "At first I designed more anomalies than 'normal' babies. Not intentionally, of course. Loudin was so angry at me. I asked for more Geneticists to help—older ones with more experience. But he insisted that all of us working in the State be young, fresh out of school."

"Because he planned the Nuclear War and he knew you'd be the only survivors." That fact still makes me feel ill. Kristie's reminder to never forget what happened that day stays with me, will always stay with me.

"Yes." James places his hands in his lap, hands that have helped create life and helped destroy it. "I didn't know that at the time though. I promise."

"But why didn't you leave with Kristie and the others, when they knew there were pockets of survivors left?" I run a hand through my hair. "Why stay and keep doing this?"

"We didn't know the effects of the Nuclear War on the survivors." He stands and moves behind his chair, then grips it for support. "We didn't know how far the radiation carried. Even though people survived, we had no idea what those people looked like. The effects of the toxins could have affected every cell in their bodies. They could have been sterile. Or if they weren't, they could have only been able to produce children with severe disabilities."

"But they didn't. They produced people like Dallas and Alex. And so many more."

James's Adam's apple bobs in his thin neck. "That is miraculous. Truly."

"But you didn't believe in miracles."

He lowers his head. "I believed it was possible that the only way to ensure the survival of the human race was here, in this room. I was suddenly vitally important—Loudin needed me."

"But he needed the others too."

"Yes, but the others didn't have anyone here that Loudin could use against them."

I swallow hard. "Your father."

"Yes." He presses his lips together. "As long as I did what Loudin asked, he would allow my father to remain alive."

"John was kept locked up in the lowest level, only allowed to interact with people scheduled for annihilation." I stand, knocking over my chair. The sound echoes in the silent room.

"I thought it was best."

"*Loudin* thought it was best."

"And I believed him." His shoulders slump. "I believed everything he said. I believed in his ideas and his plans."

"But it's been forty years." I pick up the chair and set it back on the ground, but I remain standing. "How could you have gone along with him for that long?"

"There was always another project, another plan." James does not look at me. "I love research. I love this laboratory. And I got to spend all my time here, doing what I loved. And in doing that, I was preserving mankind, helping to save the earth. I thought we would be revered throughout history, that our legacy would carry on for thousands of years. It was a heady thought."

"But now?"

"Now I am ashamed." His eyes close. "Ashamed that I ignored my parents and listened to Loudin, ashamed that I lived my whole life pretending there is no God when everything I did— everything I worked with—told me otherwise."

"So you are no longer a follower of Loudin."

"No. Never again." James's eyes open. "He has to be stopped. I see that now. And I know how to do it."

CHAPTER 27

What are you doing?" I watch as James taps on his communications pad.

"Shutting down my laboratory."

"What?" The lights on the cooling appliances turn off, making the glass in them look more like mirrors than windows. "Why?"

"I refuse to create another generation." He looks lighter, his smile wide, eyes glowing. "There is no need."

"But is it right to destroy all of these?" If these are the ingredients for life, locked away in these appliances, are they not valuable?

"These represent a continuation of the State." James lowers his communications pad onto a table. "Destroying these is the first step toward destroying the State."

Destroying the State. "Can we really do that?"

"I can do *this*." He motions to the now-silent appliances. "But I need your help."

"How?"

"As soon as Loudin sees what I have done, he will kill me."

"No—"

James raises a hand to stop me. "Watching Kristie die changed me. It made me realize there are worse things than death. Continuing to do what Loudin wants—*that* is worse than death. I gave my soul to that man forty-five years ago. It's time to take it back."

"Your father would be so proud of you."

He blinks back tears. "I have time. Loudin won't know right away what I've done. The specimens will thaw while he is gone. I will turn the appliances back on before he returns. Nothing in them will be viable, but he won't know that."

"How long until he realizes it?"

James places his hands on the desk. "He wants very much for a new generation to be born in the next year. But he is also very focused on all the survivors."

"With the Athenian pharmaceuticals, he can control the survivors." Not that I want him to find that formula or make it work. "He could repopulate the State with some of them."

"He has discussed that." James sits back in a chair. "But they lack the training and conditioning you all have."

"Yes, but that training takes years—couldn't he apply those same years to training the survivors?"

"You want him to do that?"

"Of course not." Loudin needs to be stopped, but we need time to develop a plan. "But as you said, it will keep him occupied and it will keep you alive."

"I told you, I don't care."

"But I do." John would not want his son to sacrifice himself. "Besides, we need you here. You know what Loudin is doing. You can tell us."

"He doesn't trust me."

"No, but he needs you."

James leans his head toward the appliances. "He *thinks* he needs me."

"Then let him keep thinking that." We can do this. We can stop Loudin. I feel more hope than I have since I have arrived in the State.

"What about the people he is bringing back? Do we allow them to be given the drug?"

"Don't worry about that yet." I wave off James. "He has to get the formula and find a way to reproduce it before he even can go out to the other surviving colonies. Hopefully we can stop him before then."

"And how will we stop him?"

"I don't know." I look at his communications pad, fear replacing my joy. "You are sure he can't overhear us?"

"Yes, I'm sure." He lifts his pad and taps on it. The image of this room fills the screen. It is empty. He taps again and the image of a medical chamber is on the screen, a lump underneath the sleeping platform. A machine beside it shows a heartbeat. "This is what Loudin sees if he taps into the quarter's cameras."

"Won't he know he is being tricked?" Loudin always seems

to know everything, to be steps ahead of everyone. "How can we be sure he doesn't suspect us?"

James taps the screen again and I see the aircraft. Loudin is sitting in the front, a Monitor beside him.

"There are cameras everywhere." James winks.

I look back at the screen and watch as Loudin directs the Monitor to follow the flight path to Athens. He then walks to the rear of the transport and sits next to Alex. "Right now I have Thalli in a room wired for electricity. You step one foot out of line and she will pay. Do you understand?"

Alex nods, and my heart constricts at the look of pain and horror on his face.

"It has taken me four and a half decades"—James watches the screen—"but I have finally learned that Loudin is *not* God."

"But he thinks he is." I want to crush the smug look from Loudin's face.

"Not for long."

CHAPTER 28

T ake her to Pod C."

James is in the room where I have been "sleeping." I snuck in here while the Assistants were diverted with a project James assigned them. The cameras are now live, and if Loudin is watching, he is seeing me being woken up by two large Monitors to be taken to Pod C to join the others.

I stand on the transport as we return to my childhood home, and I think of the time I took a transport just like this to New Hope, so many weeks ago. I pray for Alex, returning there now with Loudin in an attempt to find the formula, reproduce it, use it against people all around the world. Against us. I swallow down fear that rises into my throat.

I look up at a panel far above me, and I see a glimpse of the sun shining down, blue sky surrounding it. How I long to be there. Music plays in my mind and I close my eyes. It has been so long since I have heard music, played music, so long since I have held an instrument in my hands. I am overpowered with longing to do what I was made to do. God never seems as close as when I am playing, my prayers never as complete. So much has happened, so much that I want to play, to express through my fingers, channeling my thoughts and feelings, my prayers and fears, into my violin, the piano, anything.

The transport lowers itself to the ground in front of Pod C. The flowers that used to line the walkway are withering, their reds and yellows now a yellowish-brown, crisp at the edges. Even the grass is neglected, patches of brown showing through what used to be lush green.

"Thalli." Berk rushes from the entrance to the pod and lifts me into his arms. "Where have you been? Are you all right? Did he hurt you?"

"I am fine." I can barely speak, he is holding me so tightly. I don't mind though. I love the feel of Berk's arms around me.

"I was so frightened." He releases me and we enter Pod C. I smell food being prepared in the cooking chamber, see a Culinary Specialist bending over the cooking appliance.

"We need to talk." My gaze goes to the Monitor behind me. "Alone."

"There is no privacy here." Berk sighs. "You know that."

I turn my face so only Berk can see me. I mouth, *We are safe.*

Berk raises his eyebrows, but he follows me down the hall, into the isolation chamber. His forehead crinkles a little as his lips press together—he must be recalling our last conversation here, the one where I told him about Athens and Alex, the one Loudin listened to that started all of this.

My heart drums a rapid rhythm. What if James's work on the camera in Pod C wasn't effective and Loudin can see us? But James's words play again in my mind. *Loudin is not God.* He doesn't know everything, doesn't see everything. He can be defeated. He can be outwitted.

I draw in a deep breath. Then exhale. I will trust James's work, and I will do everything in my power to work against Loudin so he cannot do to others what he did to my friends from this pod, what he did to Kristie.

"Where did you go?" Berk closes the door to the isolation chamber and takes my hands, lacing his fingers through mine. "I wanted to look for you, but we were surrounded. I was worried Loudin was taking you with him to Athens."

I pull Berk to the couch and we sit. He pulls me into his arms, my back against his chest. "James found me."

"Where were you going?"

"I was trying to find the aircraft and stop Loudin."

"And then what, Thalli?"

I lean my head back against him. "I don't know. I just wanted to stop Loudin. To be honest, I wanted to kill him for killing Kristie."

"I know."

I turn into Berk, holding on to his waist, burying my head in his chest. "I hate him, Berk."

He runs a hand through my hair, down my back. He says nothing, and for several minutes, we sit there. I alternate between grief and rage.

"You said we're safe?" Berk breaks the silence, pulling back and looking into eyes I know are swollen and red.

"James did something to the cameras."

"Disabled them?"

"No." I think of the image of me lying in a sleeping platform, attached to medical equipment. "He made it so if Loudin looks at us, he will see us here. But he won't see us *here*. I don't know how to describe it."

"He has it on a loop." Berk smiles. "Brilliant. For how long?"

I feel the warmth of that smile all the way to my toes. "I don't know."

"Tell me everything then." He pulls me back against him again.

I want to just enjoy his nearness, this moment, but there is too much to say, too much to plan. I fold my arms over Berk's, though, and breathe in his scent. "James destroyed the ingredients for life stored in his laboratory. He refuses to create another generation."

Berk's breath catches. "Loudin will kill him."

I explain that hopefully Loudin won't know, that James will plug the appliances back in so they will appear to be working. I tell him that Loudin wants to use the Athenian drug on survivors he plans to bring back to the State from other parts of the world.

"We cannot allow him to do that."

"I know." I sit up and turn so I can see his face. For a moment I forget what I was going to say. He is so handsome. I want to stop time, to stare at him for hours. But I cannot. "We have to make sure the formula fails. I am hoping Alex will find a way to prevent Loudin from getting it, or at least change some of the ingredients so it doesn't work."

Berk's face darkens at the mention of Alex's name. There is still much about that relationship we have not discussed.

"If Alex"—Berk says the name as if it tastes bad on his tongue—"cannot prevent Loudin, then what?"

If Loudin arrives here with the formula, how long will it take for him to recreate it? If that is all he is focused on, then it could be completed in days. But if it's not all he is focused on . . . "We need to create a distraction."

"A distraction?"

"Something needs to go wrong." I stand from the couch and pace. "Something big. Something that is more important to Loudin than the formula."

"What's more important than that?"

I stop and turn to Berk. "The State."

He leans forward. "Of course. This is everything he has worked toward. When anything is wrong with the State, he gets frantic."

"Like when the oxygen levels were too low?" He sent us aboveground precisely because he wanted Kristie found and brought back here in order to fix that.

"And the power outages." Berk stands. "He had me work for weeks figuring that out."

"And did you?"

"I worked with Dr. Williams to reconfigure the solar panels so they would convert the energy faster."

"Could you undo that?" Plunging the State into darkness would certainly stop Loudin.

"No." Berk runs both hands through his brown hair. "He

had us establish backup power sources to prevent that from happening again."

"Hey." Dallas's loud, accented voice comes muffled through the door. "What are you two doing in there?"

Berk opens the door and Dallas enters, followed by Rhen.

"Thalli comes back and you don't even tell us?" Dallas leans against the door. "We were worried too, you know."

"I'm sorry." Berk's hands fall to his side. "I'm glad you found us though. We could use your help."

We explain the situation to Dallas and Rhen. Dallas starts pacing as soon as I begin talking. He is all over the room, constantly moving. Rhen, however, is completely still, sitting on a chair, her eyes looking at an invisible spot on the wall. I know her mind is processing all of this, sorting it, trying to find a logical solution, a plan. Subverting the plans of the State's founder goes against all she was taught, growing up here in Pod C. But being intelligent, logical, finding solutions to problems—that is who she is.

"You said James was able to make cameras show what is not actually happening, right?" Rhen looks from the wall to me.

"Yes."

"What if we used that technology to confuse him?"

"Keep going." Dallas is beside Rhen, his love for her evident in the way he looks at her.

"We have time while he is away, correct?"

"A day—two at most," Berk says.

"What if we recorded ourselves—entering the Scientists' quarters, going through the halls and the laboratories, causing problems?"

I smile as I realize Rhen's plan. "And we play those recordings when he returns."

Dallas lets out a loud laugh. "Loudin goes running down to wherever he thinks we are, ready to yell and scream at us, and he finds nothing but an empty room."

"We only have to have two recordings, three at most." Rhen shrugs her thin shoulders. "Just enough for him to know something is wrong."

"It is fitting." I imagine the scene. "He has spent his life manipulating others' minds. He deserves to have his mind manipulated."

Berk stops us with a hand in the air. "But then what? He'll find out and he'll punish us—maybe even kill one of us. And all we have done is postponed him."

"What's your idea?" Dallas's tone reveals a protectiveness toward Rhen.

Berk bristles but continues. "I don't have one."

"But you shut Rhen down?" Dallas places his hands on his hips. "Nice."

"I understand what Berk is saying." Rhen's hand is on Dallas's shoulder. "But this will allow us to have time. If we distract Loudin with the video, we will know where he is going. And we know he will bring his Monitors with him, especially if he thinks we are destroying something valuable. When he goes to stop us, we can be in place to confiscate the formula and destroy what he has begun."

"That might be the hottest thing I have ever heard." Dallas wraps a thick arm around Rhen's tiny frame.

"I agree—it's a good short-term solution," Berk says. "But even if we can confiscate the formula—and if he hasn't already made a copy of it—he'll still be Loudin. He'll still be working to find a way to control the people he brings in. If it's not with the drugs, he'll just use what he knows: cerebral manipulation. But he'll still accomplish what he wants to accomplish."

I step to the center of the room. "There's only one way to stop him."

Three sets of eyes are on me, but they all know what I am about to say.

"We have to kill Loudin."

CHAPTER 29

We cannot do it. We cannot commit premeditated murder. No matter how justifiable, no matter how despicable Loudin is, none of us can be the one to end his life.

The four of us have been in the isolation chamber for hours. We left briefly to eat so the Culinary Specialist would leave. The Monitors are all gone—except for the two stationed outside the pod to make sure we don't try to escape. We could have returned to the living area, but the isolation chamber feels safer, more protected.

We have run through myriad ideas. Many of them excellent, all of them ending with Loudin dying and the residents of the State—the world—being free. But we cannot execute those plans because we cannot execute Dr. Loudin.

"I keep telling you guys," Dallas says. "I'll do it. I'll kill the man with my bare hands."

Rhen places her hands on her slim hips, her blond ponytail bobbing with every word. "No, you can't."

"He killed my grandmother, Rhen," Dallas roars.

We have watched him go through so many emotions in the past few hours. From calm and loving to angry and hurt and back again. These emotions are natural, we all recognize that. But we also see what he does not: he is not thinking clearly.

"I won't allow you to add guilt to your grief."

"You won't *allow* me?" Dallas takes a step closer to Rhen, his large frame dwarfing hers. "You're my mother now?"

"We both know what happens when decisions are made based on emotions," I say. "We can't act on our anger. We can't give Loudin that kind of power over us."

Dallas releases a breath—so like Kristie in that moment—and he sits on the sleeping platform, head in his hands. "Fine."

"Let's go back to Rhen's idea—fake some videos to throw Loudin off track and we can nab the formula." I look to the others.

"But then we antagonize Loudin." Berk shifts in the chair. "He could choose to kill one of us as punishment."

"As opposed to just killing us for some other reason?" Dallas raises his head. "The guy is like a lit cannon—he can blow anytime, for any reason. We can't worry about making him mad. It's too late for that. We just have to stop him."

Rhen leaves the couch and sits beside Dallas. "We have

been up too long. Our brains do not function well when we are tired. Let's get some sleep and talk again in the morning."

"But we still do not have a plan." I lean my head against the back of the couch. "And we don't have much time. Loudin will be back, and then what? He just makes the formula, uses it on us first, and we forget everything, become just another one of his projects, his slaves? We cannot allow that to happen."

"Rhen is right." Berk stands. "We should sleep. And pray. John told me that God gives wisdom to those who ask for it."

"We sure need it." Dallas scratches his face. "It'd be nice if he sent down one of those lightning bolts to just wipe Loudin off the planet too though."

"I think you are confusing the Designer with one of the mythical gods of the ancient world." Rhen walks to the door. "I have not read anything in the Scriptures that says God throws lightning bolts."

"I was joking, babe." Dallas laughs, his mood changing once again. "But I sure do love hearing you talk like that."

Dallas and Rhen discuss the relevance of joking during a serious conversation as they walk into the hallway. I am happy for them, happy they found each other, happy they can help each other through this.

I stand from the couch and blink. I am exhausted in every way—my body, my mind, my spirit. There is so much to process: Kristie's death, James's destruction of his laboratory, Loudin taking Alex to retrieve the formula for a drug that will allow him to control any non-State citizen.

"How are you?" Berk is beside me, his voice quiet.

I shake my head, too full of emotion to speak what is in my mind, in my heart.

Berk pulls me to him and holds me. He doesn't say anything. Though Kristie is not his mother, I know he is grieving for her, missing her. He spent more time with her than I did, in New Hope, while I was away in Athens. And he has also spent more time with Loudin—my father—than I have. He knows just how intelligent Loudin is, how calculating, how driven.

I tighten my grip around Berk's waist and try, for a moment, to forget everything else that is happening. My muscles relax, though my heart quickens—not out of fear, but because I am near Berk. Every nerve seems to tingle, my whole body feels warmer, more alive when I am with him.

I love Berk. I love him with everything in me, and I want nothing more than to be with him forever, to have his arms around me every day of my life. I want what John had with Amy, the committed love he spoke of, the wedding and the life. Children. I want everything I was always taught was "primitive." I lift my head from his chest and look into Berk's eyes, eyes that have seen me since birth, that have watched me play and hide my differences, eyes that have always loved me for who I am.

Yes, Berk loves me. I see it. I feel it. He lowers his head, and I feel as if I am about to float away, that I am somewhere above, watching what is happening. His face is inches from mine, and I close the gap, my lips touching his in what is the most glorious feeling I have ever experienced. My arms are around his neck, and I rise on my toes so I can deepen this kiss, say without words what is in my heart, what has always been in my heart.

I discover that music can be made with no instruments at all.

CHAPTER 30

I cannot sleep. Every time I close my eyes, I see Berk, replay our kiss in my mind. I feel like little Nicole—I want to run and jump and scream and laugh. I want to find Berk and kiss him some more, kiss him forever. I want to run away from here, forget all of this, and just be with Berk.

I feel guilty for feeling so much joy when so much is wrong in the world, when Kristie is dead and Loudin is plotting terrible things and all of our lives are in danger. But I cannot stop this joy, and I don't really feel guilty. I feel guilty because I don't feel guilty and I think I should. I laugh at that and quickly cover my mouth. I don't want to wake Rhen.

I just want to pause time, like a video can be paused on a learning pad, so I can remain back there in the isolation chamber, in Berk's arms. John told me that God delights in giving good gifts to his children. Berk is a good gift. A very good gift. And I feel God's pleasure in receiving that gift, in knowing that he is mine.

Loudin and Kristie may have provided the ingredients from which I was created, but the Designer created me. He did a beautiful job creating Berk. I know, in the deepest part of me, that Berk and I were made to be together. I think I have always known that, from the time we were children when we would play and fight. I knew it when, before Berk was taken to the Scientists' quarters when we were twelve, he carved our initials in the floor. I knew when I saw him again, outside this pod, right before all of this started.

Love for the Designer fills me. He has seemed distant, but this reminds me that he is here . . . he is working and planning, even when I don't see it. I can trust that he gives good gifts, that he is good. As John said over and over, "God is love." He has given us emotion, he has given us love, and he has shown us how to demonstrate that love to others.

What of Loudin? Could he be changed by love too? Is he beyond the reach of this emotion? I sit up in the sleeping platform and breathe deeply. Maybe we are wrong in our approach, wrong in thinking he must be destroyed. Maybe the reason none of us can kill him is because that is not the answer. Love is the answer.

I get up, slip into shoes, and walk into the dark living area. Soft lights shine through the windows, artificial lights that mimic stars. But those lights cannot compare to the real stars.

I have seen them, bright spots of white on a black sky, millions of them, so far away, yet still visible, still shining. Loudin is like those artificial stars—he is trying to mimic the Designer. But he cannot. Like those lights, he will one day burn out, be replaced. He wants to be God, but he is not God. And he is most definitely not love.

But he has loved, and he has been hurt by love. Could he be healed by it?

Could I love Loudin?

The thought turns my stomach, makes dissonant chords strike in my mind. Loudin has done so much to hurt me and the people I care about. He is a murderer, an egotistical tyrant.

But what was it Kristie said as she was dying? *"Remember who you once were. You can be that man again."* He wasn't always like this. Kristie said as much in New Hope. Kristie loved him once.

Could I love him?

I look out the window at the lights that mimic the stars. I never knew how false those were until I saw what was real. Loudin has spent so much time creating this false world that he has forgotten what is real. He has come to believe what is false.

Perhaps I can remind him of what he has forgotten.

CHAPTER 31

T hat's your plan?" Dallas is shouting, but no one stops him. They are all looking at me like I have developed an ancient disease. "You're going to be *nice* to Loudin? Why don't we just walk into his lab with knives and kill ourselves in front of him?"

"James told me that Loudin is proud of me." Proud of his DNA in me, but still . . . "Somewhere beneath that pride and that self-centeredness is love. If I can get past all of that, maybe I can get him to see truth. Maybe he can change."

"Ever heard the term *psychopath*, Thalli?" Dallas's voice is slightly lower, but it rings with conviction. "A person who feels nothing and thinks only about himself, who will do anything necessary to get what he wants. That is Loudin. You look inside him and all you'll see is evil."

"But he is human." Words from the Designer's book fill my heart. "And humans are made in God's image. So Loudin is made in God's image."

"That may be true." Berk's green eyes almost undo me. I can see the battle raging in them—he doesn't want to hurt me, but he cannot agree with me. "But there have been plenty of men throughout history—and in the Designer's book—who choose to behave in ways that are not loving."

"What about Paul?" Rhen speaks up. "I've been reading about him. He was a terrible person. He hated the early Christians, and he was responsible for persecuting them. But Jesus spoke to him, and Paul was changed so radically that he traveled all over just to tell people about the Savior."

I want to hug Rhen, but I do not. I look at Dallas and Berk, trying to interpret the looks on their faces, the thoughts in their heads.

"It's a nice thought." Dallas crosses his arms. "I'll give you that. Do I think God can change Loudin? Sure I do. He has changed all of us. It isn't that I doubt God. It's Loudin I wonder about."

"I'm tired of trying to think up ways to trick him." I sigh. "I'm tired of being chased and pretending and plotting. It doesn't feel right. It never has. But being honest feels right. And loving feels right. That's how John lived. I never heard him say anything bad about The Ten, and he could have. He loved his son, even though his son had basically abandoned him. He cared for those who could give him nothing in return. We have been trying to think like Loudin all this time, to stay ahead of him. But we should have been trying to act like John."

"I don't like it." Dallas shakes his head. "I'm sorry, Thalli. I know you mean well and all, but you are giving Loudin more credit than he deserves. We know how he feels about love. We saw what he did to the one woman he cared about. There's no changing a man like that." He walks out of the room.

Rhen and Berk are silent. I want one of them to speak up, to agree with me. I want Berk to take me in his arms and kiss me and tell me he knows how powerful love is, and that love will break through Loudin's tough exterior. But Berk doesn't move.

So I do. I leave the room, the pod. I go outside and tell the Monitor I need to visit the performance pod. He communicates to another Monitor, then trails behind me. Ordered to guard me, no doubt, to ensure I don't run off again, don't hurt anyone else.

I start out walking, but then I break into a run. Not because I am trying to escape the Monitor, but because I am trying to escape my thoughts, trying to outrun my emotions. I feel like I just opened myself up back there, in front of my friends, in front of Berk. I was exposed, heart and soul, and they just looked on, spectators at a performance.

The doors to the performance pod open. The building smells clean—obviously a Sanitation Specialist has been here recently. The instruments shine from their slots. I should feel joy at seeing all of these instruments—friends I have known my whole life, who have listened to my secrets and my longings. But they don't have the same appeal they used to. So much of me has changed. I no longer feel like the Musician of Pod C. That is not my identity anymore—but what is?

I sit at the piano and play what has become my favorite song, "Jesu, Joy of Man's Desiring." As play, I recall John singing the words to this song for me.

Jesus, joy of man's desiring,
Holy wisdom, love most bright;
Drawn by Thee, our souls aspiring
Soar to uncreated light

I keep playing, thinking of John and Kristie, their souls soaring to the uncreated light, their being present with him, whole, full of joy. I pray for Loudin, that he would be drawn to this love, that his soul would aspire to it.

I close my eyes and pour my prayer into my fingers. I cry because I can't help it and because I can, and I should. Emotions are not to be hidden. These tears are a testament to the fact that I am human, I am made in God's image, not in Loudin's. I am more than he planned me to be. And he can be more . . . he can be better.

When I open my eyes, I see Berk sitting in a chair, facing me. I finish the song and lift my hands from the keys.

"Beautiful."

"I know." I caress the keys. "It is my favorite song."

"I wasn't talking about the song." Berk moves to sit beside me on the piano bench. His lips find mine, and I forget everything but the glorious feel of Berk, the taste and smell of him.

He pulls away—too soon—and rests his forehead on mine.

"You disagree with me." I hold his hand in mine, tracing his knuckles with my finger. "About Loudin. You don't think he can change."

"I want to agree with you." Berk sits back, and I look into his face, so handsome, so conflicted. "But I know Loudin. I've lived in the Scientists' quarters for five years. I've watched him. He is the leader and he knows it. The other Scientists defer to him. He really does think of himself as God."

"But he's not."

"I know." Berk brushes a strand of hair from my forehead. "But look what he has done—he created this world. It was all his idea. He hired all of the Scientists that came. Have you noticed they all have similar personalities? They do what Loudin says. They'll question him occasionally, but not for long."

"James said he was so happy to be doing what he loved, he didn't even think about what Loudin was doing."

"Exactly. They're all like that. Focused on their science."

"And Loudin sees that as a positive trait—we were all designed to be focused on our jobs." The Ten were considered "superevolved" according to our learning-pad lessons. They were better than the average human. "But he was just looking to be obeyed. That's still what he's looking for with the survivors."

"He has spent a lifetime becoming who he is." Berk presses an A flat on the piano and the sound lingers in the air. "I believe God can change him. But I don't believe he will want to change."

"I want to believe he will." I begin to play, my fingers moving over the keys, finding chords and rhythms. "I want to believe he will be like Paul, like Rhen said, that he will turn from what he is doing and will follow God."

Berk is silent, and I continue to play, my hopes, my prayers, my love all being poured into this instrument. As I play I feel the Designer's nearness, his comfort. I finish and lean into Berk, closing my eyes and continuing the prayer that was begun on the piano. The room seems to echo with the notes I played. It seems to be filled with the Designer, every inch, every crevice. I am filled with him too. I am ready. For what, I do not know.

"He's back." Dallas enters the performance pod. "Loudin just landed."

CHAPTER 32

Alex looks like he has been beaten. His entire face appears bruised, his right eye is swollen shut, and he is holding his right arm against his body, his left hand protecting it. He limps painfully into Pod C in front of Loudin, who is wearing a smile that makes the hairs on my neck stand, the flesh on my arms crawl.

"What happened?" I reach for Alex, but I am afraid to touch him, afraid I will cause him further injury. So I gently place a hand on his shoulder and walk with him to the couch.

Loudin reaches into his pocket for his communications pad. He lifts it up, the sickening smile still plastered on his face. "It seems like the folks there in Athens are a bit unhappy with their king."

Alex says nothing, his expression distant, as if he cannot hear what is happening, isn't really here.

"What did you do to him?" Dallas's entire body is tense, and I fear he will try to hit Loudin. Rhen must share that concern because she places herself between Dallas and Loudin.

"I didn't do anything." Loudin waves the communications pad in the air before returning it to his pocket.

"Alex, man, say something." Dallas sits next to Alex, who remains impassive.

"Aren't you going to ask about the formula?" Loudin arches an eyebrow. "Did I get it? Will I use it? How did it go?"

Loudin is mocking us, and he is hiding something. Something so terrible that it makes Alex ill and brings Loudin joy.

"Please, sit." Loudin motions to the couches and chairs in the living area.

My curiosity is replaced by dread. I know, deep within me, that whatever Loudin is about to reveal is horrible, that I would rather not know. But ignorance is not an option. I sit in the chair nearest Alex on the couch. Rhen sits beside Dallas, and Berk takes the chair beside Rhen. Loudin taps on his communications pad and the wall screen lights up. I see the entrance to Athens. People have gathered by the city gate, looking at the aircraft that has brought Loudin and Alex. And someone else. I lean forward, watching the screen as the third person emerges from the conveyance.

Nicole.

Dallas stands. "What are you doing with my sister?"

Loudin pulls out his weapon and motions for Dallas to sit

down. He lowers himself back to the couch with reluctance, but he is leaning forward, his eyes focused on the screen.

Nicole's brown eyes are wide as she cringes. She reaches for Alex's hand, and he holds it, helping her down.

Loudin faces the camera. "I had my Engineers design this—the camera is on a tiny platform that can follow us. I knew you'd want to see what is happening. So here we are: Athens."

Loudin moves away, and I see the faces of the people—most are confused. Frightened. They have never seen this aircraft, and if they know of Loudin, it is through conversations they may have had with the people of New Hope. He has never been there, never interacted with the Athenians.

With a look from Loudin, Alex clears his throat. When he speaks, he does not sound like himself. There is no music in his voice. It is monotone, like a poorly made recording of the real thing. "People of Athens, it brings me great joy to be here today. I have missed you, and I look forward to returning soon to rule in my father's place."

The people nod, confusion lining their faces.

"This"—Alex motions to Loudin with his free hand—"is Dr. Loudin, founder of the State. I have spent time in the State with him. It is a wonderful place, and we have much to learn from the advances they have made. Dr. Loudin hopes to bring some of you there with us very soon."

A few people step back, some murmur. A voice from the center cries out, "What is he doing here? What does he want from us?"

Several in the crowd echo those questions and shout out more. I recognize some of the guards from the palace. They move forward, their weapons drawn.

"King Alex." The guard's deep voice silences the crowd. "Are you safe?"

The look Loudin gives Alex is filled with poison, and his gaze goes from Alex's blue eyes to Nicole's brown ones. My hand goes to my throat. "No."

Dallas is up again, but the video continues and Rhen pulls him back onto the couch beside her.

"I am well." Alex lies, protecting Nicole, who presses herself as close to Alex as she can, her small body shaking. "Please put your weapons away. I want to assist Dr. Loudin in his pursuit of a peaceful union between Athens, New Hope, and the State."

So many lies, lies I know Alex would never have agreed to speak. Which was why Loudin took Nicole. He knows Alex would not allow an innocent child to be harmed. He was counting on Alex's humanity to accomplish his plan.

"Please allow us to pass, and please inform our esteemed scientists that we wish to speak with them in my father's . . . my . . . chamber in one hour."

The camera switches to that room, and my mind is filled with images of the last time I was there. The king was dead, Peter was dying, Alex was much like he is now—stunned, silent, mourning.

The bloodstains have been cleaned, new bed coverings replaced the old ones. New window coverings as well. All is black, Alex's preferred color, making the room seem even darker. The sun shining through the curtains appears gray and muted. Loudin is sitting in the king's chair at the far end of the room. Alex remains standing, his face still impassive. Nicole is still beside him, trembling.

Two women enter the room. One is about ten years older

than I, her dark hair short, her dark skin smooth. The other woman is older, around King Jason's age, I'd guess. Her hair is almost entirely gray and hangs down to her shoulders in slight waves. Her eyes are light brown, and they look at Alex with concern.

"You wanted to see us?" The older woman's voice is deep, a rich sound that echoes in the room.

"Dr. Loudin would like the formulas to the pharmaceuticals you have created."

The younger woman stands straighter. "Sir, you ordered us to destroy those after your father was killed."

"I know." I see a flicker of what looks like hope on Alex's face. "But I am confident that you kept a copy, or that you recall their makeup."

The older woman looks to the younger, an unspoken message passing between them. "We agreed that those drugs were dangerous."

Loudin's jaw muscles flex, but he remains quiet, allowing Alex to negotiate.

"Of course. But Dr. Loudin is a brilliant Scientist, and his desire is to see what we have developed here, to see what else can be made from them. Perhaps medicines that can cure some of our diseases."

The younger woman raises her shoulders. "I'm sure you have better equipment in the State. It would be wonderful to find more cures . . . if you really think it is safe to reveal these formulas."

I want to scream, "*No!* It is not safe. Do not give Loudin those formulas." But this is a recording, and I know the outcome. No amount of shouting can change what I am seeing.

"I trust Dr. Loudin and his fellow Scientists." Alex seems to choke on those words. Loudin comes behind him, and Nicole's arms wrap around Alex's waist. "Please give us the formulas."

The older woman pauses, her eyes shrewd. She knows what is happening. She sees that Nicole is being threatened and that Alex is being forced to ask for this. "I have destroyed all the physical copies, but I do recall the formulas."

"Excellent." Dr. Loudin smiles. "Please type them here on this. And as I am sure there are ingredients that only come from this area, I would request that you have someone gather them for me."

"Do exactly as he asks." Alex emphasizes the word *exactly*, and I shrink back into my chair.

The older woman takes the communications pad from Loudin and turns it around.

"You should recall these," Loudin says. "I'm sure you were young when the War occurred, but even children had older models of these communications pads."

"Of course." The older woman smiles. "I played games on them."

"Exactly." Loudin's tone changes to that of a friend. "What is your name?"

"Alayne."

"Beautiful name." Loudin sounds like John. The juxtaposition is revolting. "This, of course, is a more advanced version of the technology of your childhood, but you will find it comes back to you. Like we used to say, 'It's like riding a bike.'"

Alayne laughs. "I haven't heard that in a while."

"No bicycles here?" Loudin widens his eyes in mock surprise.

"King Jason wanted us to reflect ancient Athens." Alayne is

tapping on the communications pad, her earlier concern seemingly vanished. "So no bikes."

"Chariots?" Loudin leans over, watching her type.

"Of course." Alayne's smile is bright, and she looks at Loudin with appreciation.

"So you have horses."

"This *is* Texas." Alayne winks.

"I haven't seen a horse in decades."

"Do you ride?" Alayne looks up from the communications pad.

"Grew up in Nebraska." Loudin takes a deep breath. "My grandpa had several horses on his farm."

I listen, fascinated. Is Loudin telling the truth, or just trying to win Alayne over so he ensures she types in the correct formulas? Or both? I try to imagine him as a child, riding horses on a farm. I cannot conjure the image.

"You're welcome to take one out for a ride," Alayne says.

"I'm afraid my riding days are over." Loudin puts a hand on his lower back. "But I may come back another time and just take a look at them. Beautiful creatures, horses."

"So you're planning to return?" Alayne looks up from the communications pad.

"Of course." Loudin walks to the window, pulls back the black covering, and surveys the courtyard. "Now that we no longer need to stay below in the State, we plan to explore the world again."

"Can you go anywhere in that jet?"

"We can."

I watch, confused and disgusted, as Loudin explains how the aircraft works, what fuel has been developed for it, and how delighted he is to find survivors around the world. I am even more disgusted that Alayne apparently believes it, all of it.

"I would love to see Europe." Alayne looks over what she has typed into the communications pad. "My parents went to Germany on their honeymoon. They have such lovely pictures from that trip—the castles and the mountains. Stunning. Did any parts of Germany survive?"

Loudin pretends to be thinking. "No, I don't believe we have seen indication of life there. There does seem to be a pocket of survivors in Romania though."

"That's too bad." Alayne sighs. "What I wouldn't give to have seen one of those quaint little villages."

"A terrible thing, the War."

I want to jump up now. Rhen must notice because she shoots me a warning glance. Loudin is responsible for the destruction of those "quaint little villages," and he acts like he feels bad they did not survive. How can this woman not see that Loudin is manipulating her?

"Can I take this to my office?" Alayne lifts the communications pad. "I am having trouble recalling some of the formulas."

"Of course." Loudin smiles. "May I come with you? I'd love to see your facilities."

The camera turns off, and the next scene is New Hope. The people there are crying, hysterical, angry. They are running toward the camera, rage in their faces. They are all saying one word over and over again.

"Nicole."

CHAPTER 33

The camera turns, and I see Loudin carrying a limp, blood-soaked Nicole in his arms. Her eyes are wide, frightened, and unmoving.

"Nicole." Dallas runs to the screen, as if he could break through and reach his sister. He bangs his fist against the wall screen until a Monitor comes behind him and places a needle in his neck. He slumps to the ground, but I do not notice where he is taken. I cannot take my gaze off the screen, off Nicole.

"I tried to stop him." Loudin is yelling over the crowd, his eyes large and sad, though I know that sadness is fabricated.

"But Alex was in a rage when we left New Hope. He thought I was trying to take over his throne. I was his intended target."

The people stop, their eyes going from Loudin to Alex, whose hands are bound behind his back, a piece of fabric covering his mouth.

"It happened so fast." Loudin's voice breaks, and he looks down at Nicole like he actually cares for her. "He came at me with a knife, and this sweet, brave girl tried to stop him. She ran up to him, and he . . . he killed her. Slashed her throat. He didn't even show remorse. Told me I was next."

Alex's eyes are wide, and he shakes his head back and forth. Of course he didn't do this. Surely the people of New Hope know that much about him.

"Just like his father." Someone in the crowd yells, and others join in.

"Thankfully, one of the guards came to my rescue." Loudin pulls Nicole closer to him. "Alex was subdued before he could hurt anyone else. But it was too late for Nicole. I just wanted to take her for a ride in our aircraft. She looked so sad when I arrived. I wanted to make her happy."

I scan the crowd, looking for Carey. Where is he? He'll know Loudin is lying, but Carey is nowhere, and the crowd is getting more and more angry, looking at Alex like they want to kill him, tear him apart.

And then they do. One man breaks through and throws a fist in Alex's face. Alex, bound and gagged, cannot fight back, cannot tell them what truly happened. The wall screen goes black and Loudin looks at us, the smile even more nauseating now that I know what he has done.

"Just a reminder that I *will* complete the goals I have set for myself." Loudin's smile finally disappears. "In case you were thinking of challenging me or attempting to stop me."

I swallow hard. I thought James hid us so the cameras wouldn't record our conversations.

"Don't look so worried." Loudin's laugh is short and high pitched. Like a single note being pushed out of an oboe. "I didn't listen in on you. This time. I was a bit preoccupied, as you can tell. But I know you. I know how you think. I will always—always—be a step ahead of you, and I will always get what I want."

Before Loudin walks out the door, he looks at each of us, his eyes boring into ours. None of us looks away. None of us says a word. And when he leaves, his Monitors follow. None of them stays behind. He isn't even concerned about us being alone, doesn't feel we need to be watched.

"Where is Dallas?" He is not in the living area, and I was too focused on the wall screen to notice where he was taken. "What did Loudin do with Dallas?"

"He's in his cube," Rhen says. "The Monitors took him there after one of them administered the sedation drug. His vitals are fine and he is resting."

I move to the couch where Alex is still sitting, staring at nothing. "What happened?"

"You saw what happened." Alex's voice comes out in a whisper, damaged, I am sure, from his beating.

"Nicole . . ." I don't think I will ever be able to forget the image of her lying dead in Loudin's arms. "Why was she even there?"

"Carey is sick." Alex wipes his face with his hand. "Really sick. I don't know what's wrong, but Nicole was sad when we arrived without Kristie. She wanted to see her grandmother, and she wanted Kristie to see Carey. She cried when I told her Kristie wasn't with us."

Fresh pain fills my heart. None of them deserves this.

"Loudin offered to take Nicole on a ride with us to Athens. He was acting so kind—like he did with Alayne. Nicole came along gladly, and the people were so grateful. They love your family." Alex looks at me.

My family. Kristie. Nicole. Dallas. Carey. Family I put in danger by escaping to New Hope to begin with. Guilt battles with grief, but I push them both aside because I need to hear the rest of the story. I need to know what happened to Nicole.

"But as soon as the aircraft took off for Athens, Loudin pulled out his weapon and pointed it at Nicole. He said I better make sure he got the formula, or Nicole would be killed just like her grandmother was killed."

Poor Nicole, having her life threatened by her grandmother's murderer. Hearing of her grandmother's death like that. She was so young, so full of life and joy. I don't know if I can hear the rest. I want to run away, hide, bury myself somewhere. This is too much.

"So I made sure he got the formula, and the ingredients to make it." Alex bites his lip. "I tried to do just what he asked. I swear I did."

I put my arm on Alex's back and pull him to me. "I know you did. We saw it. You did your best to protect her."

"But I couldn't protect her." Alex takes a ragged breath, and I feel the pain, the aching in every muscle.

"What happened on the way back to New Hope from Athens?"

"Loudin talked the whole way back about what he will do with the formula." Every word seems to take monumental effort. "He is going to make it stronger, engineer it to be permanent and not temporary. If he can't do that, he'll put it in the water so everyone ingests it every day. That way, when he brings people here from all over, they'll do what he says. He wants to control the world, Thalli. He wants everyone out there to be just like everyone in here."

Knowing this already doesn't make hearing it any less frightening.

"I fought with him." Alex's bottom lip shakes, and I tighten my hold on him. "I told him he can't do that. It's wrong. My people deserve to be free. Everyone deserves to be free. I said I wouldn't let him go through with this."

Alex begins to sob, and we all wait in silence until he composes himself again.

"He said if I tried to stop him, then he'd . . ." Alex closes his eyes and shakes his head. "He'd kill every person I loved while I watched him do it."

I lower my head onto Alex's shoulder. I know what happened next. "And then he killed Nicole."

Alex nods, unable to speak.

Rhen leans forward. "And he blamed you to set himself up as a better leader, so he can return to New Hope and take people from there to use here."

"Yes. They hate me. And they'll tell the Athenians too."

"Carey will suspect the truth," I assure Alex. "He knows Loudin."

Alex shrugs. "I don't know if he can communicate or not. And even if he can—you saw how angry the people were. You think they're going to believe him? After they saw Nicole?"

"Surely they will." I refuse to believe the people in New Hope will side with Loudin. They are better than that. Smarter than that.

"People believe what they see." Alex speaks so softly I almost miss it.

I turn as heavy footsteps come down the hall. Dallas enters, his face red, veins bulging in his neck. He pushes me to the side and grabs Alex by his shirt, ignoring the cry of pain from Alex as his arm is jostled.

"How could you?" Dallas yells, and none of us is strong enough to pull him away from Alex. "How could you let that man kill my sister?"

I see movement outside our window. Loudin is looking in, smiling.

CHAPTER 34

Berk finally pries Dallas away from Alex, but not before a wound on his cheek is reopened, blood dripping down onto his shirt. Dallas is still fighting, lunging toward Alex, desperate, I am sure, to undo what we just learned, to erase it.

I understand how he feels, the pulsing anger directed at Loudin, who has so little value for life, so much arrogance. I want to do to him what he did to Nicole. All thoughts of forgiveness and love are gone.

"It's not his fault." Berk says this over and over again as he holds Dallas tightly in his arms, his face red with his attempt to contain the larger man.

Rhen steps in front of Dallas, and he seems to deflate like a punctured ball I once saw in New Hope. He sinks to the floor, and Rhen follows him, Berk still holding on.

"Dallas, it isn't anger you're feeling." Rhen holds his face in her hands. I feel myself clinging to her words as well, wanting the calm she possesses. "You are upset, and that is natural. Allow yourself to feel grief."

"Shut up."

I have never seen Dallas speak to Rhen like this. Even she leans back, unsure of what to say.

"My sister is dead. My grandmother is dead. My grandfather is sick. My parents are hundreds of miles away. I can't do anything. I can't stop this man. I can't be sure the rest of my family won't be murdered. You have no idea how that feels."

Rhen swallows hard and moisture pools in her eyes. "You're right. Of course. I don't know how that feels."

Dallas shakes Berk off and walks back down the hallway, then shuts the door to his cube with more force than necessary. The rest of us are silent, Dallas's words hanging in the air.

Alex wipes the blood from his face, then runs his hands through his curly blond hair. "I know how he feels."

I take Alex's good hand and lead him to the cooking chamber, then make him sit in a chair at the dining table while I find medical supplies. I put salve on the cuts on his face and arms. I wish I could bring healing to his heart as easily as I can deliver it to his body. But Alex is crushed. I see it in the slope of his shoulders, in his inability to look me in the eye. I wash my hands and fill a glass of water.

"Can you eat?" I set the water on the table, but Alex doesn't reach for it.

"I'm not hungry."

"It's not your fault, Alex." I place my hand on his and he pulls it away.

"I was right there, Thalli." He hides his face in his hand. "I was a foot away when Loudin killed her. If I had just reached out, grabbed the knife . . . I didn't know. One minute I was yelling at him and swearing he'll never hurt my people. The next minute she was gone. I watched her die. It was like standing over my father that day, seeing the life leave him. But Nicole was innocent. Completely innocent."

I pull a chair beside Alex and wrap my arms around him. He stiffens at first but then relaxes and folds his good arm around me in a grip that almost takes my breath away.

"The people think I did this." Alex's tears wet my shirt. "They think I am a murderer. I know that is minor compared with Nicole's death, but . . . I love those people. I want to lead them. I hoped I would be able to when this was over."

"You *will* lead them." I rest my head on Alex's. "They won't believe Loudin's lies."

"They already did." Alex leans back in his chair, his crystal-blue eyes shining with grief. "They wanted to kill me—if Loudin hadn't called them off, they would have. I wish they did. He promised them he would deal with me. He has no intention of letting me ever return to Athens."

"We're going to stop him, Alex." I force his eyes to meet mine. "We're not letting him win. James is working with us. Berk and Rhen are some of the smartest people in the State. And you know strategy."

"But none of us is capable of murder. He is. So he wins. He got the formula because he was willing to kill Nicole. If I had known he was going to kill her anyway—"

"You would have done the same thing." I need him to see this is not his fault. I don't want him blaming himself for Loudin's actions. "You are a good man, Alex. You're not like him—you wouldn't allow an innocent person to die."

"But I did." Alex turns away.

"No, you didn't." I reach for his face and gently turn it toward me.

Berk walks in. Sadness weighs on his face and something else—jealousy? But I cannot process that now because Alex needs me. And we need Alex. He has to release himself from this burden—for his own good, but also for ours.

"Do you want me to call in a Medical Specialist?" Berk's voice sounds strained.

"No." Alex stands, biting his lip. "I'll be all right. Let's just figure out how to stop this madman before he hurts anyone else."

"Exactly what I was thinking."

A loud tone shatters the room—the signal that we have an incoming communication on the wall screen. We walk into the living area, and Loudin's face fills the screen.

"No rest for the weary, I'm afraid." He is speaking to us the same way he spoke to Alayne in Athens. It is sickening. "I am still preparing to travel down to South America. So much to do. Thalli, I'll need your help with a little gift I am preparing for the folks we'll visit. A transport is on its way to pick you up."

My legs suddenly feel too weak to hold me up. Berk's hand grasps mine, and the warmth of his support staves off the fear that was rising within me.

"Alex." Loudin's gaze goes to Alex standing behind us. "You'll come too, of course. We'll need your linguistic skills."

"I'd like to assist." Berk squeezes my hand.

Loudin narrows his eyes. He has a slight, satisfied smile. "No, Berk. I don't have need of you. Yet. Just Thalli and Alex. They'll be spending lots of time together, working side by side. We wouldn't want you to distract them from their work, would we?"

Berk releases my hand and takes a step forward. "Dr. Loudin—"

The wall screen goes black, and the door to our pod opens.

"Transport for Thalli and Alex." The Monitor motions toward the door.

CHAPTER 35

Alex and I have been in the Scientists' quarters for three days. Despite Loudin's claims, we haven't worked together much. I have been given a musical assignment. Music, he says, is a universal language, so it is my job to learn some musical pieces he found from Ecuador to speak peace to them before he exits the aircraft. Then Alex will take over as translator.

The original trip has been modified, he said, and there isn't as much need for us to work together on this. I think of our time working together in Pod C, before Berk, Rhen, and Dallas arrived. Before Alex was used by Loudin. He was different then. Still grieving his father and sister, but without the weight he carries now.

I do not know where Alex is or what he is doing or how he is faring with his injuries sustained in Athens. I am more concerned, however, with the damage done to his spirit than his body. The bruises will heal in a few days, but the guilt over Nicole's death will take much longer. And the fear that his people believe him to be a murderer just adds to the burden he is carrying. I wish Loudin would allow us to work together, to be together. Alex needs me.

I wish I could refuse to do this, to defy Loudin. But he was clear that disobedience would result in the immediate annihilation of Dallas or Rhen. He means that. And though I know he could still choose to kill them even if I do all that he says, my love for them, for life, prohibits me from acting on my desire to disregard Loudin's instructions.

My mind goes back to John, to his words to me. From the beginning, he told me I have a purpose. We all have a purpose. But am I fulfilling mine? Am I doing enough? John did—he died having fulfilled all that the Designer wanted him to do. He never seemed to doubt, never seemed to question. He just loved and lived and prayed. He was always praying.

But I don't pray. I can't. I don't want to pray, I want to yell at God. I want to know why people like Kristie and Nicole have been allowed to die. Why Loudin is allowed to keep winning. Where is his power? Why isn't he stopping Loudin? It isn't fair.

I am not like John. And if the Designer wanted me to be like him, then wouldn't he help me? Wouldn't he show me my purpose and demonstrate his power over Loudin?

I close my eyes and push these thoughts from my mind. I cannot answer those questions now. I cannot keep thinking about them or I'll become as moody as Dallas. So I turn back to the music on my communications pad. This is a different type of melody. And I have not found the right sound on the synthesized keyboard Loudin brought into my room. I do not enjoy this type of instrument as much. I like a piano to be a piano, a trumpet to be a trumpet. But it is fitting that Loudin wants a false version of the real thing. That is exactly what he is—a false version of the real God. One who wants to be obeyed but not to love, one who wants to receive but not to give.

My fingers play the notes on the pad, but my mind wanders. My heart is not part of this music. I cannot escape into it . . . I cannot enjoy it. If this works the way Loudin plans, then the music I am recording will lull the survivors in this village into believing Loudin desires peace. He'll speak to them the way he spoke to Alayne. And they will believe him. And if the Athenian formula works the way he wants it to work, then those people will become just like the rest of the residents of The State—single-mindedly focused on completing whatever tasks Loudin assigns them. No questions, no arguments, no feelings. They won't even realize they've left families behind, left children and homes and memories.

Removing my hands from the keyboard, I sigh. Sometimes, if I am completely honest, I long for that forgetfulness. I wish I didn't know so much, didn't feel so much. I ache with grief for Kristie and Nicole, for Helen and Peter. I worry about Dallas and his anger, Alex and his guilt. I miss Berk so much that sometimes I cannot even take a full breath.

A Monitor opens the door. "You have a visitor."

Since we have been back, Monitors have replaced Assistants in taking me to and from locations. I feel like a child again, with the Monitors' disapproving glances and raised eyebrows.

This one checks my work every night to make sure I accomplished the tasks Loudin assigned. She purses her lips together now, seeing me with my hands in my lap when they should be on the keyboard, perfecting this song.

"Thalli." Alex enters the room, and as the Monitor closes the door behind him, I rush to him and take his face in my hands.

"How do you feel?" His face is still bruised, but the swelling has gone down. There are broken blood vessels in his eyes, making the blue seem darker.

"Much better now." Alex pulls me to him with one arm, the other still in a sling next to his body.

I lay my head on his shoulder and close my eyes. I have missed him. More than I realized. What Alex and I have is different from what Berk and I have. I cannot fully comprehend that difference. I cannot put it into words. But Alex and I have a connection I don't have with anyone else. Together we have endured what no one around us can imagine. I have come to share Alex's burden for the people of Athens.

When I open my eyes, I see Berk. His face covers the wall screen. The look in his eyes is a mixture of sadness and anger, a look similar to the one on his face when Alex and I left three days ago.

"Berk." I pull away from Alex, but Berk says nothing. He just stares at me.

Loudin's voice breaks through the silence, his face in a small window at the top of the screen. "See, Berk, I told you they were getting along very well, didn't I? Safe, happy, together. Nothing to worry about."

The muscle in Berk's jaw twitches, but he remains silent.

"Such a caring group. Rhen and Dallas, Thalli and Alex. So

you can see, Berk, you can come work for me and know your friends will be well taken care of."

I look at the wall screen. What is it Loudin is asking Berk to do? And why is he trying to make him feel separated from the rest of us?

Berk turns and walks away. The wall screen fills with Loudin's face. "I would like to leave for South America in two days. I will give you two a few more minutes together, but then you must get to work. There is much to be done."

The wall screen goes black, and I sit in a chair. "Berk thinks we are together."

"Would that be so bad?"

I look into Alex's face, and all the conflicting emotions I have had for weeks resurface.

The silence drags on, and Alex sits on my sleeping platform, his head down. "I guess it would."

"No." I move to his side and place a hand on his knee. "It's just . . . complicated."

"Of course." Alex shakes his head. "How could you ever love me? How could anyone?"

"Don't say that." I take his hand in mine. "John would say you are loved by the Creator of the universe. Deeply, completely loved."

"John would say?" Alex stands, his shoulders tense. "Why should I care what John says?"

"Because he lived out the truth of that love better than anyone I have ever known. He lived here, alone, for forty years, trusting that the Designer had a purpose for him. He lost his family. All but James, and James basically disowned him. John could have become bitter and angry, but he clung to love, to God."

"I don't want to be alone." Alex's arms hang heavy at his side. "I have lost everyone—*everyone*—I care about. Everyone but you. You were the hope I was clinging to, Thalli. If you would just stay with me, help me, my people might accept me back. And even if they didn't, I'd have you."

I walk to where Alex is standing, but I keep my hands in my pockets, unsure of what to do or say, how to reach him. I do not want to cause him more pain. He has endured so much.

"I love you, Thalli." Tears pool in Alex's eyes. "I have loved you since the first time I saw you, coming in on that transport like some kind of queen. Like *my* queen. I never thought I'd marry for love. I mocked my sister for wanting that. I fought my feelings for you because they seemed out of place for royalty. But I couldn't help it. The more time I spent with you, the more lost I became, the more sure I was that I would do anything, go anywhere, if you would just be with me."

Alex lifts a hand to my face and traces my jaw with his fingertips, the movement so soft, so tender, I close my eyes.

"Please, let me try, Thalli. Give me a chance." Alex's forehead is on mine. "I know I don't deserve you, but I need you."

I feel Alex's breath on my face. The door opens before I have a chance to speak. James is standing there, only his head visible through the doorway.

"*You need to come with me.*" He is mouthing the words, and I have to step closer to understand them. "*Now.*"

CHAPTER 36

One of the Scientists-in-Training from Pod B died." James has us in his office, the cameras on a loop so Loudin won't know we are here. "It happened last night. Dr. Loudin is frantic."

"He was just on my wall screen." I recall his smug face, no trace of fear evident. "He didn't seem frantic then."

"He is an expert at masking his emotions." James raises an eyebrow. "But, believe me, he is quite upset."

"Go on." Alex nods to James.

"The Scientist, Magnes, was one of the most promising. He had been trained to replace Loudin."

"But he's Pod B." That is the generation just above us. "What about the Scientists-in-Training from Pod A?"

James rubs a hand over his head. "The first generation didn't develop the intelligence we had hoped. They were the first ones to survive—we lost so many before them, you know."

Kristie told us of the dozens of babies who were born with significant malformations and mutations—"mistakes" made by James as he tried to perfect the genetics for what would be the generations of life in the State. "I know."

James sighs. "None of them had the potential to be Scientists."

"So Magnes was important?" Alex leans forward in the plastic chair.

"Very." James folds his hands on his desk. "He was Loudin's right hand. He aided Loudin in his cerebral studies. He was running the lab in Loudin's absences. Loudin told Magnes things he didn't tell anyone else."

"What happened?" People born in the State don't die. Some are annihilated, but natural death? That is unheard of. James's work in genetics ensures that our bodies will live for a hundred years or more before shutting down.

"Aneurysm." James's voice is quiet.

"What is that?" Because diseases are not part of the State. All we were ever taught was that they were part of the primitive world.

"It's basically a weak area in an artery, like an air pocket. Magnes's burst, and he experienced a subarachnoid hemorrhage."

"What?" Alex and I ask together.

"A burst blood vessel in the brain." James lays his palms flat on the desk. "I can only do so much. I am a Geneticist, working alone. I have Assistants, but no one else. I didn't know—"

"No one blames you, James." I have never seen him so agitated.

"Loudin blames me." He looks up. "You should have seen him. How could I have missed that, he asked. This was Pod B, second generation. There should have been no complications. I thought for a moment he would kill me right there in the autopsy room."

"He won't kill you." I want to calm James, to help him. "He needs you."

"Not when he finds out I destroyed everything in my lab." James closes his eyes. "Which won't be long. He wants me to begin working now on samples, to make sure this doesn't happen again. He wants to see results when he returns from South America."

"We won't let him do that." I think back to our plan of leaving Loudin in South America. But he will not allow himself to be in a position to be left. Even if we found a way to disable the aircraft's communication with the State, he would still find a way to stop us. Just like he brought Nicole with him to Athens to make sure he got what he needed, he will use Alex and me to make sure he returns from South America safely. He knows we will not allow each other to be hurt.

James lifts his hand in the air. "I did not bring you here to discuss how you might prolong my life. I am telling you this because he is weak right now. He feels like control is slipping from him. He has felt that in some degree for months—since yours and Rhen's testing."

"Why?"

"He didn't understand it. He saw what happened, the breakthrough between conscious and subconscious, but the testing wasn't his idea."

"It was Berk's." I tell Alex because he knows nothing about those events.

"He pored over that test, trying to make sense of it, and he couldn't." James rubs his eyes. "That's why he insisted on sending you to find Kristie. He needed to know what it meant."

"I thought he wanted Kristie to repair the oxygen."

"Yes, but that test was part of the solution." James waves his hand. "The bottom line is, Loudin wants to be able to understand everything that happens. He needs to be in control. And when he isn't, he gets upset. But he also gets sloppy."

"Sloppy?" I look to Alex, who is smiling.

"My father was like that," Alex says. "As a kid, I knew I could get away with anything when Father was battling for control."

"Exactly." James leans forward.

"So we have an opportunity to act now, while he is distracted." Alex is thinking—I can tell from the way he focuses on a far-off point, how he nods.

"After Magnes, Berk was Loudin's protégé." James looks at me. "He had great plans for Berk, you know."

"Until he got involved with me." Berk's decision to help me cost him his potential for leadership in the State.

"No, Loudin saw the benefit in that." James taps his fingers on his desk. "He wanted Berk to help you escape."

Alex strikes the desk with his hand. "That's why Berk showed up on the screen in your room today."

"What?"

"When I came in and you hugged me, Berk was there, watching." Alex stands and paces. "And when we left, Loudin made a point to let Berk know we'd be here together and he couldn't come. He's trying to make Berk jealous, so he'll get over you and return to him."

Understanding fills me. "He wants Berk to replace Magnes."

"And, ultimately, to replace him." Alex nods.

"Nothing is more important to Loudin than his legacy." James stands. "And nothing is more important to his legacy than for this State to continue as it has been, according to his vision."

"So what do we do?" I ask James.

"Don't. Give. Loudin. Control. Don't give him what he wants."

"And what does he want?" Alex leans against the wall.

"He wants the five of you to fight among yourselves. He wants you, Thalli, to be so focused on keeping both Alex and Berk happy that you don't use your intellect to fight against him."

"What about Rhen and Dallas?" Loudin tried to kill Rhen once. I know he will do it again.

"They are leverage," James says sadly. "They'll be the first to go if you don't do what he wants."

"And what is that?"

"Right now"—James points a finger to the ceiling—"it's going to Ecuador and returning with survivors."

"So we should fight him on that?"

James looks at Alex for long seconds, then turns his gaze on me. "You should fight him on everything."

CHAPTER 37

just can't finish it today." I play a chord on the keyboard.

"*Can't* is not an option." Loudin throws my communications pad on my lap. "This is your assignment, and you will complete your assignment."

"I miss Berk." This is true. While I may need to fight Loudin, I have determined not to lie. "If I could see him, I'm sure I would be more productive."

The veins in Loudin's neck are bulging, and beads of sweat have appeared on his forehead. "You will not dictate to me what you will or will not do. I need this music recorded by the end of the day. We leave for Ecuador tomorrow."

"I'm sorry, Dr. Loudin." I rub my temple. "I'm out of practice, you know, with all the moves. I need more time to perfect it."

"Perfect is unnecessary." Loudin lifts the communications pad and places it back on the stand above the keyboard. "These are primitive people."

"Like the ones in New Hope and Athens?" I bite out.

"Exactly." The glint in Loudin's eyes makes my stomach lurch. "They neither need nor expect perfection. I simply want music that will be familiar to them so they know we are peace seeking."

"But you aren't peace seeking." I stand from the stool so I can look Loudin in the eye. "You are the exact opposite. You want to go into their peaceful world and disrupt it. You want to take fathers and sons and mothers and daughters away from their families and turn them into your version of a perfect human."

Loudin stares at me, his jaw twitching. He breathes loudly and when he finally speaks, his voice is low, quiet. "I want to save them from themselves. They are corrupted, just like you were corrupted by spending time in the villages. You and Berk both."

"Corrupted?" I roll my eyes. "Being around people who love and care for one another, who treated us like family—you think that is corruption?"

"You were drugged, Thalli." Loudin takes a step closer. "You were forced into an engagement and then framed for murder. You were placed in a dungeon. I heard it all when you were in the isolation chamber talking to Berk."

I am disgusted at how much he knows, how little privacy I really have. But I will not give him the upper hand. That is what he wants. "And how is that different from the State? You expect complete submission, just like Jason. The pods are our dungeons. We do what we're told or you kill us."

"It is a small-minded person who believes those comparisons are accurate."

"Then I am small-minded."

Loudin leans in to me. "You are not my only Musician."

That thought entered my mind too. "So why don't you use one of the others? Have them record this, take them with you to South America."

Loudin throws a hand down on the keyboard.

I hear the answer to my question in his silence.

"Because you need me there to make Alex do what you want." Seeing Loudin angry makes me feel strong. James is right. He is sloppy. "You need us."

Loudin looks me right in my eyes, his gaze frightening. "I. Need. No one."

My feelings of strength fade. Loudin may be deluded and arrogant and homicidal, but he is still human. "Then I am sorry for you."

Loudin laughs and takes a step back. "You? Sorry for me?"

"You are missing out on something beautiful." I cannot imagine life without love. Without friendships. "We were made to love others."

"You were made to make music." Loudin points to the communications pad. "You have lost sight of your purpose, spending time with those people."

Those people. How dare he call Dallas and Kristie and Nicole—my family—*those people.* I want to shove him to the floor, kick him until he looks like Alex looked when he returned from

New Hope. I will never fulfill his purpose for me. I'd rather die than give him that satisfaction.

The wall screen comes to life, and I see Rhen, eyes wide, blond hair out of her signature ponytail. A Monitor has her gripped in his arms, a weapon raised to her neck.

"It seems," Loudin says to Rhen, "that your friend does not wish to complete a task I have assigned for her to accomplish. She seems to believe she can refuse or reason with me. Foolish assumptions, Rhen, would you not agree?"

Rhen doesn't speak, but her eyes speak for her. She is frightened, unable to move from the Monitor's grip. Where are Berk and Dallas? They would fight against this man if they could . . . which means they can't. They are subdued too. Panic grips my throat, my muscles.

"I will give you just one more opportunity, Thalli." Loudin speaks to me, but he continues to look at Rhen on the wall screen. "Sit at the keyboard and record this music, in its entirety, without delay or error, or Rhen will be disciplined for your rebellion."

I sit at the keyboard and straighten the communications pad holding the music. "All right. Just don't hurt her."

"Much better." Loudin powers on the keyboard once again, and I play every note, every rhythm, exactly as it is written. Loudin looks on, as does Rhen, still in the grip of the Monitor, still being threatened. She is not released until I finish. The screen goes black, and Loudin sends the music from the keyboard to his communications pad.

He has won.

This time.

CHAPTER 38

S olitude.

The worst possible punishment.

Loudin knows this, and that is why he has left me here, in this room, in this hallway, completely alone. No communications pad. No wall screen. Nothing but silence.

I have spent three days in this room in the Scientists' quarters, the room where I was first placed when I was taken. John's old room is down the hall. I cannot get there—this room is locked. And even if I could, John is not there. The memories would be painful. But I would rather have the pain of seeing that room, smelling it, touching John's things, and remembering him there, than to sit one more minute in this white room with its white walls, devoid of sound, empty of life.

I have prayed, recited the pieces of the Designer's book I recall. I have hummed music, replayed past conversations in my mind. Anything to escape from this reality. But I am still here. And peace is as elusive as noise.

And, lately, what has come to mind are the possibilities of what may be happening while I am here. Has Loudin gone to South America without me? Did he kill Rhen? Has he perfected the formula? So much could go wrong, and I can do nothing but sit here. And as I sit, I wonder if there was more I could have done that day I recorded the music. Could I have stopped him? Should I have refused to play, made him wait?

But I couldn't have. I have gone over this in my mind a hundred times. If I hadn't played it, he would have killed Rhen. But he may have killed her anyway.

I groan, and the sound bounces around the walls. I have to stop. These thoughts will only plague me, and I have no answers. Only the same questions, over and over again.

I hear a click and I race to the door. It is unlocked! I pull it open before it can lock again, and I look to the right and to the left. Which way? Who unlocked it and why and where should I go?

Berk.

I need to find him, to know he is all right.

Resisting the urge to stop in John's room, I run down the hallway and into the stairwell. My muscles wake as I push them up the stairs, toward the entrance of the Scientists' quarters. I don't know if Berk is still in Pod C, but I do not know where else to look.

I open the door that leads into the main lobby. It is quiet. Still. I do not see any Monitors. In fact, I do not see anyone.

I walk out the glass doors. They slide open, allowing me into the area I used to call "outside." I cannot call it that anymore. Although there is grass here and flowers, I am fully aware that it is not outside. We are still trapped in the State, oxygen pumped in, water filtered in. I feel trapped, even here.

And I feel alone.

It is unusual—no Maintenance Specialists, no Botanists, no one is here. Barely ten steps into my trek toward Pod C, I hear the door slide open, my name being called.

Alex.

I run to him. His bruises have faded to yellow and his eye is no longer swollen. His smile, though, does not reach his face. He motions me back into the Scientists' quarters, and I follow him through the lobby and onto an elevator. He presses Level H.

"Where are we going?" My ears pop as the elevator races down.

"We're going to see James." Alex speaks quietly. "He'll explain everything in his lab."

I wonder what "everything" there is to explain. The elevator slides open, and I rush down the hall after Alex. When the door opens to James's office, I wrap my hands around my body. I had forgotten how cold he keeps it here.

"Thalli." Berk is here, and I drop my arms so his arms can encircle me, the warmth he brings making me forget all about the temperature in the room, the people in the room. I want to freeze this moment and hold Berk, look at him, know he is all right. But I sense the urgency in his tense muscles, how he pulls away too quickly and puts a hand on my back to guide me to a chair by James's desk.

I look around and see Rhen and Dallas. We are all here in James's office. How? "Where is Loudin?"

"He is undergoing testing." James smiles. "Under the advisement of our Medical Specialists. We want to make sure he is completely healthy. We don't want what happened to Magnes to happen to him."

"But didn't he go through testing right after Dr. Spires died?" I remember Loudin was concerned after that. He ordered all the Scientists to undergo extensive medical testing.

"Yes, and Magnes was part of that." James shrugs. "Obviously we missed something."

"What about you?" James is one of The Ten. Surely he had to go through the testing as well.

"Loudin couldn't allow all of us to go at once, could he?" James leans forward. I have never seen his eyes so light. "He, of course, is first. As is Dr. Williams. I'm in the final group."

"What else happened while I was gone?" I look at my friends, all gathered around James's desk, looking relieved. "And why was I locked in that room for three days?"

"A day and a half," Berk says.

"What?" I know it was three days. I slept twice, through the night.

"You were there a day and a half." Berk puts his arm around the back of my chair. "It probably just seemed like three."

Did Loudin drug me or manipulate the surroundings just to torture me? I was sure three days passed.

James clears his throat. Of course. How long I was in the room is of no consequence right now.

"Everything is on hold while Loudin is being tested." James's voice sounds so like John's right now it makes me ache. "No drugs being manufactured, no preparation for the trip to South America. No surveillance."

"Are you sure?"

"Absolutely." James's smile is wide. "I have spoken with some of the Scientists over the last few days. I told them about Kristie, about you. I warned them that Loudin's plan to bring other survivors here would only serve to further inflame his megalomania."

"You went to the other Scientists?" My heart feels like it has stopped beating. "They'll go straight to Loudin."

"I went to the Scientists I knew would be sympathetic. Several were like me—close to going with the other five all those years ago. I stayed because Loudin threatened my father. They stayed because they were scared or because they thought maybe Loudin was right. But, like me, they have watched him change over the decades, and they don't like who he has become."

"Why didn't you go to them sooner?" We could have had an army in place to fight Loudin before he killed Kristie and Nicole. The thought makes me nauseous.

"I had to be sure." James sighs. "Like you said, they could have gone straight to Loudin. I couldn't risk that. I dropped some hints about my concern. They shared concerns of their own. It took time to be able to speak freely."

Time in which people I loved were killed. Berk must sense my rising anger because he touches my shoulder and leans over, his voice soft in my ear. "He is helping us, Thalli. He knows Loudin better than any of us do. We can't change what has past. We have to look to the future."

"All right." I swallow hard. "So now what?"

"We have three Scientists with us. Four including me."

"But Loudin has five." My math skills may not be superior, but even I can deduce that Loudin still has the majority. "Not to mention the other pods and the other Scientists-in-Training."

"Dr. Llanes is responsible for the transports." James taps on his communications pad. "She is going to make sure your trip to South America cannot happen."

Berk smiles and nods at James to continue. "Dr. Wheeler is the Medical Expert. He'll be taking extra time on Loudin's exam, making sure he is completely well. The testing will continue for at least another three days."

"And the other one?"

"Dr. Ferguson is working with another Scientist to perfect the Athenian drug."

I bite my lip. This seems too good. Is it wrong to doubt that this is all coming together this way? "So we can be sure that it will not be perfected."

"Exactly."

"We can stop him." I stand and look at the others. "We can really stop Loudin."

I see excitement in my friends' eyes as we plan the next step.

CHAPTER 39

Y ou make it so easy." Dr. Loudin is behind me, pulling
something from my head. I try to move my hands, but
they are restrained.

The fog of sleep—or something else—lifts, and I assess my
surroundings. I am in Loudin's laboratory, strapped to a chair.
A screen in front of me has the image of James at his desk, smiling. The last thing I remember.

I am fully awake now. And horrified. Loudin wasn't being
tested. He was setting us up. Now not only are my friends in
danger, but also the Scientists who would have come to our
aid.

Loudin releases the straps on my arms, but he leaves my legs restrained. "That is not footage from a camera."

I look at the screen again. Of course it is footage. What else could it be?

Realization takes root in my stomach, pushing bile up into my throat. I swallow hard to keep from vomiting.

"This old dog has many new tricks." Loudin laughs at a joke I do not understand. "This is my newest—yours and Rhen's work with the music was a breakthrough in so many ways. I already developed the technology to watch dreams, though that is dull stuff down here. Most of you don't even dream at all. Did you know that? Some of the anomalies that came through did. You, of course, had phenomenal dreams."

I am disgusted to know how often and for how long Loudin has been inside my brain, exploring when I didn't even know.

"And the Progress simulation." Loudin is speaking more to himself than to me. "Introducing new ideas to your brain. It was brilliant. And quite convincing."

My eyes burn as I remember Stone and Asta, April and Hope—people I thought were real, memories that were programmed by Loudin to determine if I had the ability to leave the State.

"But could I introduce an idea into your brain and have you dream of it?" Loudin is pacing, his arms punctuating his words. "I can access memories, sure, but that takes so much time, so much to sift through. I needed to know specifics. What do you know, what do you want, what do you hope?"

I feel naked, violated. No word or thought or action is beyond his grasp. The thought is revolting.

"And I was able to discover just that. You want to beat me.

You want my Scientists to assist your plans. It would be some-what humorous if it weren't so mutinous." Loudin stops and bends down so his face is close enough to mine that I can smell his foul breath. "That will never happen. I have told you before that I will always be a step ahead of you. Now do you believe me?"

I refuse to respond. I will not give him the satisfaction of hearing the fear in my voice.

"You see what this belief in a higher power does?" Loudin straightens. "Nothing. It does nothing. Belief in me, however, now that will change your life."

I glare at him.

"I have plans for you, Thalli." Loudin's corruption of the Designer's words makes the blood in my veins feel like ice. "I will use you to do great things. I'm not ready to give up on you just yet, though I could. And I would be justified in it."

I close my eyes. I cannot stand the sight of this man.

"Every time I am in your mind, I am amazed. It is beautiful, really, so complex, so much going on all the time. It was dif-ficult to get you to focus on the scene I created. You wanted to go to the stairwell with Berk, the palace with Alex. It just never stops, does it?"

I open my eyes. As he speaks those dreams, I recall them. He is right. My mind rarely rests. I wish it did. My mind has given him far too much, and he will take more from it. I want to shut it down, but I cannot.

"Useful information, all of it." Loudin raises an eyebrow. "Alex or Berk? Berk or Alex? Sure, you love Berk. But Berk can live without you. Can Alex?"

Loudin is mocking me, trying to make me angry. I will not allow him to manipulate my emotions. I pray for calm, for my lips to stay shut, for the Designer to intervene. How long will he allow Loudin to be victorious?

"We'll talk more about that later." Loudin pulls a chair in front of me and sits. "It's true, Magnes is gone. All those years of training, all the knowledge. Gone. But I devised a way to save the information in the brain. Like saving a video on a communications pad. I can download the contents of a mind. It's genius, of course. I perfected that in the weeks after Spires died. Couldn't lose another one like that. I didn't tell anyone though. Didn't want them all knowing they were expendable."

"Why are you telling me?"

"I want to give you an opportunity." Loudin leans back in the chair. "That brain is valuable, as I have said. It truly is unique. I can't even get to all that's in there, it moves so fast, knows so much. Those feelings you have muddle things up, confuse facts with fiction. If we can just get it under control, you could, one day, be one of us."

"One of you?"

Loudin straightens. "A Scientist."

What is he doing? More tricks? Or is this a dream? I reach to the back of my head, checking to see if I am under a simulation.

Loudin's laugh is forced. "You are awake."

"You hate me."

"True," Loudin responds quickly. "But, unlike you, I do not allow my emotions to guide my decisions. You are valuable."

"So was Kristie," I yell.

"True." Loudin stands and sighs. "But she was old. She outlived her usefulness, lost it when she left the State to return to the primitive world."

"Yet you sought her out when you couldn't fix the oxygen problem."

"One final use of her skills." Loudin dips his head. "But she was not the same as she once was."

I keep my lips clamped together.

"You are in danger of becoming like her. I want to save you from that fate."

"I want nothing more than to become like her." A family, love, a lifetime of memories in a place that is hers. How I long for that.

"When will you see that you have been deceived?" Loudin raises his voice.

"When will you?" I shout back.

Loudin stares at me for so long I have to look away. He stays there, standing in front of me, unmoving. When he finally speaks, it is quiet.

"Do not throw away your potential. You want to be stronger. I see it in you. It's in your dreams. In your emotions. I can help you harness that, achieve it. I am willing to give you a chance to be like me, to study with me and lead with me. I am giving you the opportunity to rule the world. What do you say?"

I could say yes. I could play along to try to trap him. I could say yes and mean it. I could be like Alex and wait for the chance to be a better ruler than my father.

"Never."

CHAPTER 40

Have you ever observed an autopsy, Thalli?" Dr. Loudin leans over the body of the dead Scientist-in-Training, Magnes. "It is fascinating. This one will be slightly different. He has been, shall we say, 'on ice' for the last few days. I have been working on some other projects and couldn't get to him right away."

Loudin is cutting into the dead man's chest as he talks, as easily as he would cut into an apple, talking as he makes a Y incision on the torso.

"You can watch the screen if you'd rather not see it happening live." Loudin points with his elbow to the wall screen at the far end of the laboratory.

"Why am I here?" I move away, wanting to rid myself of Loudin's proximity and of the noxious smell coming from the corpse.

"We're moving into the next phase of your education." He steps aside as a Medical Specialist opens Magnes's chest cavity. "You need to know more about human anatomy if you are to assist me in my projects."

"I do not want to assist you." I force myself to look at Loudin, his arms deep in Magnes's body.

"So you say." He pulls an organ—kidney?—from the body and lowers it into a waiting steel bowl. "But I refuse to give up on you. You'll thank me some day."

I keep silent. Loudin seems to be ignoring my words anyway. I have told him dozens of times that I do not want to be a Scientist-in-Training, yet he is training me, holding me here on this floor, making me read notes on the communications pad about his cerebral studies. Making me watch an autopsy. Has he finally lost control of his brain? It would be ironic, this man who made the brain the focus of his life work. But I fear he is in complete control of his brain, and he is attempting to be in complete control of me. I cannot escape him. I do not know what is going on outside this floor. He does not answer my questions about Berk, Rhen, Alex, and Dallas. I am afraid to ask about James. I do not know how much Loudin knows about him.

"The heart." Loudin holds it up, and I look at the real thing— the image on the screen is large and grotesque. "Look closely. There are no feelings here, no love. It is simply a muscle. A vital one, no doubt. But still. Not something to make decisions with, not something to stake your future on."

Loudin drops the heart on a shallow tray and orders the

Medical Specialist to take it to the scanner. Soon the image of the inside of the heart is on the screen.

"Perfectly healthy." Loudin shakes his head. "A result of living in the State, being formed here, eating our food, breathing our air."

He stands beside me, removing the plastic gloves covered with blood and throwing them into a waste receptacle. "I performed the autopsy on my father when I was still in medical school." Loudin points to the screen. "His arteries were full, so clogged that his heart just stopped beating one day. But he had a poor diet, he was a drunk, there was a history of heart disease in his family. All the odds were stacked against him. He was barely fifty when he died. It's a shame he didn't live to see me become the man I am today."

He is speaking of my grandfather. I find myself wanting to know more, in spite of his obvious dislike of the man he called father.

"What was he like?"

"What was he like?" Loudin's eyebrows come together. "He was a fool. An angry fool. He lived for the weekends, for the bar down the street. He missed my science fairs and my graduations because he didn't think they were important. Wanted me to play football, like him. Thought I was weak."

I want to ask what science fairs, graduations, and football are, but I don't want to stop him. Loudin never speaks like this.

"But I showed him. I became what no one has ever become— the new world leader. And I have corrected the wrongs people like him brought into the world. I overcame my genetics, found ways to evolve past them. I am a better human than my father was. And I am making sure all subsequent humans are better. In every way."

I want to disagree, but he is being so open, I choose to swallow my retorts, keep to myself that he is far more like his father than he may choose to believe.

"Look at this heart." Loudin again points to the screen. "Really look at it. Memorize it. Clean, clear, strong. No defects."

"Extraordinary."

"But it's not." Loudin turns to me. "It's quite ordinary here. The science was in place before the War, but we perfected it here, with our genetic manipulation and our oversight, to ensure every person born here would have a heart just like this."

"Oh."

He pulls up other organs—lungs, intestines, spleen—all, he says, in perfect condition. I find myself pulled into his enthusiasm, imagining what he was like before the War, wondering what he would have been like had he not turned into the man he is now. He could have done so much—saved people like his father perhaps, made lives better.

"I want you to remember all this." Loudin points to the trays of internal organs spread around the room. "Because the next autopsy will be on an earth dweller. You'll be amazed at the differences in his organs."

I feel the room sway. "An earth dweller?"

"Yes." He washes his hands at the cleaning station. "We have one here that is of no further use."

"W-we do?" I grip the back of a chair, not trusting my legs to hold me. Surely he isn't going to annihilate Dallas. He wouldn't.

"Yes, it'll be interesting to see how the air and diet above affected him." Loudin turns to me. "What his heart looks like, compared to Magnes."

I cannot speak. My mind is racing, trying to figure out a way to save Dallas, to get him out of here.

"Yes, yes, an interesting specimen, indeed, your Alex."

I fall into the chair. "Alex?"

"Consider it a gift from me." Loudin winks at me. "Saves you from having to decide between the two boys."

CHAPTER 41

You can't annihilate Alex." I find my voice, and my feet. I rush to Loudin's side, then stand on my toes so I am eye to eye with this monster.

"Cannot?" Loudin laughs and takes a step back. "Of course I can. He has served his purpose."

"What about the translating?"

"I didn't really need him for that." Loudin shrugs. "As I mentioned, I can transfer knowledge from one brain to another. I can give you his memories if you like. Keep a little piece of him with you always?"

I close my eyes. This cannot be happening.

"I admit, I was upset when Magnes died," Loudin continues, as if I am an Assistant or a camera recording his words. "I hadn't thought to transfer what he knew. He was healthy. I needed to concentrate on the minds of the remaining Scientists. We are getting older. Our bodies, even with the advances, aren't as strong as yours.

"It caught me off guard. And I do not like being caught off guard." He presses his fingertips together. "But that will not happen again. We will work harder to train our remaining Scientists. We'll make the necessary adjustments, and the State will be what it has always been."

I run to the door. I have to find Alex, warn him. Berk and Rhen helped me escape. We can help Alex.

But the door is locked. Loudin hasn't even moved. Even his Assistants remain where they are, completing their tasks, uncaring, unmoved by Loudin's plans.

"Don't worry." Loudin sits. "I'll give you some time with him before I bring him here."

If he expects me to be grateful for that, he is terribly mistaken.

"He's just down the hall now, being prepared for the cerebral transfer. I'd let you watch when I perform that, but I fear your emotions would cause him to be disturbed, and I need absolute calm during that."

Alex is nearby. That is good—I can get to him. I can get him out of here. God will not allow Alex to be killed, I am sure of it.

But God allowed Kristie to be killed. And Nicole. And the billions of people before them, people whose only crime was that they lived on earth and not in the State. I don't understand why the Designer allowed evil to reign. John said evil is a result of the sin that man brought into the world. But still, God is greater than man. I wish he did not give us the choice to rebel against him, that men like Loudin could not do what they have done.

"Where is Alex?"

"He is in John's old room. Fitting, don't you think? Go ahead." Loudin taps on his communications pad and the door unlocks. "I am sure you can find your way there without any assistance."

I barely register the hallway, the elevator, the rows of doors as I go to Alex. Does he know? Am I the one who will tell him? Loudin won't annihilate Alex. I will make sure of that. But how do I prevent it? What do I do?

I am at the door, and I have no answers. John's room looks exactly the same as it always has: colorful, with a multi-patterned bedcovering and floor covering. A thin layer of dust coats the worn furniture. Alex is on the couch, head in his hands. I walked to this door so many times and saw John in that same position. Sometimes on his knees. Always praying, praying, hoping, believing. He never gave up.

The door makes a slight groaning sound and Alex looks up.

He knows.

"Thalli."

I have never seen him look so defeated. "We're going to get you out of here."

"No."

"Loudin isn't going to do this."

Alex sighs. "Of course he is."

There is a blankness in Alex's eyes, a look that is familiar. The look he had when he was drugged by his father.

"He has given you the Athenian drug." His pupils aren't dilated, but I am sure I am right.

"No, he is still working on that."

"How do you know?"

"He took me to the lab." Alex's voice is so small, like he has already given up, died inside. "They can't quite figure it out. Something isn't working."

"That's wonderful."

"It is."

"They need you." I want to shake Alex out of this lethargy, move him. "Loudin needs this drug. Or he thinks he does. He doesn't want to bring anyone back from above without knowing he can control them."

"He isn't bringing anyone back from above." Alex lowers his head back to his hands.

"What?" I push his hands away, force him to look at me.

"He's been watching the other places like he watched us." Alex closes his eyes. "Too many deep-seated traditions, he says. Their way of life has reverted too far back. Too much trouble to try to reprogram them."

"That's good news." I put my hand on Alex's shoulder.

He shakes it off, stands, and walks to the other side of the room. "No, it's not good news." The blank look in Alex's eyes clears, replaced by fear. And resignation.

"What is going on?" I stay rooted to this spot.

"He's going to kill them." His eyes fill with tears. "Again. He's rebooting the nuclear warheads and aiming them for all the remaining villages around the world. He's going to finish what he started, and this time he is making sure there are no survivors."

CHAPTER 42

cannot speak. My mind is racing. My heart is racing. Loudin wants to destroy the world? Impossible. He cannot do that. "We have to stop him."

"We can't stop Loudin." Alex sinks onto the sleeping platform.

"Of course we can." I walk over to him. "What is wrong with you?"

"I'm useless, Thalli." Alex lies back on the pillow. "I deserve to die."

I don't have time to convince Alex he isn't useless. I need

him to get up and help me. "No one deserves to die. Tell me what you know and we can plan from there."

"I've told you what I know." He closes his eyes. "Just go. Let me sleep."

Why is Alex acting this way?

"Remember Peter?" His voice remains quiet, but something has changed.

"What?"

"Remember Peter? He was an Athenian."

"Of course I remember Peter." He loved Helen, Alex's sister. He escaped Athens and came to New Hope, but he returned after Helen died. He killed King Jason and was killed himself as a result. I'll never forget walking him to Helen's room, cleaning his body after he died. "Stop thinking about that. You're not going to die."

Alex lifts one eye, a slight movement I almost miss. "I'm not thinking about that."

I move to the side of the sleeping platform and lower myself beside Alex. There is something more he is trying to say. This room, of course, is monitored, our conversation monitored. "What are you thinking of?"

"My sister never should have told him what she did." Peter escaped through a secret door known only to the royal family. Alex and I know that, but Loudin does not.

I push Alex's hair from his face, taking time to think, to plan. How do we do that when we are watched so closely?

Alex opens his eyes. "He was right about one thing though."

"What's that?"

"He was right about love." Alex looks at me, and the emotion in his gaze takes my breath away. How can he transition from apathetic to passionate so quickly? And what does this have to do with escaping?

Alex grabs my wrist and pulls me toward him. "Would you grant a dying man his last wish?"

His face is inches from mine, his gaze is on my lips, and I start to pull away. He tightens his grip, raises an eyebrow slightly.

"Alex."

He leans forward, and before I can stop him, his lips are on mine. But this isn't a kiss. Alex is speaking quietly. "There is another way out. There has to be. Find it."

Alex weaves his hand in my hair and kisses me in earnest. He pulls away and closes his eyes, a small smile on his face. "Peter died a noble death."

Is Alex playing a part now? Giving a clue? I don't know how to respond.

"He was my subject, and he did what I couldn't do. Even he was better than me."

"You are a good man."

"You'll forget me within days." Alex sighs. "You and Berk will be down here with Loudin, and you'll forget I ever existed."

Is the exit in Loudin's laboratory? Does Berk know about it? I want to ask Alex, but he is right—we have to be aware of every word that comes out of our mouths. We have to pretend, to make Loudin believe we are helpless. But we need to plan like Peter did, finding ways in and out, defeating the man who would defeat everyone else if given the chance.

I stay for several more minutes, Alex sinking deeper into what appears, even to me, like a man resigned to death.

I remind Alex again of the Designer's Words, of what I

know about life and our purpose. I tell him what John told me so long ago, what gave me hope when I was facing annihilation: "Death is only the beginning."

Alex looks into my eyes and cradles my face with his hand. "I would like a new beginning."

CHAPTER 43

I am back in my room in the Scientists' quarters, still thinking about what Alex said—what he didn't say—and what to do about it. What other way out is there? I know there is the exit on the top level. That is where the aircraft is kept, where we left when Loudin took us to New Hope. But that is heavily guarded, by Monitors and electronics. It would be impossible to leave that way. Of course, we left that way when Berk, Rhen, John, and I escaped. But that, we now know, was because Loudin allowed us. He planned for it. We need an escape route that can go undetected by Loudin.

I am pacing the room, thinking of how to save Alex. I do not know how much time he has, and I do not know how to contact Berk and James without alerting Loudin. This room is locked anyway.

But then the lock clicks and the door opens. Loudin enters, his gait slow, measured. He sits in a chair and smiles at me, then motions for me to sit too. I fold my arms across my chest and glare at him.

"You're upset with me." Loudin purses his lips, as if he is truly upset at this fact.

"You want to destroy the world." There's no use in pretending he didn't hear my conversation with Alex.

"I want to protect the State."

"By killing innocent people." Images of people being burnt, bleeding, dying from another Nuclear War fill my mind.

"*Innocent* is such a subjective word." Loudin shrugs. "I believe your God says that no one is innocent. Isn't that right?"

"That's why we need a Savior."

Loudin spreads his hands. "Or eternal punishment."

"God loves people—Jesus is proof of that." Is there any point in telling this to Loudin? "He came and sacrificed himself for the people of the world."

"Sacrifice is subjective too." Loudin raises an eyebrow. "You believe your Jesus' sacrifice benefited humanity, correct?"

"Yes."

"Still, he died." Loudin leans forward. "He was killed— murdered. Correct?"

I don't know what Loudin is trying to say. "Yes, but by people who chose not to believe him."

"And what would have happened had he not been killed?"

I pause. I wish John were here, or even Rhen. They could answer this. I feel like no matter what I say, it will be a trap.

"He had to die." Loudin answers his own question. "To save poor, sinful mankind, your Jesus had to die. Isn't that what your holy book teaches?"

"He died in our place." I recall how emotional John became when speaking of this. "He took the punishment that we deserve."

"So now you won't die?"

"No . . ." I hate how flustered I am. How unsure I sound. "I mean, yes. My body will die. But my soul will live forever. And so will yours."

Loudin waves my words away. "We've gotten off topic, I'm afraid. My fault. Let's return to the fact that Jesus *had* to die. Can we agree that this is what the book teaches?"

"Yes." I sink down on the sleeping platform.

"Then there are times when death is necessary." Loudin has a satisfied smile on his face. "Times when even your God acknowledges death is the only possible solution to the world's problems."

"So you think you are God?"

Loudin laughs. "Thalli, have you forgotten everything you learned? There is no God. That belief is primitive, kept in place by people like John Turner because they want to believe they will have more than just a few insignificant decades on this earth."

"But isn't the reason you've established the State because *you* want to live on after you are gone?" I stand and walk toward Loudin. "You want to be remembered and revered. You want to be worshipped."

"Yes." Loudin stands from his chair. "But I want that because I want this world to become better, to shed the ridiculous notions that have held us back. To allow mankind to revert to their pre-War state is a sin, to use your terminology."

"So you know better than any other human on this earth?" I cannot stop my voice from rising.

"I most certainly do." Loudin matches my volume. "Death has always been necessary for mankind to move forward. The fittest survive, the weak do not. The longer we try to hang on to the weak links, the longer it will be before we move past who we are now to who we can be."

"And who is that?" I see a vulnerability in Loudin's eyes I have never seen before. He means this, truly thinks he is doing what is best for the world.

"Thalli, it's you. You became more than what we designed you to be. Your brain functions in ways I have never seen, ways I can't even explain. If you would just discard this ridiculous faith, you could be great."

I hate to admit this, even to myself, but he makes sense. It's easier to think of Loudin as evil and destructive and arrogant than to think of him as a Scientist who wants to make the world better. He is right about one thing—both he and God cannot be right.

"But I have felt God, experienced him." How can that be explained?

"Chemical reactions in your brain. A slight flaw in your makeup, but not damaging. Unless you choose to follow those reactions instead of logic. If you choose to believe what you feel, then you will eventually become no better than John and Alex."

"Both good men." I spit these words out, reminded that in

Loudin's reality, imprisoning one and killing the other is perfectly acceptable.

"Actually"—his tone changes and he returns to the chair—"I wanted to speak to you about Alex."

I return to my sleeping platform and sit. I think I might agree to anything if it would save Alex. "Yes?"

"You care about him." It isn't a question. Loudin saw me with Alex in his room, and he probably watched the kiss. "I don't think I realized how deeply you cared for him."

"He is a good man. He would be a good ruler."

"He will have no place to rule, Thalli." Loudin lays his palms on his pants. "That is not negotiable."

"They are good people."

"You really must strike words like *good* from your vocabulary." Loudin sighs. "Such primitive descriptions. And we have determined that moving on from our primitive heritage is expedient."

"*You* have determined that."

"I believe that in time you will as well." Loudin's eyes soften. "And though I do believe our people here are an improvement upon those born naturally above, I can admit there are exceptions."

"And you think Alex is an exception." Though I do not like how he came to this conclusion, I do have hope.

"I do." Loudin dips his head. "Raised to understand leadership, trained in some of the ancient arts we have lost here. He could be useful. And he brings new DNA, new potential for life as we develop the next generation."

"So he can live?" I lean forward.

"That is up to you."

"To me?"

Loudin taps the tips of his fingers together. "We have all the humanity I want here right now. In fact, we might have too many. Pod A is not as productive as I'd like. I will likely annihilate them soon. I have found that smaller populations are better. Quality, not quantity, you know."

My stomach clenches. He speaks of killing people like he would of wiping dust from the surface of a desk. But I suppose, in his mind, it is the same. "What of Alex?"

"As I said, Alex could be useful. And you care for him. That is acceptable. But you also care for Berk. Isn't that right?"

"Yes." I swallow past a lump in my throat. Will he tell Berk that I kissed Alex? Is Loudin trying to drive us apart?

"And Berk is also quite useful." Loudin purses his lips. "But I do have the ability to store information now. I could go into Berk's brain and record what he knows. I could even transfer that knowledge to Alex. I could, effectively, combine your two loves. Wouldn't that be convenient?"

"What are you saying?"

"I am saying that I want you to choose—Berk or Alex?"

"Choose?" I blink several times.

"It is simply not in the best interest of the State to keep them both." Loudin stands. "So I will let you choose—which one can you just not live without?"

"You can't do that." I rush to Loudin, whose hand is on the door panel. "You can't make me choose between Berk and Alex."

He turns to me. "Of course I can. And, believe me, you will thank me someday. This will aid you in becoming who you should be."

"What if I refuse?"

Loudin leans against the door. "Then I will make the choice for you."

I run my hands through my hair. This cannot be happening. There must be another solution.

"I will give you something though." Loudin's eyes light up. "Privacy."

"Privacy?"

"For the next twenty-four hours, I will not monitor you, nor will I contain you here in the Scientists' quarters." Loudin smiles. "You have my word. Talk all you want, about whatever you want, wherever you want. Try to plot against me. I think it will be fun to see what you come up with."

"This is a game to you?" My head aches with all he has said.

"No, not a game exactly. More of a meeting of the minds, as we used to call it. I want to show you that my mind will always win. And you, unless you choose to fully embrace what is true, will always lose."

"How do I know you won't be watching me?"

"You don't believe me?" He shakes his head in mock surprise. I stare at him.

"Fine." Loudin lifts his hands. "I will be undergoing the procedure to have my memories stored. It will take a full twenty-four hours. During that time I will be sedated."

"So the other Scientists will watch us." I am not a fool.

"I will turn off all surveillance." With a click, the door opens and Loudin steps out. "Have Berk check if you doubt me."

"I will," I say to Loudin's back, feeling the back of my head to make sure this is not another of his simulations. It is not.

"But don't forget." He turns around. "You must make your decision by this time tomorrow."

CHAPTER 44

What kind of crazy, sick game is he playing?" Dallas hits the wall in the living area at Pod C.

As soon as Loudin left, I grabbed Alex—whose room was unlocked, just as Loudin promised—and took him with me to Pod C. Berk had been sent back there, and Rhen and Dallas hadn't left.

Rhen pulls on her ponytail. "In his mind, this is not a game. It's an opportunity to further test Thalli's intellect while also forcing her to make a decision that will make her think like Loudin. And that, ultimately, is his goal—to turn her into his successor."

"That won't happen." I rub my eyes. "Neither of you will die. We'll show him we can win. We can find a way out."

"Can't we just go out the way we came in?" Dallas points outside. "If we're all free, then let's take that spaceship thing and just get out of here."

"We checked there first." Alex frowns. "He has disabled it."

"So fix it," Dallas says. "That's our best bet."

"It would take too long." Berk looks at Alex like he is an enemy, and I know I am the reason for that. But we don't have time to fix that either.

"And Loudin would just kill us with the nuclear bombs he is assembling."

I realize as Berk, Rhen, and Dallas look at me with wide eyes that they have not been informed of Loudin's latest plan. I give them a brief version, wave away questions, and bring us back to the assigned task. "We can worry about that later. Right now we have to find a way to convince Loudin that we need both Alex and Berk alive."

"We cannot reason with him." Rhen's voice is firm. "We must act."

We spend the next four hours discussing and rejecting plans. Nothing we can think of is something Loudin wouldn't anticipate. Or discover. With him alive, none of us is safe. But killing him remains something none of us can consider.

I glance around the room. Everyone else looks as tired as I feel. "We need to sleep."

"We can't sleep," Dallas growls. "We have less than twenty hours. We need every minute of that time."

"We won't be able to come up with anything if we don't sleep though," Alex agrees. "But just for a few hours."

"Three." Dallas stands.

"Four." Rhen looks into Dallas's face. "We need solid sleep in order for our brains to function at peak capacity."

"Fine." Dallas walks toward his cube. "Four. But not a second more."

Rhen goes into our cube, but I stay behind. As do Alex and Berk. The boys stare at each other, their gazes reflecting what Loudin would surely term as primitive thoughts. Even their stances look animal-like. I do not want to be the object of division between these two.

"Aren't you going to sleep?" Berk keeps his gaze locked on Alex.

"Aren't you?"

"I was hoping to speak to Thalli for a minute." Berk's jaw twitches. "Alone."

"She needs to sleep."

"Don't tell me what she needs." Berk bites the words out.

"Enough." I step between Alex and Berk, a hand on each boy's chest, my eyes on Berk's eyes. "I'm exhausted. We'll talk later. All right?"

The muscles in Berk's chest flex. "Fine."

Neither boy moves, so I walk away, hoping they will follow my lead and not kill each other right here in the living area.

Rhen is already asleep. She has always been able to go to sleep quickly. Even as a child, Rhen would close her eyes as soon as the Monitor turned off our lights. I would hear her soft snore before the Monitor moved to the next room. I, on the other hand, have never slept easily. My brain races with questions, images float in and out. And now, even as physically tired as I am, I am mentally wide-awake. I lie on the sleeping platform for what seems like hours. When I check the time on my communications pad, though, I see that only ten minutes have passed. I cannot stay here.

I slip on my shoes and ease open the door, then walk through the living area into the cooking chamber. I sit at the table. I do not want food or water. I want answers. There were no answers in the living area. I hope a change of scenery will bring new ideas to light.

"Can't sleep either?" Berk is leaning against the wall, his light-brown hair mussed, his feet bare.

"No." I put my hands on my face. "I'm sorry, Berk."

"For what?"

"For all of this." I cannot look at him. "For putting your life in danger. For Alex . . ."

He is standing beside me, his hand on my shoulder. "Is Loudin right?"

"About what?" I look up at Berk and, as always, my heart beats faster. Even in the shadows, he is handsome. Achingly handsome.

"Do you care for him?" Berk speaks softly, but hurt laces every word.

There is no way to answer that question without hurting Berk. And I don't want to hurt Berk. I want to see him smile, to laugh with me like he did when we were younger. I want the easy friendship we always had, the closeness that resulted from that friendship.

His face relaxes. "Let's go for a walk."

"A walk?" I look into Berk's eyes to make sure he isn't losing touch with reality.

"A walk outside the pod at night." Berk grabs my hand and

pulls me to the door. "We've never been allowed to do that before."

"But you don't even have shoes on."

"So?" His white smile seems to glow in the darkness. The earlier tension is gone. He caresses my knuckles with his thumb, and I decide I'll go anywhere with him, anytime.

I slip out of my shoes, leaving them at the door as we walk out. There are soft lights beneath the sidewalk that provide just enough light for us to see. Everything looks different in this light though. I used to look out the window at night, at the State under cover of darkness, and wonder what it would be like to see it all, without a Monitor telling me where to go, without a predetermined location where I was expected to arrive. In the quiet of this moment, the State seems beautiful. And, in spite of everything, it is home. My home.

I lean my head on Berk's shoulder and we walk until we are below the viewing panel. I tilt my head and see the moon—full and glorious and so far away. I am a prisoner here, trapped underground.

I close my eyes and remember seeing the moon from the hill in New Hope. It seemed close enough to touch. The air smelled of dirt and flowers, of animals and life. A tear escapes my eyes as I pray that God helps us discover a way to save that village and all the other villages, to save Berk and Alex. I pray that the Designer is real, that what I believe isn't, as Loudin argues, just a primitive idea invented to make me feel more important than I really am.

"We'll see them again." Berk points to the moon.

"Are you listening to my thoughts?"

Berk pulls away so we are standing facing each other. His

hands frame my face, and he leans his forehead onto mine. "I know you, Thalli. I watched you in New Hope. I stayed behind when you went to Athens—against my advice—so you could save the people. You love them."

I cannot speak. I can see the faces of those in New Hope and in Athens, people who deserve a future, freedom. "But this is so much more complicated than just stopping an arrogant king."

Berk steps back, his hands sliding to my shoulders. "We know complicated, don't we?"

I don't want to laugh. It seems out of place here, now, with all that is happening. But I can't help myself. And it feels good. Our relationship has been nothing but complicated since we were children. "Remember when we used to race at recreation and the Monitors would get so angry?"

"I remember you would get pretty angry too." Berk smiles. "Because I always beat you."

I take a step back. "You did not always beat me. When you did, it was because you cheated."

"Cheated? Me—a Scientist-in-Training? I would never break any rules."

Berk looks so handsome, smiling, remembering happier times, reliving our shared memories. I should continue to keep this moment lighthearted. But I can't. Because those moments are behind us, and I don't know what lies ahead. I only know I need to enjoy this moment. So I choose to enjoy it.

I step forward, lift myself up on my toes, and touch my lips to Berk's. His lips melt into mine, and his arms wrap around my waist, lifting me off the ground. I reach around him, my hands in his hair. I forget everything—there's no trouble, no fear, no doubt, no chaos in the world in this moment. There is only Berk and me and so much love that my chest feels too small to hold my heart inside.

We finally pull apart, both breathless. Berk pulls me to the ground until we are both lying side by side, looking up at the moon, fingers intertwined, our breaths matching. I feel weightless, like I could float right up to the top of the State, through that panel, and out into the world. I close my eyes again and fall into a contented, dreamless sleep.

CHAPTER 45

Wwhat did you do to her?" Alex is standing above us, his face red.

I sit up, straightening my hair, rubbing my eyes. Berk and I fell asleep under the moon. But now the moon is almost translucent, the black night sky is a purplish-pink. And Alex is here, wondering what we were doing.

"What do you think he did?" I stare into Alex's eyes.

His face turns an even deeper shade of red.

Berk sits up, his shoulder brushing mine. "Neither of us could sleep, so we took a walk and ended up out here, talking, and then we fell asleep. That's all."

"We are in the middle of a crisis, with a countdown going on for one of our lives." Alex's blue eyes have deep circles beneath them. "We need to be focused now."

"And we agreed that we'd all be more focused if we slept." Berk pushes himself into a standing position. "So we slept. Did you?"

"No." Veins protrude on Alex's neck.

How can I be so selfish? My actions are causing more problems when I need to be helping with a solution.

Rhen and Dallas come up behind Alex. Rhen looks perfectly awake, her hair pulled back, blue eyes shining. Dallas is holding Rhen's hand and wears a determined look.

"All right, you three." Dallas sits on the grass and motions for us to do the same. "Enough of the fighting. We have to be united here."

Alex says nothing, but his lips are pressed together as he sits in the grass next to me.

"Let's start again," Rhen says. "Think of anything you know that could help. If we compile all the facts, we can determine a clear direction."

"We have to think like Loudin, though." I lay my palm flat in the grass, spreading my fingers and allowing the blades to fill the spaces between them. "Because we know he is going to try to think like us."

"Thalli's right." Dallas chews on his bottom lip. "So what is he thinking? What's he planning right now?"

"He's working on rebuilding nuclear warheads to attack the remaining survivors." I close my eyes against the images that thought brings to mind.

Rhen folds her legs beneath her. "He's also working to develop a new generation here."

"But he doesn't know that James has destroyed that possibility." Alex leans into me as he speaks.

"Are you sure he hasn't found that out yet?" Berk leans closer, too, and I feel suffocated.

"I doubt he knows." Rhen glances toward the Scientists' quarters. "If he did, he would be focused on replacing the ingredients for life."

"How would he do that?" I ask.

"He would harvest them from the remaining members of the State." Rhen states this so calmly, but the idea makes me ill.

"That's exactly right." Berk nods. "So he thinks James is still working on a new generation."

I clap my hands together. "Pod A!"

The others look at me as if I spoke in another language.

"Loudin told me he is thinking of destroying Pod A. He says they lack the intelligence that Pods B and C had."

"But Pod C is empty." Dallas's eyebrows come together.

"He annihilated Pod C," Rhen says softly. "To conserve oxygen."

"That's ridiculous."

"Cruel is a better word." I will never forget discovering my entire pod—everyone I grew up with—was wiped out simply because they were breathing air that Loudin needed. "And he is prepared to annihilate Pod A."

"But that would only leave one generation." Even Rhen is confused by Loudin's logic, confirming my suspicion that he is functioning more on a desire to make his legacy greater than to protect the State.

"He wants only 'superior' beings here." I think of the people

I know in Athens and New Hope, people Loudin would see as inferior but who are far better than he ever was. "He'd rather have a smaller population, filled with geniuses who function at their peak, than have individuals who are less than perfect."

"People like me, you mean?" Dallas raises his eyebrows.

"And me." Alex shrugs.

"But Loudin is one of us." Dallas's face is turning red. "He was born like we were. He wasn't made in some lab—no offense. Isn't he less than perfect?"

"Loudin is deluded." Rhen puts a hand on Dallas's knee. "He believes he was born as an anomaly—but a positive one. He thinks he is an advanced human and that, as such, he can determine the best future for the rest of mankind."

"Seriously?" Dallas looks like he wants to stomp off and hit Loudin. Part of me wishes he would.

"But we can use that to our advantage." I lean in. "He wants to leave behind a 'perfect world,' right?"

The group nods, and I continue. "And with the medical advancements in place, he has the potential to live another fifty years."

"What?" Dallas interrupts. "He's already, what, seventy something?"

"Yes." Berk runs a hand through his hair. "But he is healthy and well monitored. As we saw with Dr. Spires and now Magnes, the possibility of sudden death still exists. But barring an unexpected event, the life expectancy down here is estimated to be one hundred and twenty years."

"So Loudin, potentially, can oversee three or more generations before he dies." Rhen pulls on her ponytail.

"Exactly." My pulse is pounding. "Pod A isn't perfect, so they can be replaced with generations who will be more advanced, according to Loudin's model of perfection."

"How does this help Berk and Alex?" Dallas shakes his head.

"Because." I look at each person in the circle. "It will take every one of us to take charge of their annihilation."

"What?" Everyone stares at me with wide eyes. Berk and Alex lean away from me, horrified expressions on their faces.

"How much more time do we have?" I stand, wiping debris from my pants.

"Sixteen hours." Rhen's answer comes quickly, as if she has been keeping a countdown in her head—which she probably has.

"Excellent." I pull Rhen up and the others follow. "That should be enough time to get rid of all of Pod A."

The group does not move, so I walk ahead without them. "Are you coming?"

I walk quickly, feeling hopeful, excited, and determined. I have a plan, and that plan will save both Berk and Alex. I just hope the others won't try to stop me.

CHAPTER 46

peek in Dr. Loudin's laboratory before heading to find James. Just as he promised, Loudin is sedated, wires protruding from his brain while several Assistants hover around him, checking his vitals. Dr. Williams is seated at Loudin's desk, tapping on her communications pad and occasionally looking up at the wall screen.

No one notices me, and no one has stopped me as I entered the building or wandered around in it. Berk checked the cameras before we left yesterday, but I needed to see for myself that we truly are not being monitored.

"All right," I say to the others. "Let's go."

Rhen, Dallas, Berk, and Alex haven't spoken since we left our spot in the grass. I would like to believe that though they don't fully understand my plan, they are willing to trust me. We take the elevator to James's laboratory, and I rush in there, finding him in conversation with another Scientist.

"I understand Dr. Loudin's desire to see the new generation begun." James is speaking, his back to us. "But there is much to be done before the fertilization process can commence."

"May I help you?" James's eyebrows are raised. We, of course, are not supposed to be on familiar terms. Nor should we even be here without permission or a guard.

Berk steps forward. "Dr. Turner, we were sent by Dr. Loudin to observe your work today."

The other Scientist, Dr. Llanes, turns around and looks at each of us.

"Ah yes." Thankfully, James pretends well. He smiles at Dr. Llanes. "Excuse me. This has to do with another project Dr. Loudin has assigned. I assure you I am doing the best I can with what I have, and the problem of the next generation will be solved very soon."

"All right." Dr. Llanes taps on her communications pad and walks to the door. "I just want to make sure you know how urgent this is."

"I do." James ushers her out the door and waits to speak until we hear the tone that indicates the elevator doors have closed.

"Thank you." I follow James back to his office where the six of us sit—Alex, Berk, and me on the couch, Rhen and Dallas on chairs, and James behind his desk.

"One moment." James taps on his communications pad. "Interesting . . . the cameras are all disabled. Did you do that?"

I quickly explain to him Loudin's "game" and our time frame. I also explain my idea.

"It is risky." James speaks after a long pause. My friends are silent too, having heard the plan for the first time themselves. "But I think it is possible. What of the logistics?"

I bite my lip. "I was hoping you could help with that."

James taps on his communications pad again, tossing the images onto the wall screen so we all can see them. I discover that while ideas come easily to me, turning those ideas into reality is much more difficult. For Rhen and James, however, details come naturally, and I join Dallas in being an admiring onlooker as they take charge and make the plans that will, hopefully, save the lives of Berk and Alex. Among others.

With twelve hours left, the six of us split up. James, Rhen, Alex, and Dallas go to Pod A. Berk and I remain in the Scientists' quarters. Though we have much to do, Berk stops me before we get to the elevator, taking my hand and pulling me through a door leading to the stairwell.

"I need to say something." Berk draws me close to him and his hands cradle my face, his green eyes searching mine. "Just in case this doesn't work."

"It will work." I try to step back, but he refuses to let me.

"There are no guarantees." His voice is whisper soft against my cheek. He leans his forehead against mine and closes his eyes. "And if it doesn't, I want you to know it's all right."

I wrench myself from his grasp. "Don't even talk like that."

"We need to be realistic, Thalli." Berk does not move closer to me, but the look in his eyes creates an intimacy that feels like arms wrapped around me. "I have learned much from you and from John. I know there is more than this life. And I am prepared. If my life ends today or tomorrow, I am ready. Alex is not. If you have to choose, choose him."

Tears sting my eyes, and I blink them back. "I am not going to choose. I'd die before I saw either of you killed."

Berk comes forward now, and I do not fight as his arms pull me in. His lips touch mine in a movement so tender, so perfect, that every other thought flies out of my brain. It is just Berk and me and no one else. We kiss longer than we should, but neither of us can pull away, neither of us wants to end this moment, knowing, as reality slowly begins to bring me back to this building, that we may never get a moment like this again.

I lower my head, catch my breath, and close my eyes to capture this feeling. I swallow hard, then look back up into Berk's eyes, seeing the feelings I have—the feelings I have always had—mirrored there.

"I love you, Thalli." His eyes are moist, making the green in them even brighter, the gold flecks seeming to float, suspended like stars. "I want you to know that. No matter what happens."

CHAPTER 47

We are back in the cremation chamber. James has brought all of Pod A here—a feat only he, as one of The Ten, could accomplish. My stomach feels heavy, my mind racing with all the potential ways this plan could fall apart.

With only six hours left before Loudin is finished with his "procedure," we do not have time for any mistakes, any changes to the plan.

"The pharmaceutical is working well." Rhen's gaze scans the row of people, standing still, eyes slightly glazed.

Though I hated to do it, we needed to drug them. We could not take the risk that anyone in Pod A would question us or fight or—worse—alert one of the Scientists. It was difficult enough removing each of them from their assigned tasks to bring them here. But they are here, and we have very little time to place each one of them in the cremation chamber.

As the shelf to hold the body slides out, I remember Kristie lying there peacefully, almost like she was asleep. I recall the smell that escaped as she was pulled in, her body consumed. Gone. I swallow hard and pray this is the right choice.

One by one, the first generation of people born into the State are laid on the shelf and pulled into the white cremation cylinder. They blink, confused but submissive, and close their eyes when they are told to do so. The shelf goes in and the panel lights up. After several minutes, the next person is laid on the shelf and the process starts again and again.

I examine each face to see which one is my brother. I cannot be sure. My sister in Pod B looks very much like me. But there are several in this group who could be him. Does he have Loudin's lighter complexion and eyes or Kristie's darker skin and brown eyes? I cannot tell if any of them have dimples like me because none of them smiles. And why would they? They are being led to their deaths. I am placing my brother, whoever he is, in the cremation chamber. I cannot even tell who he is, cannot discuss our shared heritage. I can only keep moving the line forward.

It is difficult with just James, Rhen, and me. But the younger men were needed for the other part of our plan. So we do our best, sweat pouring down our faces as the room gets hotter and hotter. My eyes sting as sweat drips into my eyes, but I am bringing the next person—we only have seven remaining. Almost there. But I do not feel joy at that. I do not even feel relief. Fear is gripping me. So much could go wrong. We have no way of knowing if the plan is actually working. And when Loudin discovers what we have done, he could annihilate us all.

James looks as if he will fall over. Bright-red spots on his face and neck reveal just how overheated he is.

"Maybe we should stop, just for a moment. You need water."

"We're almost there." Even his voice sounds parched. "We can't stop yet."

Rhen is as pale as James is red, and I am sure I look no better. We are spent. But there are only five remaining. We must carry on.

"If Loudin felt that Pod A was defective"—Rhen pulls her hair back into a ponytail—"why did he not annihilate them instead of Pod C when the oxygen levels were low?"

James wipes his forehead with his hand before speaking. "Because he wanted Thalli to suffer. He wanted her to hate him so she'd be more motivated to escape."

This man and his "plans"—I want to crush him and his plans, destroy him the way he destroyed so many others. He sent me to the annihilation chamber knowing I'd be rescued, and he killed my pod just to make sure I'd continue with that escape?

I need to move, to work. "Let's finish this." I go to grab the next person in line and see there are four now, not five. I am so tired, so emotional, that I lost count. I rub my temples. *Just focus, breathe.*

James leans his palms against the chamber as the shelf slides in. He is panting.

"James, you need a drink." I will not allow him to refuse. "Rhen and I can handle this. Go. We'll be fine while you're gone."

I can see that while he wants to argue, he does not have the strength to do anything but nod. He knows I am right. Besides, we need him for the cleanup. We're not finished when the final member of Pod A enters the cremation chamber. We still have the final portion of our plan to complete.

The next member of Pod A seems to be more alert than the others. Her eyes are wary and she is hesitant. I fear the drugs are wearing off. I look to Rhen, who speaks with a calming voice.

"We are here at Dr. Loudin's request, as Dr. Turner's Assistants." Rhen takes the woman's hand and pulls her toward the cremation chamber. "You will not feel any pain, I assure you, and in moments you will experience freedom like you have never known."

The woman remains stiff, pulling away from Rhen as she pulls the woman toward her.

"Should I give her more medication?" I check the bin we used to transport the drug from the pharmacology laboratory. "Ten doses remain."

Without taking her gaze off the woman, Rhen says, "That would be a good idea."

I snap the vial into the syringe and hand that to Rhen. My hand is not steady enough to administer the shot.

Rhen slides the needle into the woman's arm so quickly I barely notice it has happened. The woman jerks away, but within seconds, she is calm again and willingly lies on the shelf.

This is how King Jason got people to do what he wanted. It is what Loudin does. Now me. Us. We are becoming like those men to beat them? I shove away the guilt. There was no other way. Every other solution created more problems. This solution solves problems. If we had more time ... maybe.

Rhen holds her hand out to me, and I have nothing to give her. The vial and the syringe. The next person. I get back to work.

The man on the shelf closes his eyes, and Rhen presses the button.

Nothing happens.

I check the chamber, and it has stopped humming. The room feels slightly cooler. Something has gone wrong. Maybe it has reached its capacity. None of us knew how many people could be placed in the chamber in one day. That was a concern James voiced. But with the chamber not working, we have no way to complete the task, and no way to communicate with Berk, Dallas, and Alex.

Rhen's hand goes to her mouth. I follow her gaze and see the last member of Pod A holding the door open. There were five left. I was right. She must have left the floor. And if she left, there is only one place she would have gone, one person she would have found.

And there he is, storming through the door.

Loudin.

CHAPTER 48

W hat have you done?" Loudin sways, apparently not fully recovered from the sedation. The woman from Pod A woke him before his full twenty-four hours were complete.

"As you stated." I try to remain as calm as possible. "Pod A is unnecessary. So I have sent them to the cremation chamber."

Loudin's gaze darts from me to Rhen to the chamber. I am thankful James is not here. I pray he hears the commotion and returns to his laboratory before Loudin discovers he was part of this.

"Where are Berk and Alex?"

"They, along with Dallas"—Rhen speaks slowly—"have left the State."

"What?" Loudin seems to shake off the remnants of the sedation. "Impossible."

"It would be pretty hard to kill them if they aren't here." I shrug.

"Fool," Loudin shouts. "I have nuclear bombs aimed at every surviving village. You have already condemned them to death."

"You haven't completed the work on those bombs." I say this with far more confidence than I feel. "We have time."

Loudin's face reddens. "You think you can do anything?"

"I think we already have."

"You've annihilated a worthless generation." Loudin motions to the chamber. "And you've sent off young men who will die anyway."

"But they were sent off alive." I fold my arms to prevent Loudin from seeing my hands shake. "And you have not been in their brains. You've lost what they know. And if you set off the bombs, that information will be lost forever. Then what? You admit Berk is important, his training is important. Alex, too, though he isn't State born. You said yourself you want to know what he knows."

Loudin laughs so long and so hard that I want to go over and shake him, make him stop. I expected anger, outrage, even a threat on our lives. But not laughter.

"Did you really think *that* would hinder my plans?" Loudin wipes tears from his eyes. "Oh, Thalli. I truly expected more from you. I give you twenty-four hours, complete freedom, and this is your solution?"

His voice betrays him. I hear the change in tone, the slightest tremor in his speech. He is bothered by this. He just refuses to acknowledge it. He wants me to believe he is not surprised by what we have done.

Taking a step closer to the cremation chamber, Loudin frowns. "I thought you were opposed to mass annihilation."

"I am. But you're not, and you argued quite convincingly for its necessity."

"And you have come to agree with my conclusion?" He cocks his head and arches one eyebrow.

"This was my idea." I motion to the chamber.

Loudin says nothing, but he steps to the rear of the chamber, then presses a panel that sounds a long tone. Part of the chamber slides open, revealing the interior.

"Interesting." Loudin looks inside. "No remains are in here."

I turn to Rhen, whose eyes are wide.

I swallow hard and point to the wide tube that extends from the top of the chamber. "It is designed to bring all the ashes to the surface, is it not?"

"It is warm in here. But not quite warm enough." Loudin leans his head inside the opening. "No flames. Just enough heat to make people sweat. Why would you need them to sweat, Thalli?"

I bite my lip.

Loudin looks up and sees what I saw when I came here hours ago—a tube that goes straight to the surface. A tube wide enough to pull people through—if they are slightly wet. And if there are people above with a rope to help pull them through.

"Where. Is. Pod A?"

Rhen steps around the chamber to stand beside Loudin. "They are on their way to New Hope."

"With Dallas and Berk and Alex." I wipe sweat from my forehead.

His lips twitch. "You lied to me."

"No." I draw out the word. "Not exactly."

"You told me you cremated Pod A."

"I told you I placed them in the cremation chamber." I tilt my head to the side. "And I did."

"So you used the time I gave to allow your young men and Pod A to escape?"

There was no other option. "You were going to kill them."

"I will still kill them." Loudin's voice reverberates around the room. "You have delayed their deaths. You have not saved them."

"Not yet. But I will."

Loudin laughs. "Ah, my dear, your time is up. You will get no second chance. And you most certainly will not win."

I stand as tall as I can and meet Loudin's fierce gaze with one of my own. "Watch me."

CHAPTER 49

I push past Loudin, past the Monitors, and run into the hallway. Loudin is shouting behind me, but I caught him unprepared. And though I don't know where I am going or how long before I will get caught, I run, praying that Rhen is able to get away too, that Berk, Dallas, and Alex got away and aren't still above, waiting. I pray their communications pads worked and that they saw Loudin come in, that James was able to repair the aircraft and it is miles away, headed to New Hope. I pray they can gather an army from there and return, as planned, to the State and defeat Loudin.

I rush down the stairs, almost tripping in my haste to put as much distance as possible between Loudin and me.

As I reach Level C, the lights that line the stairwell flicker out and go black. I can see nothing. Reaching my hands in front of me, I inch forward, feeling along the wall until I find the door. I press it open—the hallway is as dark as the stairwell.

James.

He must have seen what happened and cut off the electricity. I turn back around in the stairwell and feel my way back to the stairs. I need to find James, plan the next step.

It will be days before Berk, Alex, and Dallas are back. They have to convince the people to come with them, and then they'll have to take several trips to bring them all back. We need an army of people—enough to overpower The Ten and Pod B, who will be working with The Ten.

I bang my hand against the wall. I want to move faster, but it is so dark, and I don't want to fall. So I feel for every step with my heel, keep a hand against the smooth wall.

The darkness around me seems to sink into my heart, my mind. What if we fail? What if the people of New Hope and Athens refuse to come? What if they still blame Alex for Nicole's death? What if something happens to them on the way there? What if Loudin completes the nuclear bombs before they return?

I have to stop, my breath is coming too fast, my heart feels like it will jump out of my chest. The plan sounded good when all of us were together, when Berk was at my side and the people I loved were nearby. But I am alone now, and if they are hurt—or killed—because of this plan, my plan, I do not think I can live with myself.

I sink to a stair and lean my head down, trying to catch my breath. John said God always keeps a remnant. He will never allow his name to be forgotten, no matter what man tries to do. What if I am that remnant? What if I become John—the only believer in the State after the second Nuclear War, relegated to a room in the depths, only allowed to speak to those scheduled for annihilation? Tears sting my eyes. Is that the purpose God has called me to? Is he going to allow Loudin to keep doing what he wants, to keep destroying what is good and living as if he were God?

I don't want to believe that, don't want to think of myself isolated from everyone, living on memories of Berk, but growing old without him. I don't think I have the strength to be like John. Fresh grief and renewed respect for this man engulf me. I wish he were here. I wish I knew what to do. I close my eyes and take another shaky breath.

"I can do all things through Christ who strengthens me."

The words come into my mind like a projection on a wall screen. I see them, large and bright, and the words bring light back into my soul, fill my heart with music. A loud, pulsating major chord.

"I can do all things through Christ who strengthens me."

I sit up. I cannot do this alone. I cannot face the possibilities alone. I don't have the strength. But in Christ—the Designer, the Savior—I can do all things. I can have his strength. I am not alone.

"Yea, though I walk through the valley of the shadow of death,

"I will fear no evil:

"For you are with me;

"Your rod and your staff, they comfort me."

The words that John gave me replay in my mind. I know I can trust the Designer. I have walked through the valley of the shadow of death before, and he has brought me out. Even when I have not felt him near me, he has been here. He is always here. No matter what happens, he will never leave me.

Confidence in him pushes out all fear, all doubts. I do not know what will happen. I do not know if my plan will work. But I know his plans are perfect, and I will trust him. I may be weak and scared, but I can be strong in him.

I stand back up, my heart rate back to normal, repeating with every step: *"I can do all things through Christ who strengthens me."*

CHAPTER 50

feel a door, but I have lost count. Is this Level D? F? I need to find James. I push open the door when I hear footsteps on the stairs above me. I pull away from the door, look up, and see a slight glow in the distance. It gets brighter as the footsteps get closer. I am so relieved to see something that I freeze, my eyes on the light, willing it to get brighter so I am not plunged back into the darkness again.

But then reason takes over—that light could be from a Monitor, or from Loudin himself. Though it is possible it could be Rhen, and I would like nothing more than for it to be her, it is far more likely to be a foe than a friend. I turn and see that I am on Level D, so I need to take two more flights before I can reach James's office.

I move as quietly and as quickly as I can. I do not want to alert whoever it is that I am here. If it is Rhen, she will know to go to James's laboratory. If it is not Rhen, I do not want to give my destination away.

The footsteps are loud and heavy. Not Rhen. They are also fast—they can be because the person running has a light to guide his way. He doesn't have to feel along the walls with his hands, touch each step with his heels like I do.

I am finally at the door of Level F, but my pursuer is too close. If I open the door, he will see me, he will know where I am going. I have to protect James. So I keep going. Slowly, staying close to the exterior of the staircase so I cannot be seen.

A door clicks open. My pursuer is going onto Level F. I move to the edge of the staircase and look, but the man has gone through the door. I cannot see who it was. I head back upstairs, count to ten, and open the door. Peeking my head through, I see the door to James's office glide shut.

I walk along the edge of the hallway, still quiet. The man in the office could be Loudin. Or a Monitor. I do not want to alert anyone to my presence until I know who is in there.

I stand flat against the wall beside James's door and lean slowly toward the window. I see a shadow, a glimpse of blond hair. A black shirt. My heart explodes in my chest and I push the door open.

"Alex?"

He turns around and his blue eyes fasten on me.

"What are you doing here?" Did the aircraft not work? Did

Pod A refuse to get on board it? Did the portable oxygen tanks malfunction? Did we really kill the people we were trying save?

"We couldn't leave you here."

"We?" I look around.

"Berk is here too."

"What?" I put a hand on my chest, as if that could slow down my heart. "Why?"

"We didn't want you and Rhen to have to face Loudin alone."

"But who's flying the aircraft?"

"Dallas."

"Dallas can't fly that." I picture the aircraft crashing into the ashy ground. All those lives lost. No army coming to help us.

"Berk programmed it to fly by itself." Alex walks to me and tries to hold my hand, but I pull it away. "All Dallas has to do is press some buttons when he's prompted. He can do it. They'll be fine."

"But you won't be fine." I wrap my arms around myself. "Berk won't be fine. And what about the people in New Hope and Athens? Dallas is going to convince them to come here all by himself?"

"He'll have Carey."

"If Carey is alive."

Alex sighs. "I tried to talk Berk into going, but he refused."

"Then why didn't you go?"

"They hate me, Thalli." Hurt fills Alex's eyes. "You didn't see their faces when Loudin told them I killed Nicole. They wanted to kill me."

I did see their faces—on the wall screen in Pod C. But I know what Alex is saying. He is afraid they'd be so focused on him and what happened when he was there last that they'd refuse to listen to anything.

"Where is Berk?"

"He's going to Loudin's laboratory." Alex says this as an apology.

"No." I move toward the door. "He can't. Loudin will kill him."

James stands from his desk. I didn't even notice him sitting there. The light from his communications pad shines from the surface of the desk, throwing odd shadows on his face.

"I am tracking him." James points to his communications pad. "And I am tracking Loudin."

"What is Berk doing?"

"He's trying to see how far Loudin has gotten with the assembly of the nuclear warheads."

"How can he do that when there is no electricity?"

"Dr. Loudin has backup generators in his office," James says. "He is never without power."

I walk to his desk. "Where is Loudin?"

James points to a red dot on the screen. "In the hallway of Level A."

The red dot is rooted in one spot. "He's not moving?"

"Berk was able to sedate him right after the lights went out." James smiles.

"When did you plan all this?"

"I saw the woman from Pod A leave, and I anticipated what would happen next." He sits back down. "So I communicated with the guys above, told them to leave. Alex and Berk refused, and I didn't have time to argue. So I gave them both a job."

"So Berk is going to disable the nuclear bombs?" I place a hand on my stomach.

"No." James shakes his head. "It is a bit more complicated than that. We need to know what Loudin knows. Then we'll plan the next step from there."

"But if Loudin finds out you're helping or that Berk and Alex are here, all your lives will be in danger."

"So we don't let him find out," Alex says. "That's part of my job."

I look from James to Alex.

"They're going to be headquartered in Pod A." James pulls a small object from his desk. "Loudin will disable all power to that pod now that it is empty, so they will be safe there. They can't have communications pads or they will be detected. But they can have this."

Alex takes the object and places it in his ear.

James continues, "This is old technology. We used it before we had all the functions on the communications pad we have now. It is a device that will allow communication—Alex and Berk will be able to hear us, and we will be able to hear them."

"And Loudin won't know?"

"No." James shakes his head. "Old technology doesn't show up on the security grid. Most of the Scientists got rid of theirs years ago."

"You didn't?" I look at the object—translucent and tiny, it will fit perfectly in our ears and no one will ever notice it.

"I used it to keep tabs on my father." James shrugs. "I didn't want the others knowing. They'd think I was weak. Dad didn't even know. He didn't have one. I hid the transmitter on the back of his chair."

I do not know what to say to that. Part of me is hurt—how John would have loved to speak to his son. Another part is relieved to know James cared, that he wasn't ever completely obedient to Loudin.

"I didn't listen all the time." James presses the tips of his fingers together. "I couldn't stand to hear him pray. I'd hear him asking God to open my eyes, and I felt such rage that he clung to that faith even after everything he loved was destroyed."

"Not everything." I look down at James.

He sighs. "I am ashamed now. And it's too late to do anything about it."

"It's not too late." I lay my hands on his desk. "He would be proud of what you're doing. His prayers are being answered."

James's eyes fill with tears. He clears his throat. "Yes, well. There is much to do. Thalli, you can't let Loudin know Alex and Berk are here. Carry on as if you believe they made it to New Hope."

"All right."

"Alex, go straight to Pod A." James stands. "You know where that is?"

Alex laughs. "Right before Pod B?"

"Exactly." James's mouth tips at the corners. "Berk should be there soon. I told him I couldn't give him more than thirty minutes before I needed to restore the electricity. As it is, Loudin will know I shut it off. And he is already suspicious of me." He places the object in his ear, and Alex and I follow.

"What will he do?"

"Don't worry about that, Thalli." James walks to the door with us. "I know how to work Loudin."

"How does this work?" I push the listening device into my ear.

"It is motion sensitive." James pulls on his earlobe. "This turns it on and off."

I pull my earlobe and hear static, then I hear James's voice in my head. "Now go. Quickly."

CHAPTER 51

Thallium." Loudin's voice is in my pocket—my communications pad. I push the listening device deeper into my
ear canal, and I pull my earlobe so James, Alex, and Berk
can hear Loudin.

"Dr. Loudin." I pull the communications pad up to eye level,
ignoring the tones from the elevator telling me I have reached
the top floor.

Rhen is on the screen, fear filling her eyes. Loudin is behind
her, bony hands wrapped around Rhen's neck.

"What are you doing?" I ram my finger into the panel on
the elevator, willing the cube to move faster to the bottom
floor—Loudin's laboratory.

"I could ask you the same thing." His eyes are bloodshot.

"What's happening?" Alex is in my ear.

I swallow hard. "Why do you have Rhen?"

"I will ask the questions." Loudin's voice is hard. "Who sedated me?"

I hold my breath. Berk sedated Loudin, but I cannot say that.

"I did." Rhen speaks, and I am once again grateful for her intelligence, her quick thinking.

"And what did you do during the time I was out?" Loudin glares at me.

The elevator tone announces that I have finally reached the bottom level. An eerie tone, adding to the mood of this floor.

"I am coming to your laboratory."

"Don't." Rhen squirms in Loudin's hold.

Ignoring Rhen, I race down the hallway and open the door to Loudin's laboratory. He is near the back wall, and Monitors grab me as soon as I enter.

I try to shake them off, but they are too strong. "Get off of me."

"Thalli." Alex's voice is so loud in my ear, I worry that the Monitors will hear him. "What's wrong? Do I need to come there?"

"No." I speak without thinking. Loudin jerks his head up. I struggle again, addressing the Monitors. "I said no. Let me go. I won't leave. Not without Rhen."

The Monitors drag me to Loudin and force me against the wall. It holds me, like the chair Loudin had me in before we left for New Hope. My arms and legs are attached to the wall. I do not even have time to try to fight them.

Rhen is placed in a chair against the wall across from me so

I can see her. Her neck is red from where Loudin was gripping her. Loudin stands so his gaze is on both of us, his weapon back in his pocket.

"Did you really need to restrain us?" This is more for Alex's benefit than mine. I know the answer.

"Did you really need to sedate me?" Loudin raises his eyebrows.

"As long as you plan to destroy the world, we are enemies." Adrenaline rushes through my body and I lean forward, trying to release myself from the magnetic grip of this wall. But it is useless.

"I do not have enemies." Loudin laughs. "Enemies are for the primitive world. Our world is united in mind and in purpose. If you cannot determine to share that mind and that purpose, then you are not an enemy. You are dead."

The words hang in the air. I know they are true. I have seen him kill those who oppose him, those who are of no value to him.

"You have more power over him than you think." James's voice is soft in my ear, but it fills me with confidence. I think of the Designer, of music. I refuse to allow fear to overwhelm me.

"Then kill me," I say. "Because I will never share your purpose."

Loudin walks toward me, standing so close I can see the thin blue veins that line his temples. "Oh, believe me, I will kill you. But you will watch your friend die first. And then you'll watch this world you love destroyed, along with the people you love."

Everything in me wants to give up, to give him anything he wants to save the people I love. But I cannot give up. I pray for strength as I face Loudin, my gaze never leaving his. "Fine."

"Good girl." I can picture James clapping, and I stifle a smile.

Loudin steps away, a hand on his lower back, reminding me that despite all the medical advancements, he is still old, still human. "You are more like me than you realize."

The fact that this man is my father disgusts me. But it may very well be what has kept me alive. James says Loudin sees my anomalies as proof that his DNA is powerful. He wants me to be like him, to carry on his legacy. "I know how like you I am."

Loudin's nostrils flare. "Kristie told you."

"If I am different, it is because the Designer—God himself—made me different. To accomplish *his* purposes."

"There is no room for me and your God in this State." Loudin puts a hand in his pocket.

"Then we do agree on something."

Loudin pulls the weapon out and lays it on Rhen's neck. She convulses against the wall.

"No." I am screaming, pushing myself forward, but frozen in place.

Alex's and James's voices shout in my earpiece. Then Berk's. They are discussing whether or not to come here. "No. Don't." They will be too late to save Rhen, and then they will be here, in the same position.

Rhen slumps down in her chair, her head on her chest. I blink back tears. I cannot do this. I am not strong enough to be God's remnant. I am not John.

Loudin's hand is on Rhen's neck.

"Don't touch her." I speak past the lump in my throat. I will not let him see me cry.

"I was checking her pulse." Loudin pulls his hand away. "She is alive."

I release the breath I was holding.

"For now." Loudin replaces the weapon in his pocket. "But this is a warning. She is your weakness. We both know it. Those people out there are your weakness."

"You and I have very different definitions of what weakness is." I spit the words out.

"Perhaps." He takes a step back and looks at me—like he would look at a project or a specimen under the microscope. "But I am willing to give you more time to change your definition. You would be useful, powerful. I believe in you, Thalli."

Loudin's voice is soft, almost fatherly. I am reminded how much he truly believes what he is doing is right. As much as he wants to change me to be more like him, I want to see him change to be more like the Designer. But that won't happen if I continue to argue with him.

"All right." I sigh. "What do you want me to do?"

CHAPTER 52

The wall releases me. I collapse on the floor but refuse to stay down. I stand, pulling my ear so I cannot hear what Alex, James, and now Berk are saying. They think I am insane. We had this argument days ago. They do not see the benefit in trying to reason with Loudin. They think he is too hardened to respond to kindness, to love. But I refuse to believe that. Kristie saw good in him once. She believed he could be good again. I will choose to believe it as well.

I watch as Rhen is taken out of the room.

"Don't worry." Loudin nods to the door. "She will recover. As long as you cooperate."

I wait until the Monitors have left before I speak. "Don't you ever feel lonely?"

"Loneliness is an unnecessary emotion." Loudin taps on his communications pad. "It clouds our judgment. Productivity is key."

I grew up hearing that statement. It was repeated in our lessons, enforced by our Monitors.

"How do you know you're right?" I do not follow Loudin into his office, forcing him to turn around.

"I am a Scientist. And my science tells me that all truth can be observed. Scientists before me spent years observing this world and coming to conclusions based on those observations. Some of those conclusions were that emotion is part of a survival instinct man has developed. Emotions were necessary in the past, mostly to ensure the procreation and care of our species. Since we have developed the technology to allow for procreation without the assistance of emotion, we no longer need it."

"So we do not need to be cared for?"

"Not in the emotional sense." Loudin frowns. "Generations need food and education, clothing, that sort of thing. Because studies show that human touch is important for the development of infants, we do permit the Monitors to spend time each day with new generations, holding them, so they can integrate well into life here."

"So they can be productive."

"Exactly."

"And then what?" I lean my head to the side. "A whole world of orderly, productive people who never feel joy or love or even sadness? That is your definition of perfection?"

"Perfection is unlikely." Loudin smiles. "Even with me. But better. This world can be better when we shed the superfluous."

"But you loved Kristie. You created children with her."

"Not in the primitive way." Loudin frowns deeper.

"But still . . ." I pull my hands behind my back. "You made sure each generation had a child that was yours and hers. Why?"

"She is brilliant." Loudin clears his throat. "As am I. Offspring of two people whose intellect is so superior has great potential."

"You believe I have great potential." I smile.

"If you release the hold emotions have on you, yes."

"But my emotions are what have set me apart. Had I not been emotional, I would still be in Pod C. Or I would be dead, annihilated when they were. My emotions saved my life. Knowing I am an anomaly led you to test me and to send me above to find Kristie. Had I been born without emotions, none of that would have happened. Correct?"

"Your emotions have made you vulnerable." Loudin's jaw tightens. "I chose to manipulate them to achieve my goals. But they are no longer necessary."

"So it comes back to you knowing what is best for everyone." I raise my eyebrows. "For the whole world."

"I know you think me egotistical. But it is my logic, not my ego, I depend on. Science tells me I know what is best because I am one of the few people willing to follow science to its logical conclusions."

"Your science sounds very much like my God." I put my hands in my pockets. "We're both followers."

Loudin lifts a corner of his mouth. "That is where you are

wrong. I lead. I do not follow. And I want to give you the opportunity to lead too."

"Because you care about me." I step closer to Loudin.

"Because my tests show that you are incredibly advanced, capable of maintaining productivity here in the State."

"What if you're wrong?"

"About you?" Loudin's forehead creases.

"About everything. About science. About God. About emotions."

"I am not wrong."

"But you don't know for certain." I smile. "Even your science leaves room for doubt."

"Not as much room as primitive thoughts do." With that, Loudin waves his hand and turns back to his office. "We have delved into the realm of ideas and philosophy. While I have enjoyed the discussion, we must move on to what is important."

"What is that?"

Loudin sits at his desk and pushes an image on the wall screen—a map of the world, with green dots scattered throughout. Dots that represent people, culture, families.

"The elimination of the unnecessary."

CHAPTER 53

I pull my ear again and apparently jump into the middle of a conversation between the others on this transmitter.

"... still alive?" Alex says.

"I told you." James is speaking slowly. "I am watching them. Rhen is in a medical chamber and Thalli is with Loudin."

"Safe?" Berk asks.

"Yes." I answer their question while also answering Loudin's. He wants to know if I am willing to assist him as he prepares the nuclear bombs. "But are the bombs ready? When do you plan to launch them?"

Berk speaks at the same time as Loudin. I struggle to listen to both.

"They're only partially ready."

Berk is quiet, seeming to understand my need to hear Loudin as well.

"You still hope to stop me?" Loudin shakes his head, disappointment radiating off him.

"I still think there is a better solution. Innocent people do not need to die. They aren't harming anyone."

"First"—Loudin points to the wall screen—"they aren't innocent, as we discussed before. And second, they are procreating. These few dots will multiply, generation after generation."

"So let them."

"And when they eventually develop technology and find us?" Loudin waves his hand. "When they want to infiltrate the State and turn it back into what the world was like before? They could undo all that we have worked toward here. They could reverse our progress."

"Do you have a date in mind?"

"Soon." Loudin eyes the wall screen. "Very soon."

"The earth will be toxic again." I try another argument, anything to stop him, or at least slow him enough to give us time to find a way to sabotage this plan. "You'll never see the surface. You won't live long enough."

Loudin presses his lips together. "It is a small price to pay to save the world."

"Save the world?" I know I should remain calm, but he is making that extremely difficult.

"There is a story in the mythology you love." Loudin sits back at his desk. "I remember hearing it when I was child. God destroyed the earth in a flood because the people on the earth were wicked. He had no choice. They wouldn't listen, wouldn't change. So he started over with the only ones who would listen to him. Noah, I believe. Are you familiar with that story?"

There is no time to debate whether or not it is mythology. I simply nod, but my mind is working. A worldwide flood. God promised he would never flood the world again. Not the whole world but . . .

"That is what I am doing," Loudin continues, unaware of the thoughts in my mind.

I try to listen, but a plan is coming. It is frightening and almost impossible. But if it is from God, then it will work.

"The world needs to be destroyed so it can be populated with better people."

The door opens and Dr. Williams enters, a smile covering her face. "They have completed the warheads. We are ready."

"Excellent." Loudin walks to Dr. Williams and shakes her hand.

"Who is that?" Alex asks in my ear.

"Williams," James whispers. "I have to go."

"When can we launch?" Loudin pulls Dr. Williams's communications pad from her hands.

"Twelve hours."

Loudin tosses the image from the communications pad onto the wall screen. Red circles cover each location on the map where survivors live. The circles, I realize, are targets. In the corner of the screen is a clock. The countdown.

Eleven hours and forty-four minutes.

CHAPTER 54

need to leave." I put a hand on my head, not needing to pretend I am dizzy, but needing desperately to get out of here.

"Of course." Loudin barely notices I am here. He is focused on destroying the world. Again.

I don't think there is any way Dallas can bring enough people back in the next twelve hours to stop Loudin. It is up to us. To me.

I leave the room and take the elevator up to Level C, where I go down the hall and peer in each window, looking for Rhen. Loudin won't be observing me right now. No Monitors follow me. The Communication Specialist beside the desk in the lobby didn't stop me or ask me any questions.

What would she say—what would the others say—if they knew what was happening right now below their feet? I grunt as I pass yet another empty medical chamber. They wouldn't think anything. They'd just keep doing what they were programmed to do. They wouldn't find it appalling or terrible.

But maybe they would. Rhen was like them. Until she went above, spent time with the people in New Hope. Up there, she changed. They could change too.

If I could just get them there.

If there is a *there* to get them to.

Finally I find Rhen. She is sleeping, but I have no choice. We have to get out of here. An alarm sounds when I enter her room. I pull her out of the sleeping platform and force her into her shoes.

A Monitor opens the door and presses the panel on the wall. "You said to alert you if there was any change with the patient."

Loudin's profile is visible on the wall screen, but he does not even look up. "Let her go. She poses no danger anymore."

We leave. Posing no danger. Of course not. Escape is futile if the earth is eleven and a half hours from becoming radioactive once again. Eleven and a half hours from destroying people in Athens and New Hope—people on continents all over the world. I imagine that blast of light followed by devastation and I move faster.

Rhen is struggling to walk so I wrap my arm underneath hers and half carry her to Pod A. I am out of breath and sweating by the time we arrive, but the effort kept me from having to think too much about what is happening, and I am grateful for the reprieve.

As soon as we step up to the door, Alex and Berk rush to meet us. I turned off my earpiece on the way to get Rhen—they didn't know we were coming.

The four of us freeze for a moment. Berk and Alex stare at me in the same way. I cannot look at either of them. Rhen straightens and walks through the entry to the couch.

Pod A looks just like Pod C—same layout: living area, cooking chamber, long hallway leading to the cubes. Even the furniture is the same. But unlike Pod C, the former residents of Pod A are alive, in New Hope. At least for now.

"We have eleven hours." Saying this out loud doesn't make it any more real than it was before, but it does make it more frightening. *Eleven hours.*

"Until what?" Rhen pulls her hair back and fastens it with an elastic band.

I explain Loudin's plan to her and her face pales.

"Where is Dallas?"

"He should be safe in New Hope right now." I don't need to tell her that the army he may be assembling will not come in time to help us, nor that a bomb is pointed straight at him.

"You left him to do that by himself?" Rhen glares at Alex and Berk.

Alex waves his arms. "We had to."

"How do you know he is in New Hope?" Rhen leans forward. "He doesn't know how to fly that aircraft. He could have crashed. How dare you do that to him, just so you both could be here with Thalli."

I have never seen Rhen angry. We are all stunned. But I

break the silence, explaining that the aircraft has autopilot, that Dallas and the others will be fine. "We need to focus on these bombs right now. We have very little time."

"We won't let him do this." Alex runs a hand through his blond hair. "Berk and I have been talking. We have to kill him. We can't avoid it any longer."

"The bombs are on a computerized countdown." I pace the length of the room. "Even if Loudin is dead, his plan would still go on."

"There has to be an Off button." Alex leans on a chair.

"James would know," Berk says. "But he turned off his transmitter. I don't know where he went."

I pull on my ear and call for James, but there is no response. "Berk, can't you tap into the videos in the Scientists' quarters?"

"It would take too long." He shakes his head. "We're better off going there and trying to see what's happening."

"But if we get caught, it's all over." I glance at the door. "We can't take that risk."

"What if we split up?" Alex says. "That way, if he catches some of us, the others can still act."

"But we still don't have a plan," Berk says. "We need more information before we go storming in there."

My earpiece crackles, and I hear Loudin screaming, "You did *what?*"

"I destroyed everything." James's voice is hard.

"What do you mean, you destroyed everything?"

"Just that. I cannot create a new generation. It is impossible."

I hear a crash, like metal hitting the floor. "How dare you!"

"You are out of control, Joseph."

"And you are finished, Dr. Turner. Get him out of here."

"Turn off the bombs." James is shouting.

"Fool." Loudin sounds far away. "We can gather reproductive ingredients from those here below. You have done nothing but sign your own death warrant."

James argues about genetic difficulties, just one generation to collect from, malformations, but Loudin obviously does not listen, does not bring him back. I can no longer hear Loudin. All I hear is James's grunts, his straining against the guards.

"Do not let this happen." James is speaking quietly—he is speaking to us. "You cannot let this happen. There will be no one left. It will mean the end of mankind."

CHAPTER 55

We are running to the Scientists' quarters. We have no more time to debate whether or not this will work or even how this will work. I am praying, praying for strength in our weakness, praying for protection from our enemies, praying for victory.

We stop just before we get to the entrance of the quarters.

"I don't like this," Rhen says. "We can't just walk into the operations chamber."

"We've run out of options." Berk repeats the argument he made in Pod A. "We have to see if we can disable the countdown."

My doubts echo Rhen's, but Berk knows the computer

system in the State better than almost anyone. Before we left for New Hope the first time, he was in training to be a Scientist, and he had lived in the Scientists' quarters for five years.

Alex crouches down, then shoots off, faster than I have ever seen him go. We wait thirty seconds, as he instructed. When we enter the lobby, the Monitor behind the counter is unconscious, and Alex hands her communications pad to Berk.

"Well done." Berk taps on the pad, and I keep my head down, praying Loudin is distracted enough not to look at the monitors.

"She doesn't have access to the operations chamber." Berk looks up from the pad. "But we can get right to the door. Alex, we'll need you to help us move past the guards that are down there."

"All right."

We slip into an elevator and go to Level E. The doors slide open, and six guards greet us. We were not expecting so many. Loudin must have sent more down here. I press the panel to shut the elevator door, but one of the guards jams his foot against the opening. Another pulls me out and grips my wrists together behind my back in one large hand.

Within seconds, Rhen and Berk are trapped by guards. Alex is still fighting. He has managed to punch two guards and is grappling with a third, but there are too many.

I throw my head back against the guard holding me, and he releases my hands. I launch myself into the back of the guard holding Berk. But his back is like a rock and he doesn't move. Meanwhile, my guard has recovered and he is pinching my shoulders in his hands.

I scream and Berk bends at the waist and kicks back between

his guard's legs. The guard drops to the ground, and Berk bends down to pull the communications pad from the man's waist.

The door to the operations chamber opens, but another of the guards lunges toward Berk and lands on top of him, covering Berk's body with his own. He'll crush Berk.

I follow his example, leaving my guard on the ground, and I kick at the guard on Berk until he rolls over and Berk scrambles through the open door.

I race in the opposite direction. Rhen is still fighting against her captor. She has barely recovered from Loudin's attack. I know she doesn't have the strength to get away. But I can't help her yet. I have to draw attention from Berk so he can get inside the chamber and to the operations center.

We turned our earpieces on as soon as we left Pod A, but there is so much noise—grunts and groans from each of us—that I can't distinguish Berk's voice. I keep running until I am at the end of the hallway, then I push through the door and go down the stairs. No one follows me. I stop to catch my breath.

"Berk." I speak as loudly as I dare. "Did you make it?"

"I'm in. And I changed the code to unlock the door so the guards won't be able to come in. Where are you?"

"The stairwell." I look up—still no one has followed me. "Alex? Are you all right?"

"Run, Thalli," Alex whispers. "The guards are calling Loudin. Berk, you don't have much time. You better fix this fast."

I race down the stairs. I can't stay here. I need to get out of the Scientists' quarters. I'll be harder to track out there.

I make it to the lobby when shouting bursts in my earpiece. Loudin has found Alex and Rhen. I pray Berk can find a way to stop the countdown before Loudin enters the chamber.

Alex is shouting Rhen's name, and I want to go back and help them. Rhen is weak. She is hurt. Even Alex sounds tired.

But I go on anyway. I run out the doors as fast as I can, and I keep running, running, to the spot in the State where the cameras won't see me: the water reservoirs. I keep my head down, listening intently to the shouting, Loudin insisting someone open the door to the operations chamber. Guards' voices are muffled, but I do not hear victory in their tone.

"Berk." I am so winded I can barely speak. "Did you find it? Can you stop it?"

"Open the door, Berk." I hear Loudin in my earpiece, but can Berk hear him through the glass? "Open the door or I will blow it open. And that won't be pretty. Believe me."

Blow it open? Images of an explosion, of Berk and Rhen being hurt as a result, fill my mind. I stop. "Berk, you have to let Loudin in."

"This code is unbreakable," Berk says. "Loudin made sure no one could override it."

"You have thirty seconds." Loudin's voice fills my ear, and I relay his message to Berk, then I continue running.

I hear more shouting, metal clanging, tones sounding in a cacophony of minor keys. I am at the water reservoirs now, my hands flat against the rough sides. I look up, again reminded how massive these are. I cannot see around them, can barely see to the top.

I hear a groan from Alex that freezes my blood. Rhen shouts, but then she is silenced.

"Bring. Berk. To. Me." Loudin spits out each word.

I hear glass shatter and then I hear Berk. "I love you, Thalli."

CHAPTER 56

Nothing. After Berk spoke, the earpieces stopped working. I have tugged on my ear, pulled the device out and examined it, hit it, placed it in the other ear, thrown it to the ground, yet it remains silent. I do not know what is happening or even how much time has passed since I left the Scientists' quarters.

I want to go back to check on my friends. But I cannot. Part of me is too frightened to move, to see my worst fears realized—those I love, dead. Another part of me, one that has been praying, desperate for the Designer to perform a miracle, feels that I need to stay here. I must stay here. Why, I do not know. But I remain.

I turn back to the reservoir, walk around it. So much water is in this one, and this is not the only one. Because the water is from above, piped in from faraway oceans, it must go through years of purification before we can use it. Each reservoir has water in different stages of the purification process. Each holds the equivalent of the large lake in New Hope. An immense amount of water. If I could get the water in there out here . . . the State would flood. All of it. The computers would stop working, the bombs would not launch.

There are tubes at the top, but I cannot get up there, not without a transport. And even if I got a transport and I reached the tubes, how would I release the water?

I slump back to the ground. Impossible. This all seems impossible. My worst fear will come true—I alone will survive, trapped here like John was, with nothing but verses and memories to keep me from losing my mind.

The ground shakes, and I look out toward the Scientists' quarters and see what appears to be a crowd of people walking this way. I stand and squint—it is Loudin with several guards, a dozen or more. All to capture me?

As he gets closer, Loudin slows. Wiping the debris from my pants, I peer between the guards. I see Rhen and Alex. Berk. Loudin has brought them all here. Why?

"I offered you so much." Loudin stops six feet away from me. "The opportunity to use your talents in the State, beside me, to be a world leader. Yet you chose again and again to defy me."

"Let them go." I continue to look past him to my friends.

"Oh, I plan to." Loudin smiles. "I am letting them go above. Right now."

"No!" I will not allow them to be killed by the nuclear bombs. I cannot.

"Which is it?" Loudin takes a step closer. "Let them go or don't let them go? You seem to be confused."

My pulse is pounding in my ears, a steady beat, beat, beat, like a metronome. The rhythm steadies me, clears my mind. *God, help me!* That is all I can pray. I hope it is enough.

My gaze drops to Loudin's waist.

I see the weapon that killed Kristie. I have felt its power in my own body. Intense pain, immense power. Loudin has used that weapon to control us. He will use it again.

Unless I use it first.

Loudin sees where my gaze has gone as well. "This is for you. For after your friends have gone. I want you to watch them go, to watch the world you love so much disintegrate before your eyes. Then if you remain rebellious, I will use this on you. If, however, you change your mind, I will spare you."

"I'd rather die than be like you."

"So be it." Loudin motions to the guards surrounding Rhen, Alex, and Berk. He points above. The directive is clear.

Berk tries to push through the guards, but he is held back, his arms pinned behind him. The guards surround the three-some, each holding the arms of the one in front of him, pushing them together so none of them can move. They cannot escape. The guards move in unison, pushing my friends toward the doors of the Scientists' quarters—and from there, above.

The clock counting down the time to the detonation of the nuclear weapons fills my mind. The seconds tick with every beat of my heart. I have to do something. I have to stop this. I look back at the reservoirs.

A flash of blue in the distance makes me turn around. James. He has a weapon, and he is directing it at the group of guards. They are falling.

I lunge toward Loudin, using the momentary distraction to pull the weapon from his belt. It feels cool and heavy in my hands. This weapon destroyed my grandmother. Can it also destroy the State?

I need time to think this through, to talk to the others. But I don't have time and neither do they. I close my eyes and pray for the strength to do what must be done. Because I am sure of one thing: either the State destroys the world, or I destroy the State.

I depress the panel on the side and it hums in my hand. Loudin reaches for me, but I turn, evading his grasp. With everything I have in me, I plant the weapon on the side of the reservoir.

At first nothing happens. I lean harder against the concrete, my hand almost numb with the effort. Loudin is pulling at me, and I put my other hand on the weapon, curling my body around it so he cannot reach it.

Thankfully Loudin is weak—I can fight him off as easily I could a child. Keeping my torso against the weapon, I use my legs to kick at Loudin, aiming for his kneecaps. His hands yank at my shoulders. His desperation to pull me away gives me hope that this plan might work.

Finally the reservoir begins to shake. Loudin gives up his attempts to pull me away on his own and renews his calls for the guards.

As his hands leave my shoulders, he screams, "Stop him."

Is he talking about Berk? Alex? James? I want to know what

is going on behind me. But I cannot look. I have to stay where I am and hope the others have gotten away from the guards, that they see what I am doing and are giving me time to complete the task.

The reverberations are going up my arm and making it difficult to keep the weapon trained on the concrete. But I must. I cannot let go. I cannot fail. I close my eyes and imagine myself away from here, on a hill in New Hope, playing my violin, surrounded by my friends. The thought renews my strength and I lean harder against the concrete.

I hear a loud noise and I open my eyes. A crack! There is a crack in the concrete and it is racing up, up, up the reservoir, getting wider as it gets longer. Water begins to trickle, then spills out.

I pull away from the concrete and run to the next reservoir. I can do this. I can flood the State, disable the nuclear warheads. I can stop Loudin.

He is at my heels again, but no guards are pursuing me. I look over my shoulder. Every one of them lies on the ground. James holds the weapon out to Alex, and Alex runs to the final reservoir. He leans the weapon against the reservoir.

"Push as hard as you can," I call out to him. With a swift kick to Loudin's shins, I send the older man to the ground. I use the time to turn around and locate James, Rhen, and Berk.

They are searching the guards for more weapons.

"Run! Alex and I can take care of this. Get everyone out of here, get them above. Hurry."

The integrity of the reservoirs is already compromised. It won't take long for the strength of the water to overcome the strength of the concrete. Then the entire State will flood.

Most of the others leave, but Berk remains. He is searching for something to use against Loudin. But there is nothing he can use. Rhen pulls him toward the Scientists' quarters.

"Go," I yell. "Go now."

Berk pulls against Rhen, but she forces him away. I release a breath. He will be safe.

"You will not destroy what I created." Loudin is back up and at my neck now, his fingers squeezing my throat. If I let go of the weapon to fight him, he will grab it. That is not an option. I lean harder into the concrete.

"Thalli." Alex is beside me, the weapon at his waist. His hands work to pry Loudin's fingers from my throat.

"Kill him," I croak out.

"He's too close to you." Alex's face is red with the effort. Where did Loudin's burst of strength come from? "If I shoot him, the current will go through you too."

"Do it." My life is not worth Loudin's victory.

"Enough." Loudin releases me and reaches for Alex's weapon. His movement is so fast, Alex has no time to react, no time to stop him.

Loudin holds the weapon against Alex's neck and glares at me, his eyes bloodshot and cold. "Give me your weapon and put your hands up, or I will kill him right now."

I do as Loudin says, despite Alex's pleas to let him die. I cannot. The damage has been done. The reservoirs have been broken. The State will flood. Loudin cannot stop that.

Loudin pulls his communications pad out. "I need everyone here now, with the strongest sealing compound we have. Do you understand me?" Loudin jams the weapon deeper into Alex's neck. "This is not over."

Alex yanks the weapon down so it sits in the space between his and Loudin's chest. "Yes, it is."

Before my brain even has time to register what Alex is doing, he has pressed the panel on the weapon.

Blue light flashes between them, striking both Alex and Loudin in the heart. Both men are shaking, electricity coursing through them. Killing them.

"Alex, stop! Please turn it off! Please."

He just looks at me and smiles—a smile full of peace.

My eyes are so full of tears that I can see nothing for several seconds. The sound of water rushing around us fills my ears. It is getting closer, covering the ground behind us. Time seems to have stopped. I feel like I am already drowning. And, for a moment, I don't even want to try to save myself.

I rub my eyes, make myself watch what is happening. Alex needs to know I am here. I cannot abandon him.

The two men have fallen to the ground, their bodies rigid. The blue light creates an eerie glow around them. Loudin's eyes have rolled back into his head, and his mouth is open, frozen in a scream. Alex is still alive, still pressing that button, making absolutely sure Loudin is gone.

After what seems like hours, the blue light turns off, and Alex falls to the side, barely breathing.

I am on my knees beside him.

"Don't touch." His voice is a whisper, and his eyes look the way Kristie's did right before she died. "Run."

"I can't leave you here." I put a hand toward him, but even a few inches away, I feel the electricity on him. In him.

"It's all right." Alex smiles and my heart breaks. "Death is only the beginning, remember?"

I sit on the ground next to him, water pouring down my back, spilling onto the ground, soaking Alex's and my clothing. I don't stop looking into his eyes until they no longer look back at me.

I close my eyes and allow tears to spill down my cheeks over this man who lost so much, overcame so much, sacrificed so much. I want to carry him back, to bury him among his people in Athens. But I cannot.

I hear an explosion—part of the reservoir above me shatters, and concrete falls two feet from where I am sitting. Water pours down with such force I can barely stand under it.

In the distance, running toward me, is Berk. He is screaming my name, demanding that I get up and run to him. Escape.

I force myself to stand and I run as hard as I can, as fast as I can, until I leave the State—and Alex—behind. Forever.

EPILOGUE

Six Months Later

I am sitting at the piano in the church that John restored, in the village where I met Kristie, sixty miles from the town Alex should have ruled.

I still grieve for each of them, ache for the hole their loss has left in my heart, in my life.

I play their lives, the lessons they taught me, the sacrifices they made. The Designer uses music to speak to me, as always, and he also uses music to bring healing, a salve to my broken heart. As my fingers caress the keys, play these memories, my pain is replaced with joy. Not joy at the loss. Never that. But a joy in spite of the loss.

Each life, each death, brought me here—brought us here. They neither lived nor died in vain. As I look up from the piano, I see the church full of people—those from New Hope and those from Athens, members of the State who escaped with us. People who are here because John, Kristie, and Alex are not.

The State no longer exists. Every inch of it is underwater, all the Scientists' work—gone. I am sorry for that. But the nuclear bombs are gone, and I am not sorry for that. Rhen, Berk, and James were able to get all of Pod B out. The Scientists refused. They stayed behind and ended up buried under water, dying for what they had lived for.

The world can start over now. People like those here in this church can be free to live in the world above. We will make mistakes . . . we are not perfect. But we will live. My gratefulness for that is in the melody I play.

I finish and Gerald comes to the front. He has taken over John's role, speaking to us from the Designer's book. I sit beside Berk and his hand wraps around mine. I am home.

My gaze scans the crowd. Those who chose to follow us out of the State are slowly adjusting to life here. All of them have found ways to use their abilities to help, either here in New Hope or over in Athens. They are discovering emotions, as Rhen did, and learning to embrace the freedom they have here.

James is teaching at the school, training the next generation. The people of the State are making this world better, stronger. They are accomplishing their purposes. Some have even expressed an interest in taking the aircraft to the other pockets of survivors to learn more about them, to find ways to work together.

When we first arrived, I went to Athens, gathered the people, and told them of Alex's death. They were devastated, of course, but I told them of his heroic acts, of how his ultimate sacrifice saved all of us. Some of the artists are sculpting a statue in his honor. I promised them I would make sure he was never forgotten, and together we all promised not to treat lightly the gift he gave us.

They wanted me to take Alex's place—they still see me as his fiancée and, thus, heir to the throne. And for his memory and out of love for him, I do not correct them. But I do not want to be a ruler. I suggested Rhen and Dallas rule Athens. Together they are wise and compassionate and perfectly suited to help Athens recover from the damage inflicted on them by King Jason and his father. Though they were reluctant, the people of Athens convinced them to step into the role, not of king and queen, but as governors—rulers who seek to represent the desires of the people, to oversee but not overwhelm.

Carey is not here at the church, but he is alive, recovering from what Fluor, a survivor from Pod B, diagnosed as a stroke. Thanks to Fluor's expertise in medicine, Carey has a good chance of recovering.

Dallas's childhood home is being rebuilt, though his parents have moved to Athens to be with Rhen and him. The memories here are just too painful for them to be able to remain. So Berk and I will live there, on the farm with the horses and the orange trees. We will, hopefully, raise our children there and teach them about the world that was and the world that could be. We will teach them of the Designer, of love, of the purpose he has given each of them. We will raise the next generation in a world completely different from ours.

Gerald finishes, and I return to the piano. My fingers play the message he spoke, the Words of the Designer that we read. I play the hope that I feel. I crescendo with the expectation of a world full of possibilities.

And the music never ends.

READING GROUP GUIDE

1. Thalli felt that the Designer was very distant from her throughout much of this book. Do you think that's true? Have you ever had times in your life when you felt "ignored" by God? How did you work through those times?
2. What was your reaction to the news about Thalli's parentage? Did you suspect that connection?
3. Compare Kristie's death in this book to John's in *Luminary*. What were the similarities? Differences?
4. As you got to know Dr. Loudin more in this story, what were your thoughts about him? Tragic hero or pure villain?
5. Do you think Thalli made the right choice between the two young men vying for her heart? Why or why not?
6. How different do you think the story would have been had John still been alive?

7. How has Thalli changed from the beginning of *Anomaly* to the end of *Revolutionary*?
8. Which character do you most identify with and why?
9. If you could change any part of this book, what would it be?
10. What do you think life will be like for Thalli and the others? What would the next chapter of that story look like?

An Excerpt from *Right Where I Belong*
by Krista McGee

Chapter 1

I am leaving your stepmother."

"Let me guess." Seventeen-year-old Natalia did not fall for the woe-is-me, martyred expression on her father's face. Not again, anyway. "She is not making you happy. You've found someone else. Life is too short to be tied down to one woman."

"Natalia Ruth Montoya Lopez! You do not speak to your papa in that tone of voice."

Shame clawed at Natalia's stomach. *He's right. Help me, Jesus. What do I say to him?*

Natalia inhaled deeply. "I'm sorry. But you keep leaving all the women in your life. How do I know you will not leave me too?"

Papa turned Natalia toward him, his face softening. "*Hija.* I will never leave you. You are my daughter. My flesh and blood. But women are different. You are young and you don't understand. You fall in love and you fall out of love. Nothing can be done about that. It is part of life."

"So this is what I have to look forward to? Falling in love with a man and then having him tell me a few years later that he doesn't love me anymore? What about 'till death do us part'? Doesn't that mean *anything*?" Natalia hated the anger that kept bubbling up, but she didn't know how to stop it.

"For some it does, *mi corazón*. Your grandparents were married for forty-seven years. And they were truly happy. I have often wondered if something is wrong with me. I just cannot seem to keep that feeling. I try . . ."

"Oh, Papa, please. You do not try. I have seen this, now, three times."

"Natalia!"

She held up one finger. "Mamá—I was four. I can still remember the yelling. I would hide under my bed with the door shut and *still* hear the two of you."

"That woman had a temper." He looked out the window. "You didn't know the half of it."

"Yes, I do! I'm not saying she was perfect, but neither were you. And if either one of you had just accepted that fact, you might still be together."

Papa turned around, opening his mouth to speak, but Natalia held up two fingers and continued. "Isabelle never did anything to you. She was like a slave: cooking, cleaning, cowering in fear. I remember she'd take little Ari outside in the middle of the night just so her crying wouldn't wake you. And you kept her around for how long? Three years?"

He sighed. "Isabelle. No man can handle such a timid woman. It was nice for a while. A nice change from your mother's yelling. But then . . . there was no passion. A man cannot live without passion, hija. It was her own fault. I cannot help being a man and having a man's needs."

The image of her father and his "needs" rushed in full color into her brain, and Natalia tried not to gag. "And now we come to number three. Maureen." Natalia stood inches from him. "I think she was the best one yet. She left her home and her family. Moving from the United States to Spain was not easy. Yet she did it. She learned the language, she adapted to our culture, and still you reject her."

Natalia shook her head. "*I* have seen it coming, but I know the signs. I do not think she has any idea. You are going to break her heart, Papa. And for what? So you can do this all over again with a fourth and a fifth and a sixth?"

Natalia's throat felt like it was closing in on itself. She couldn't speak. She willed herself not to cry. *Why can't I just stay angry? It's so much easier to be angry.*

Her father had hurt her so many times that she had learned to put up a wall around her heart, hardening herself to his outbursts, his ridiculous logic. But her heart broke for Maureen. She had seen good in Papa. She had loved him unconditionally, and Natalia had foolishly hoped he would live up to Maureen's vision of who he was.

How childish that hope was.

"Natalia," Papa said, like he was explaining to a toddler why she couldn't have a cookie before dinner. "Someday you will understand. For now, help your stepmother. She depends on you."

Natalia turned and walked away, refusing to listen to any more. *God, help me stay quiet. Better not to say anything at all than to say something I will regret.*

"Natalia!"

She kept walking, out of the living room, down the hallway of the spacious apartment, into her room. She shut the door and considered locking it, but her father wouldn't come. He would yell and get angry, but he would not try to sit down and work things out. He would let her stew and then, when Natalia emerged, he would act like everything was fine, as if they did not just have an argument. She had seen this dozens of times before. Just one of many reasons why the man couldn't keep a wife.

Five years ago Maureen had come to Madrid with her company, which was in partnership with her father's. Several companies from around the world had merged. Because Maureen's position was supervised directly by Papa, they worked together often. After a few months he was bringing Maureen home to work after dinner. A few months after that he was bringing her home for good. From the beginning she had felt more like a friend to Natalia than a stepmother.

Natalia walked to her window. She took a deep breath, trying to will oxygen into lungs that felt dry and thick. Ragged breaths escaped. She pulled back the curtain to see the plaza below. Mopeds and smart cars lined up at a stoplight eight floors below. Children were playing soccer, parents were pushing toddlers in swings, fathers were pushing their babies around in their carriages. So many happy families. Natalia let the curtain fall back into place and sat on her bed, finally giving in to the wracking sobs she had held on to for so long.

I will never, ever allow myself to fall in love. I won't do to anyone what my father does to these women. And to me. Never. Do you hear me, God? Make me single. Have me travel the world or work with orphans or whatever. But don't make me fall in love. I won't do it. I can't.

℃

Natalia sat in her favorite spot at Retiro Park—a bench overlooking the small lake where couples drifted in boats and children skated along the sidewalks. She gazed at the statues of lions that guarded an ancient gazebo, the pillars reflected in waves in the waters below.

"Churros for you." Natalia's best friend, Carmen, handed her the warm pastry covered in cinnamon sugar. "And ice cream for me."

Natalia bit into the churro. Heaven. *"Gracias."*

Carmen splayed her hands in a Spanish "of course" sign and bit into her frozen treat. "Feeling better?"

"About my father's divorce? Or about his dating a woman six years older than me? Or about watching my stepmother go from a strong woman to a blubbering child?" Natalia moved her feet back as a rollerblader sped past.

"It has only been a week."

"Exactly." Natalia closed her eyes. "And Maureen just told me last night that she is leaving. Moving back to Florida."

"But you and Maureen . . . ?"

"She's like the mother I never had."

Carmen smiled sideways. "You have a mother."

Natalia raised her eyebrows. Carmen knew that Mamá was far too busy with her career to give much time to her only child.

"Poor Maureen." Natalia took another bite of the churro. "She is terrified to go back home. But she feels like staying here will keep her from being able to get over Papa. He is her boss, after all."

Carmen tossed the paper from her dessert into a trash can. "But what will she do?"

Natalia shrugged. "I don't know. Neither does she."

"She'll find something. Maureen is amazing. Beautiful, smart, funny."

Natalia nodded. Maureen had been her rescuer in more ways than she could count. She made Natalia feel important, loved, during her preteen years when she felt awkward and ugly. She spent time with Natalia.

"Who will teach me about God when Maureen is gone?" She hadn't even considered that her spiritual mentor would be leaving.

"You don't need this crutch of faith to help you." Carmen turned away and ran a hand through her long, silky black hair. "You are too smart to keep going on with this. People are talking. You used to be so well respected, but all this talk of 'salvation' and 'eternal life' is making you look foolish."

Natalia sighed. Over and over again, she had tried to explain her faith to her friend. But Carmen, like so many Spaniards, saw faith as a weakness, an embarrassing part of their history. When Natalia tried to tell her that what she had was a relationship with a God who loved her, Carmen only recalled the Spanish Inquisition and other atrocities carried out in the name of "religion."

"Natalia, think logically. There is no evidence that God exists. None. No evidence of an afterlife or a creator. Science has disproven all that superstition. Why would you go backward? You don't believe the earth is flat. Belief in the existence of God is just as ridiculous."

"Science can't disprove the existence of God any more than religion can prove it. Faith is involved on either side of that debate. But I know God exists. I have seen him at work in my life. I have seen him change me. I'm sorry you don't like the changes, but . . ."

Carmen shook her head. "It isn't that. Well, it is, I guess. I *don't* like it. But I guess if that is what you need, then I should just keep quiet and let you believe it."

"Could you be any more condescending?" Natalia laughed. "You're talking to me like I'm Ari, waiting in line to see Saint Nicholas! God is not Santa."

Carmen put her hand up in protest. "Can't you hear how silly that all sounds? An invisible Savior who speaks to you through a two-thousand-year-old book and little voices in your head?"

"I know it sounds silly to you. And it pains me more than I can say that it does. But that is all the more reason why I need Maureen. She understands." Realization hit Natalia, an almost-audible voice from God speaking to her soul. Natalia jumped up.

"What is it?" Carmen pulled Natalia back to the bench.

Peace settled over her. She knew this was from him. Of course.

"Natalia, *por favor.*" Carmen clapped her hands, startling Natalia from her thoughts.

"I need to go with Maureen." Natalia stared across the pond to a family eating a picnic lunch on the grass.

"To America?"

Natalia nodded. *"Sí."*

Carmen pulled the remaining churro from Natalia's hand. "They must have put something other than sugar on this."

"No. I mean it." Certainty settled over Natalia as soon as the words came out of her mouth. "She needs me. It's my turn to help her. I can't abandon her the way Papa has."

"What about me?" Carmen planted her hands on her hips. "If you really believe this, then should you not stay here and keep trying to get me to believe it?"

Natalia laughed. Her friend was using any tactic possible to get Natalia to stay in Madrid. "If my staying here could make you believe, I would stay. I'd sit right down here in the middle of the ground and not move an inch until you believed." She sat cross-legged on the dirty sidewalk, caring little that those passing by looked at her as if she were losing her mind. "But I can't make you believe. Only God can. So I will keep asking him to help you."

"Get up, Natalia!" Carmen whispered. "What will people think?"

"What do I care what people think? I'm leaving!"

Carmen pulled Natalia up by her wrist, shaking her head in mock disgust. "How can you be so flippant about this? Do not let your zeal over your newfound faith take you away from everyone who loves you. Please! At least finish high school."

"I know you're saying this because you care about me." Natalia straightened her jacket and dusted off her skirt. "This is my home, my people, my country. I will miss you so much. But I need to go with my stepmother. I just cannot believe I didn't think of it sooner."

"Sooner?" Carmen stood. "It has been a week."

"I need to speak with Maureen. And my father."

"Hopefully they will talk you out of it." Carmen grabbed her backpack and threw it over her shoulder. "Do not do this, *amigita*. You will regret it." Carmen stared at Natalia, shook her head, then walked off.

Natalia felt her heart breaking with each step. Maybe she *was* out of her mind. Maybe Carmen was right. Did she really want to leave everything she knew just for—?

She stopped herself. She was leaving for a God who loved her, who had sacrificed everything for her. A God who knew just what it was like to leave the familiarity of home out of obedience to his Father.

Peace washed over her in a way Natalia could never explain, an experience so intimate and amazing that all her momentary doubts vanished. God was with her in this park. He would be with her as she left. More difficulties would come, but Jesus would be there as she faced each of them.

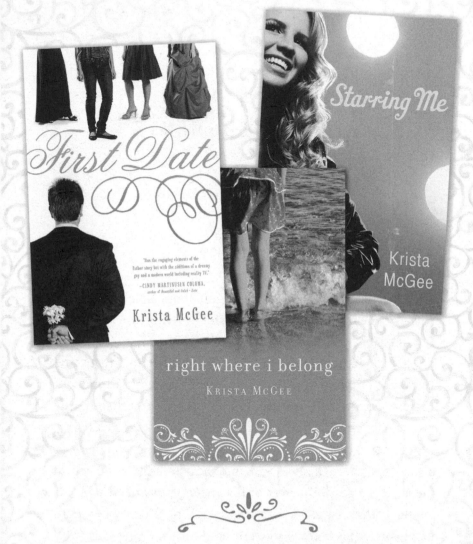

ACKNOWLEDGMENTS

I am incredibly grateful for the team at Thomas Nelson Fiction. They believed I could write this story even before I did. I am humbled by your faith in me.

My amazing agent, Jenni Burke, helped me create and tweak the proposal that would outline this trilogy. Throughout the process, my editor, Becky Monds, has been part sounding board, part cheerleader, and all friend—thanks for challenging me not to be so easy on my characters! Julee Schwarzburg, as always, saw through my messes into the possibilities and helped me see those possibilities as well. Kristen Vasgaard created this fabulous cover. Katie Bond, Laura Dickerson, and the whole marketing and sales team worked so hard to make sure this story got into the hands of readers all over the world. Thank you, thank you, thank you!

My family, as always, is my greatest inspiration and my biggest fan base. My husband, Dave, is one of the best men to ever walk the face of the earth. Our kids, Emma, Ellie, and Thomas, are the most wonderful gifts God has given me.

A huge thanks to you, my readers. Thank you for your e-mails of encouragement, for "liking" me and "following" me. I am so grateful for you.

But the reason that I write, that I live and breathe, is because of my wonderful Savior, Jesus Christ. He has made each one of us beautiful anomalies. I pray that every person reading my books knows how very special you are to the Designer, how unique and precious and valuable you are to him.

ABOUT THE AUTHOR

Author photo by Ruth Kegel

When Krista McGee isn't living in fictional worlds of her own creation, she lives in Tampa and spends her days as a wife, mom, teacher, and coffee snob. She is also the author of The Anomaly Trilogy, *First Date*, *Starring Me*, and *Right Where I Belong*.

Visit Krista's website at www.kristamcgeebooks.com
Facebook: krista.a.mcgee
Twitter: @KristaMcGeeYA